UNFILTERED

sage

CELINA | HILBRAND

Editor: Lauren Ripkin

Cover Design: Stacy Trotter

For all the dreamers – the wanderers – the romantics, and for all the people in my world who allowed me to dream.

CHAPTER *One*

I swore I'd never be here. I swore I'd never be *her* again. It's funny how life makes you break your promises.

And by funny, I mean a fucking disaster.

This place is the last memory I have before I ran—to something better, to something more beautiful than this sepia-colored culture called my childhood. I came here to photograph—or commemorate—this unwanted reunion, but even after spending a decade in war-torn, impoverished countries, I just can't seem to find anything here worth framing—all white space and no color. Without inspiration, I turn on my heel—away from the field and the memories I refuse to recollect. As I head toward my car, I hear a school bell ring. Somewhere, down there, is a girl so ready to live, so ready to love, so ready to leave—and she has no idea how broken she'll become. I want to warn her that you can travel to the ends of the earth, but you can never outrun yourself. I jam my unused camera into the disaster of my back-seat, open the front door and stop. Fingers resting on the handle, feet planted, I look up and admit for the first time in years how scared I am—afraid of whatever comes next, terrified to finish the rest of my journey—to go home.

Home.

In my 15-year absence from this white-washed town, I have been smuggled in and out of countries for work and detained by some of the most dubious governments on the planet, but still nothing is scarier than the thought of the 10-minute drive from the city limits to the outskirts of town where I grew up. I'm not sure what I'll walk into. Now that I'm so close, I sink into the dread and internally repeat the voicemail I received when I finally got service around Mumbai. "Sage, it's Mom. You need to come home—It's your brother." In over a decade no one has asked me to come home. They knew what I was running away from. They knew I would never come back—unless it was for him.

I'm startled from this silent, judgmental revelry as my forgotten ringtone sounds from somewhere in the mess of my car. After digging and finding my outdated 3s iPhone, I reluctantly answer and subject myself to the only person on this planet that could make this day a little shittier—my mother.

"Sage? Where are you? No more games."

"Mom, I'm here."

"You're here? And where might that be? Don't even start about how you're 'here in spirit'. This time that just doesn't cut it. This is different Sage . . . This—this is it." My mom chokes on the last sentence, and I feel my eyes stinging. I hold my ragged breath and count to ten before I respond.

"No, mom. I'm *here*—in town. I'm about to head out to the house."

"Don't bother. Your father and I haven't been there for days. We're staying near the hospital, so we can be here for Gage . . . just . . . in . . . case."

All I hear next is the predictable sniffle that comes with the deluge of Mom's tears. I hold the phone at arm's length expecting to wait out her weeping; however, she pulls herself together in nearly record time to tell me that they are currently in ICU room 4 and that visiting hours end at 6:00.

"Sage, you need to get here. Get here fast."

I throw myself into the car and head back onto the road.

To Gage. To the hospital. To the truth.

This trip from my small hometown to the big city hospital we frequented so often as kids is a decidedly shorter one than the flight from Mumbai to Cairo, to London, to JFK—plus the drive from New York to the sweet, sweet south. The sun is long gone and the road in front of me feels more familiar driving in the dark. Because darkness is darkness no matter where you are, and I've spent a lot of my career—my life—in the dark. The darkness found me and broke me long ago, but Gage taught me to never be its victim. So instead of trying to somehow illuminate all my own shattered pieces, I decided to flash a light on some of the most devastating and desolate people and call it a career. They give me hope. I've seen how much beauty exists within simplicity. How much good exists in war-torn, battered countries. How much strength lives within oppression. Not so surprisingly, I've found that the happiest people have the fewest possessions. It's amazing how joyful some cultures and communities are to simply be alive. Those are my favorite photos, the ones I keep for myself and rarely sell. Maybe one day I'll make an over-edited coffee table book called, *The Many Colors of Happy: A Story of Humanity in Pictures*. Then again, maybe I'll just tuck them away all for myself. These people have become my much-needed friends town after town, country after country. Many of them are in flux, on their way from hell and looking for a little grace—a place to start again. I know I'll be lucky to ever find them after the dust settles, but through their photos, I'm able to capture something beautiful. Something that changes and illuminates the little broken bits of me piece by piece.

My mind staggers like this through the dark until it floats back to Gage. I think he's the only other soul in the world who would fully appreciate my portfolio like I do. I always tell him he's far too interesting to be a history teacher. And, of course, his smart ass always responds that there is nothing more interesting than changing the fabric of history by choosing what to retell and brand on students' hearts. My brother could start a revolution with his classroom if he chose to do so. Years ago, he sent me a YouTube link to one of his lectures. Apparently, the kids had just watched Dead Poets Society in their English classes. Mix that with some role-playing and a little American Revolution, and they reenacted the entire scene of the boys standing on their desks and repeating "O Captain my Captain" to their "leader", in this case, George Washington a.k.a. Gage Gilbert. That is the color Gage brings to the world. He's meant to alter the fabric of history. Which means, I have to find a way to keep him around a little bit longer.

I pull into the visitor parking right before 5:40. I have 20 minutes to see my brother, if I'm lucky, which means I'm out of time to stall. I haven't showered since Mumbai [I know that's really gross, but in my line of work that's *not* unusual]. My hair was brushed this morning, but in all my nervous energy I have put it up in a bun and taken it down no less than a hundred times, which now gives it a limp wave and a greasy sheen. I honestly don't think I own makeup anymore, if I do, it's been roasting in this deserted car while I've been out of the country all fall. Needless to say, I'm a mess. A mess my mother would very much disapprove of, but none of these details register with me whatsoever until I walk into the upscale southern hospital and see not one, but two of my godforsaken classmates on my way up to the ICU.

They give half-hearted waves and look to be nurses of some sort who are impatiently waiting for their shifts to end. I don't remember their names, exactly, but I do remember they were there in the sea of faces at graduation. I assume they know of Gage and thus can problem solve the conundrum of why I'm here and in such a state of disarray. They graciously look away and make sure to keep their voices loud enough, so I can tell they are, in fact, not talking about me—the homeless-looking lady who they once went to high school with.

The ICU is relatively easy to find, you know, minus all the emotional baggage that attacks me on my way up. I see my dad first. He's the pillar of strength in the family—tall with a defined jaw and silver hair. He's also naturally in shape from living a busy life, but has never put a lot into his own appearance—or anyone else's for that matter. He has all of the heart of my hometown but none of the judgment. He wasn't the sort of dad that only told you how beautiful you were on Prom Night.

> I remember, when I was six or so, Gage and I were play- ing Cowboys and Indians [because back then we were much less politically correct . . . and, you know, kids] using our hobbyhorses to "fight to the death". [I should have known then that Gage was going to end up a fucking history nerd]. Even as little kids, it was obvious that Gage was going to inherit my dad's genes, and I was destined to be the spitting, yet sloppier, image of my mother who is as petite and delicate as her southern belle upbringing suggests. I was never one to go down without a fight, but Gage must have head-butted or horse-butted me in all our fighting, and my nose was bleeding all over the new upholstery. My mom yelled, and I cried . . . probably from defeat as much as from fear of my mother. Dad carried me away to help get me cleaned up in the downstairs bathroom. In that moment, he could have laughed at me or even given me tactical advice for my next horse attack. But, instead of any of those very logical reactions, he simply said, "Sage, you're stunning."

That's my dad—a man of very few words and never one to fall apart in a crisis.

I guess that's why my stomach falls as soon as soon as I see him. My personal pillar of strength—my beacon of hope—is clasping and unclasping his watch while looking off into seemingly nothing with a pair of very red-rimmed eyes. I've never seen my father cry before, but it's obvious Gage's current situation has caused just that. Rather than turn toward him and absorb whatever strength Dad has left, I make a sharp right into ICU room 4 and prepare for the other shoe to drop.

I know I'm not fully ready for whatever comes next, but knowing that and actually having the rug pulled out from under you are two *completely* different things. Gage is 100% my dad's son. He's tall and dashing with the sort of charm that is vomit-inducing. However, that is not the man I see in front of me. This Gage is pale and thin, thinner than my incredibly naturally tiny frame. I'm sure if he were conscious at this moment he would still find a way to brag about how his jeans were smaller than mine—just to piss me off. I can see him breathing—but it's obviously labored—and I can see the skeletal outlines of each of the bones peeking out behind the neckline of his loose and gaping "leisure wear" [as Mother would say]. His bold, dark locks are long gone which makes me realize this is the first time I've ever seen Gage without hair. He was born with a full head of white hair that later turned very dark. He bleached it at some point in the '90s and then went for frosted tips before donning a faux hawk in college; however, never through all his crazy styles was he ever hairless. His bony scalp even looks sick, if that's possible. Without realizing it, tears begin cascading soundlessly down my face. I fight the need to launch myself at him, to hold him tight, to share some of my strength, to bring him back to consciousness. Though, some part of me knows he isn't well enough for even my sisterly affection. With nowhere to aim this twisted surge of both anger and protection, I slump to the floor in defeat. I lash out at the walls and a cabinet and even the machines near me—looking for somewhere to place my angry confusion. I kick each stationary item with diminishing effort— silently fighting the darkness of this moment—the darkness within me.

Once my initial onslaught of anger is exhausted and while still sitting on that cold, tiled floor, I slowly turn my body back toward Gage—willing myself to confront the reality in front of me. His non-IV hand hangs loosely off the bed beside me—I'm not sure if it was like this when I walked in or if my tantrum nudged it off. It looks so limp. So frail. So dead. I reach out and close both of my tiny hands over his bigger, colder one. I gently nudge each of his fingers one at a time like I am reenacting some childhood game of 'this little piggy'.

No reaction.

I try again. This time standing and squeezing his whole hand with my added strength and leverage.

Still nothing.

"Come on," I huff at him as I grit my teeth and squeeze again in the type of bruising grip he used to tease me with when we were younger.

I lorded a lot of my age, height and strength over Gage when we were little. The 4-year age gap worked to my advantage until Gage turned eight. I was a petite 12-year-old, he was giant 8-year-old and history was rewritten. The power completely shifted all at once. Gage mostly just threatened me in order to keep my anger at bay, but on a few rare occasions he doled out enough strength to keep his threats real and effective. One such occasion was this bone-breaking handshake. It was smart, really, if you think about it. Not enough force to leave a bruise—evidence—yet it always felt like he was rolling around and smashing each of the delicate bones in my hand. His bones are the fragile ones now being rolled from side to side and still nothing—not a peep—not a flinch. This isn't my brother.

The anguish is wrenched from somewhere in the pit of me. "COME ON, GAGE!" Like a child, I begin pounding on his flimsy excuse for a mattress almost as if I were resuscitating either the lost hope or time.

"Gilberts don't give up," I squeak out through a new round of fresh tears, still pushing into the soft edges around him. His gown flaps open and closed at the collar with each shove I administer, but everything else remains lifeless and still. That's it—this is my breaking point.

I'm sure there is someone watching me—there is always someone watching through these glass-paned walls of the ICU, but I couldn't give fewer shits than I do right now. In fact, in some weird way, I'm ready for a fight. I'm prepared to unleash hell on the next person that dares to cross my path and try to pull me from my despair.

As luck would have it, a middle-aged nurse enters the small, machine-filled room upon seeing my "outburst" otherwise known as the utter collapse of my world. She cautiously places a hand on my shoulder and clucks out, "Sweetie, this is a critical unit room. You can't behave like that in here. This is an area for patients . . . who are . . . critical."

Her small, overly sugary southern voice grates on my nerves as well as her inability to have a modicum of understanding or, at the very least, a basic vocabulary. In moments like these, I can recognize the little shit shouldn't matter. And while some piece of me can acknowledge this has nothing to do with nurse no-name over here, there is a more immediate need to place blame and look for some fucking answers. How long has he been unconscious? How much longer do I get to keep my little brother? And for fuck's sake, what is even wrong with him?

How the hell did this all happen?

The insipid nurse closes in with both arms, in an effort to console or detain me, but I quickly divert her advances. I've pinned myself on one side of the bed—nurse no-name on the other side—in a weirdly silent showdown. Without flinching, I wipe the drying tears and find an eerie form of calm from somewhere deep inside. She looks from side to side. I've got her—she's scared. I move an inch—just to see what she'll do—and she shrinks toward Gage's bedside emergency button.

"Oh, I wouldn't do that . . ." I warn in a self-assured, quiet tone. I can see fear rippling off her like waves. I know it's cruel, but for a second, I enjoy this moment of control.

"What do you ww-want?" The nurse questions with a visible tremor.

"I. Want. Fucking. Answers." I yell belligerently, my anger and volume growing with each word. Then she presses the damn button. The call begins ringing to some empty nurses' station when a distinctly male voice booms with commanding authority from behind.

"I've got answers, but first, I need you to calm down and apologize to Nurse Hamilton, Sage."

My back is to him, but I know this voice. He is my darkness personified. He is my personal hell. He is all my broken pieces. So how in God's name is he here right now? My body becomes numb, and I begin shaking with violent seizures of motion. I can hear the racket behind me—multiple voices raised and cautious. I'm sure they are assessing which drugs to use on my crazy ass—or perhaps which drugs I'm using, but I can't quite reach them from the abyss pinning me down. It's a fog—no, more than that. It's dry drowning, and these circumstances—my brother, that voice—are the water seizing my lungs, rendering my breathing useless. My mom's shrill voice rises above the din, but none of it makes sense. It's all foreign and hurried and then . . . black.

Home.

CHAPTER Two

ONE.

So, it turns out your body has some seriously badass qualities. I always knew about fight or flight, but this new reboot feature is pretty cool. It's like tapping out of reality to go hibernate in your subconscious for a while. It's sort of what I imagine the upside down to be like . . . a grimmer, quieter and, most definitely, a more solitary version of reality. In this place, my thoughts are on warp speed and every sense becomes hyperaware; I can feel every vertebra that bends as he adjusts my weight and lifts me up. I can smell his day-old cologne—the same one he's always worn—as if it were being pumped into an enclosed oxygen-less room. His heartbeat is fast and steady but pounds with the deafening echo of a drummer summoning an execution at the gallows. I. Feel. It. All. I sense every piece of him, and to my complete and utter horror, I lean into it. Into someone strong enough to carry this—carry me—through hell.

Then I'm awake, switched back on, and springing from his arms like it burns me because, well, it sort of does—my pride at the very least. I stumble to the floor and find my footing only after I seriously bang my knee on one of the ugly, barely-upholstered chairs in the waiting room. Blood runs freely down my naked leg and begins to puddle in my favorite pair of canvas tennis shoes. I cuss loudly, and without excuse, at anyone in my proximity because I don't yet know how to absorb all the hate I have for myself for letting this moment happen—to me and to my baby brother.

He pushes me to a semi-seated position and begins to examine my wounds patiently even though I keep trying to flop out of his grasp like a wounded and frightened fish. My mother, who must have appeared by my side during that fine hour of mine in Gage's room, begins soothing him. *HIM*—the charming asshole she's always loved more than me.

"Brec, I'm so sorry. I don't know what's wrong with her—"

She giggles at the end of the sentence. This 50-year-old women fucking giggles then glances side to side to make sure there aren't any more bystanders to take part in her life's embarrassment—otherwise known as me, her eldest child. In hushed, angry whispers she continues for my ears only.

"—Sage, you're making a scene. For God's sake, I raised you better than this. Is that what all those filthy, tribal villages have taught you? Stop being so dramatic. I don't have time for one of your tantrums."

Fucking Home.

And like that, I'm 16 again—confined to a world of dingy, brown hues. Sepia. It's meant to make everything look aged and elegant, but to me, it has only ever felt like a murky muddiness sucking me down. I get lost in a jumble of memories, self-pity and the need to seriously fight my "flee" function and run away from my past that is currently blowing on my knee and rubbing my calf in soothing circles. Before I realize it, Brec begins counting. It was our old 'go to' when I needed to calm down— his personal reminder to think before I speak . . . or swing— whatever. And, much to my dismay, it still works. I've been told by therapist after therapist to count, to hold my breath, to inhale and exhale as a means of self-soothing and redirecting my um . . . "feelings". It's never worked, and in truth, I never really wanted it to. I was proud of my opinions—of my voice. I was proud that I was somehow able to cut through all the bullshit my childhood kept piling on me to smother me into silence. But with Brec, things were different. He was the sort of quiet that didn't feel like suffocation; he felt like comfort. And by the time he gets to ten, my breathing slows down, and I stop flopping my bony ass on that hard excuse for a chair.

How did this happen? In life, you sometimes step away from yourself and realize your personal tragedy would maybe be a perfect script for some Hollywood movie. The guy that broke you and left you in little splinters swoops in—literally—to save you at your worst moment. He then apologizes for being the world's biggest prick and begs for you to come back to him. Then, because somehow he's a freaking doctor now, he magically—and very swiftly—saves your brother all in under two hours. Roll credits.

I softly chuckle to myself at the absurdity of all of this, but it comes out a little more breathy than I mean for it to. My dad uncomfortably clears his throat, and my mom's face turns scarlet. She's had enough of this scene—or enough of being seen with me—and calls for my father to leave. Visiting hours are long over, and it's probably time for all of us to go. Instead of waiting on me, mom turns on her heel—a trait I just realize I, unfortunately, seem to have inherited from her—and calls out into the abandoned hall.

"Sage, I'll send you the address of where we're staying. I assume you did not think to reserve a place for yourself . . . see you in a bit. —And *please* brush your hair before you go out in public again. You really ought to feel embarrassed about all that," she says while haphazardly waving a bony hand over my general appearance.

Dad gives me a tight squeeze, kisses me on my head and tells me I'm still stunning. *Dad.* Thankfully, he loves me enough for both of them.

When we're left alone, the silence becomes deafening. I can see the quick rise and fall of Brec's shoulders before I realize he's laughing—most likely at me. He's always laughed in color. His eyes laugh. His eyebrows laugh. Somehow, even his hairline laughs. I hate that about him.

"Sage, you sure have a way of making an entrance. I'm glad to see you've still got that fire."

He's looking into my eyes—for meaning, for remembrance. I don't respond. Really, what is there to say? I promised myself long ago that I wouldn't reward Brec with closure, with forgiveness and sure as hell not with friendship. My eyes fall to where he is taping on the last of my bandage. He didn't even stop for gloves. I'm not sure if that's flattering, or if I should be worried about contracting hepatitis. Then my eyes fall to the other—other shoe. I knew it would be there. I had to know. Gage never clarified the details for me, but I knew when Brec left me it must be serious. And there it is—the thin piece of metal around his finger that shatters my illusions of happy—of my life lived in color.

Brec sees what I'm staring at and opens his mouth to speak, but I silence him first.

"If I wanted to know, I would have asked."

I haughtily push him away and begin to stand—pulling on a mask of righteous indifference. I gather my keys and purse, which are left lying on the tile directly outside of Gage's room. I stand shakily and look through the wall of windows at my brother—my dying brother—and tap the glass softly with just my right index finger. My breathing slows and matches his. For some reason this makes me smile, like we are still in sync after all these years. I breathe harshly on the glass and accidently create a cloud of fog. On a whim, or out of muscle memory, I draw a heart into the condensation. The tears blur my vision, but I am desperate to finish, "G & S Forever". My world feels like it is falling again—everything tilts wildly to the right—so I brace myself with both hands on the glass, unintentionally smearing my artwork. Brec's hands land on my waist in an assertive, semi-aggressive gesture. It's clear he's only trying to make sure I don't collapse again. And I appreciate the strength, but I still use my hands to remove his from me regardless.

"I promised you answers," he says quietly into the moment. "At this point, you can obviously talk with your parents, but I would like to keep my promise if you'll let me."

For shit's sake. Who is he to talk about keeping promises? I was wrong, my life isn't a Hollywood script—it's a fucking nightmare that I can't wake up from.

"My parents? How do you think that conversation will go down? I'm not interested in their blame, Brec; I want the facts. I want to know how to get Gage out of this mess. Meet me at Posies at 10:00? —Will you be off by then?"

Brec solemnly nods his assent. Then I walk away without looking back.

I have no idea why I chose Posies. Logically, it was the only place I could think of that I knew would still exist after my 15-year hiatus. Logically, I knew I needed coffee and a cranberry scone like I needed my next breath. Logically, I knew it was close and conveniently on his route back to our small home-town. Illogically, it was the place I fell in love with him once long ago.

TWO.

It amazes me how normal my mother can be when you take away her audience. I used to silently wonder why my dad never left her. You know how you see those couples that fit so perfectly together they sort of grossly look like each other? Like somehow time has morphed them into the same being and you sort of wonder if maybe they're married to their second cousin or maybe they're just arrogant narcissists? I guess, now that I really think about it, that's not so much gross as it's kind of weirdly romantic. Well, that's not my parents—at all. During my childhood, my dad became more and more amazing as my mother quickly climbed the charts of awful. It was like they were balancing on some sort of bizarre parental seesaw. To this day, they look nothing alike. But over the years, I've learned if you strip mom of her fake lashes and shellacked hair helmet, she is maybe the most fragile person I've ever met. My dad tried to show me this very fact during most of my misspent youth. He and Gage always treated mom with kitten gloves, which, in turn, made me create my own version of a familial seesaw. The more ridiculously they catered to her, the more I became her daughter of shame.

The hardest part is you never know which version you're going to run into and therefore always have to keep your guard up. I exit my car with a new change of clothes that I have to scrounge through the backseat to find.

When I arrive at the room, I find mom's teakettle on the stove in the dimly lit kitchenette. The kettle has been whistling since I exited the elevator. Two hallways away I could hear her nightly ritual involuntarily keeping everyone on the 3rd floor wide-awake and mildly annoyed. I walk to the stove and turn down her kettle. On autopilot, I pour enough for her small, well-worn "I ♡ Steamboat" mug that she has used every night since I was 11 when we took that disastrous ski trip. I quickly look through the array of teas sitting out and choose a basic earl grey to dip into the cooling water. As I go to set the cup down in front of Mom, she wakes up from her stupor and falls into my arms. Amazingly, I survive the attack with only a small rattle and a bit of spill that I quickly wipe up with the sleeve of my t-shirt. In a completely uncharacteristic move, I return the embrace and nudge my mom's head to my shoulder. For a moment, two tiny women hold each other and borrow whatever strength their bony frames can afford. My mother sniffs in what I presume to be another round of tears; however, she quickly dismantles herself from my arms and prods me through the hotel's hallway toward what appears to be the bathroom.

"For God's sake, Sage. Shower. Now."

And just like that the spell is broken.

I must admit the steam and costly bath products do help ease the tension of today and the knot in my stomach. I turn off all the lights and shower in the dark—my familiar place. I'm not entirely sure I didn't just condition my hair with some sort of lavender body wash, but who am I kidding? My hair was already greasy —now it will be greasy and fragrant which, in my book, is still a step in the right direction.

As I rinse, I start to attack the puzzle of Gage. The last time I saw him was when? —A month ago? No, about six weeks. It was only FaceTime, but surely, I would have noticed how sick he looked if something were really wrong. Wouldn't I? I mean all connections are pretty spotty in the Middle East and the image was rather pixelated, but he had hair then. Right? I'm his fucking sister—how could I miss the signs? Was I listening? What did we even talk about?

"Hey old lady! Did you finally get my now very belated birthday gift?"

"As your much older, much *wiser* sister, you really should approach me with a little more respect, baby brother. And, yes, I got the gift. It's PERFECT. Death Cab on vinyl . . . you know, before they lost their sound."

"Yeah, and the angst that you've always loved so much."

"Ben was better all angsty and high-strung, what can I say? I think adulting made him boring. Face it Gage, he lost his voice. But *this* album—gah, it's my all-time favorite."

"Plans."

"Plans."

We rambled on and on about music—how the new album doesn't even hold a candle to Ben's old stuff. We talked about Father John Misty's tour and traded names of some of our new favorites—The Family Crest [Gage] and The Wild Reeds [me]. Gage and I could talk music for days.

I remember the first time he came to visit me in New York. We spent the entire weekend laying around my shit-hole apartment listening to vinyls and critiquing them in different accents. Every new album received a new nationality of critique. It was silly, alcohol-infused fun. When I dropped him in the cab on the last morning, it suddenly dawned on me that I didn't take my brother to do any of the fun, touristy stuff. We never did Times Square or the Empire State Building. I never took him to the Statue of Liberty, a nice meal or even a freaking party. We ordered in, listened to music and drank. In a rushed apology, I promised to have a much better trip planned for him the next time; I would show him the real New York, but Gage didn't care. He said that this was perfect and couldn't be manufactured to sell on a 25-cent postcard. To this day, I don't think he has ever been to Times Square.

Two weeks later, I took one of our photos from that weekend and turned it into a postcard. On the back of the black and white close up of Gage's wily hair and crooked smile I wrote one sentence.

Keep living in color.

Love, Sage

At the time I thought it was just beautifully ironic. I hadn't really thought a lot about how Gage lived life to the fullest and how he was never afraid to feel it all. —How he truly lived in color every day.

In a flourish, mom prods through the black bathroom and the memories I've become lost in and demands to know where her PM cream is—the blue one—as if that suddenly makes me aware of where she's left her shit. Only then does she realize that the lights are out and kindly illuminates the entire room for me. Thanks, mother.

"Sage, did you hear me? I need the blue cream. The one that says PM."

Dear Lord, if she says that one more time. Yes, I know it's the blue one that says PM. Do I look like the keeper of the cream—

or any sort of self-cleaning supplies for that matter? I make one last pass under the warm water and wrap up in one of the luxurious hotel towels while my mom opens every drawer and tears the bathroom apart. As I step out to greet my mother, she suddenly turns and walks away like I've said or done something foul. I double-check that I didn't actually just say any of my vindictive retort aloud. Nope—all in my head. So, what just happened?

I catch a glimpse of my own bewildered glare in the mirror, and it all suddenly makes sense. Along with my crazy, confused stare, there are obvious tear tracks running down my cheeks. Dammit, I'm crying—again. My mom, though quite the crier herself, can't handle anyone else's emotions. In fact, I don't think I've cried in front of her since the hobbyhorse incident of '92, and even now, I do so completely involuntarily and un-aware. I stare hard into the mirror, looking through my own reflection, until all that's left is my out-of-focus mask of in-difference and every trace of my tears has dried. I dress quickly, finger-comb my hair and borrow someone's toothbrush—put that shit up if you don't want me using it—in order to fully rejoin the world of the living—or at the very least, the world of the clean.

I easily find her beloved blue fucking PM cream on the counter and toss it to her on my way to join Dad in the sitting area where I snatch away his double-malted scotch. He looks admonish-ingly amused but doesn't scold me. I like playing these games with my dad. You can push his buttons endlessly, and he'll barely be bothered. The man has the patience of a saint.

"So, Dad, what are we looking at here?"

He knows what I'm talking about. My dad just always seems to get me. I take a sip of his scotch then pass it back to him. He, in turn, takes a large pull of the amber liquid. I can see his jaw working through exactly what to say next—how much to reveal.

"Sage, it's good you're home. Have I told you that?"

He folds me into a hug, and I fully relax my wet head on the center of my dad's chest. Internally, I create and repeat a mantra: *You will not cry. He will not die. You will not cry. He will not die.* —over and over again. I blow out a deep exhale and burrow further into the couch and my dad's embrace. I attempt to diffuse my building emotions and shakily say, "So that good, huh?"

Dad kisses the top of my head and simply repeats, "It's good you're home." I check the time on my dad's wrist and unfold myself from the moment. It's 9:40. Pulling my hair into a semi-wet bun, I kiss dad's cheek and tell him not to wait up.

"Brec, I assume?" Dad offers with a slight warning to his tone.

"Yep. If he's the answer man, then I will do what I can to find some answers."

"Sage—"

"Yes?"

"Be careful—and do what you can to find some peace. Answers aren't nearly as fulfilling as peace is, dear."

"While that's probably true, peace doesn't equal a solution, Dad—answers do. Let me get my answers now. I can deal with the peace later."

I can see Dad working through what to say next. Over the years, he's had to learn to say less where my mom is concerned; he's spent a lifetime picking his battles very carefully.

"Of course. And Sage—"

I look up at him and silently plead for him not to push this anymore. I'm not sure I can discuss this idea of 'peace' any longer. It sounds and feels too much like closure—like defeat. I need my dad to be on my side. I need to know we are all going to fight whatever the hell is going on—together.

"—you're stunning," he says looking up at me from the scotch in his hand.

With a wobbly smile, I turn on my heel then pick up my bag and keys to leave. Mom calls out from her room for me to grab a key card and to make sure not to wake them when I come back. As I'm searching the entry table for this key card she speaks of, mom appears at the door with the card in hand. Her face has an oddly oily sheen to it—her beloved PM cream, I assume. Though, I can't really knock the stuff too much; it clearly works. My mom is a lot of things—beautiful, undoubtedly, tops that list.

I exit the room and close the door softly. It's colder than I assumed it would be as I enter the chilly night. I have nothing but my yoga pants and a long-sleeved NYU tee to protect me from the dropping temperature. I manually unlock my car—because it's at least as old as my absence from this shitty town—and rifle through the trunk until I find a bag of sweaters. I do my typical smell check to make sure the loose-knit, oversized sweater is clean enough and add it to my ensemble. Before I actually start the car, I smile to myself in some weird misplaced victory. I may not be able to change the fact that in some completely bizzaro turn of chance Brec is the person holding all the cards, and Gage's future, in his hands. But I sure as hell hold control over looking like a homeless, bag lady who couldn't give two fucks that she's about to meet up with her ex-fiancé— also known as her life's biggest mistake.

THREE.

Posies is charmingly placed directly off the interstate and between a local daycare and an outdated pawnshop. The signage from the highway literally reads, "Daycare, Donuts & Guns". Welcome to the south, folks. Welcome to the south. I've always loved how forgotten the place appears. Its worn chairs and curtains don't seem to be any different from when I was here last. I make my way to the counter to order the cranberry scone I have been salivating over for the last several hours, but Antonia, the owner and my long-ago confidant/questionable life coach, gives me a quick hug then ushers me to a small bistro table toward the back. Brec stands up to greet me which only serves to further grate on my raw nerves.

"Always the fucking gentlemen, aren't we?"

"Excuse me?"

"Nothing, Brec. It doesn't matter." I huff.

He clears his throat and waits for me to be seated; however, I can hear him release a pent up, shaky breath. His nervousness fuels my self-righteous anger, and I feel a small kernel of control explode within this hopeless, hellish day.

"I ordered you a cranberry scone and a dirty chai. I hope you don't mind," Brec says quickly and all in one breath.

"Of course, I fucking mind. Did you think I would come back here—to this place—and be the same girl, Brec? Who still drinks dirty chai's anyway?" —Umm . . . *I do* . . . nearly every day.

With an air of faux superiority, I pull my seat away from the table and call for Antonia. Her smile immediately makes me regret my previously bitchy tone.

"Antonia, can I have a small black coffee, please?"

She slowly laughs with large hiccups and wipes a tear from the corner of her eyes before she stops and studies my face. "Oh, you being serious, girl? Sage, since when do you drink anything without copious amounts of sugar?" Antonia banters. *"If there isn't cream or sugar in it then it's not worth fucking drinking."* She throws my old phrase back at me with a perfect impersonation of my former self. Brec laughs cautiously, but I don't have the grace to respond. Every ounce of life I have, every bit of facade I hide behind, every shade of color drains out of me in that instant. With my eyes cast toward my statuesque hands, I quietly reply, "That girl is gone. A black coffee will do." Antonia can sense the despair of the moment and knows enough not to prod. Brec motions as if he is going to reach out to me but thinks better of it and pulls his hands back to rest on the Americano in front of him. How do I know that the non-descript cup is holding an Americano with two raw sugars? Because it's Brec, and Brec is the most predictable human I know . . . I mean, other than the whole cheating on me and breaking off our engagement thing, of course.

"Sage, I don't know where to start. You have to help me a little here." Those dumb eyes plead with me to be reasonable and, unfortunately for me, all my fight is long gone.

I throw him a bone. "Gage. Let's start with Gage. How long has he been in a coma?"

"What? Sage, he's not in a coma. Shit, didn't your parents tell you anything?"

I exasperatedly look at him. Of course, they didn't tell me anything. My family is firmly built on a foundation of half-truths and ignorance. It's like he doesn't know us at all.

"Okay," he says as if he is preparing for a big game. He cracks his neck, and his entire demeanor changes. He somehow, suddenly, becomes taller, brighter, stronger. Brec leans into the table to speak in a conspiratorial tone and begins.

"Gage is under doctor-directed sedation."

I point at him and he nods.

"About three months ago, Gage reached out to me about some cranial scans. He didn't tell me who they were for, but he asked me to look at them and give my professional opinion."

Brec takes a drink and slows down to choose his next words more carefully.

"Sage, they were—bad. The scans showed several aggressive gliomas pressing on both his retinas and lymphoma in his ventricles. Anyone with these scans would not be fully functional; in fact, they would likely not be mobile. The fact that Gage was still employed, driving, being a dad and hiding his symptoms was nothing less than . . . well, the amazing man he is."

I just stare at him while he waits for me to process all of this. If I knew where my phone was, I would get it out and start yelling at Siri to explain this shit to me. I'm positive that I've never heard of a 'glioma' or any other '-oma', but I immediately jump to the only possibility that makes any sense.

"So . . . we're talking cancer? You're a cancer doctor? A, um, what's it called—oncologist?"

"No. Not exactly. I am a neurologist, which makes me more qualified to understand what these tumors are doing not only to his brain but to his body as well. I'm working with a team of oncologists to help offer Gage the best care and knowledge to make decisions for . . . what comes next." Brec trails off into the vagueness of his last sentence. He looks away from me toward the wall and begins to spin the stupid band on his left ring finger as he says, "And yes, Sage, we're talking cancer— aggressive cancer."

The brown world of home suddenly turns a cloudy red.

"So, you've known for three months! THREE FUCKING MONTHS, BREC? How could you? You bastard. You spine-less—"

"YES." He shouts back at me but quickly calms himself down. "And Gage has likely known something was seriously wrong for over a year. These tumors come with extreme symptoms. Maybe, at first, he could have chalked it up to his multiple sclerosis, but the seizures and rapid deterioration of memory, sight and brain function . . . he hid it from you, from all of us, for a reason, Sage."

You would think that a person as small as I am would run out tears. I realize our bodies are something like 60% water, but I assume most of that goes to our more vital organs—not a direct path to our tear ducts. Yet here I am, crying, in front of the one person I promised I'd never allow to see me broken again. Brec stands and bends down to me. He wipes my tears, and I stub-bornly jerk away from him. He uses his strength and the wall at my back to pin me down and engulf me in him. My breathing becomes erratic and there is suddenly not enough oxygen in the world. I'm gasping—pulling at Brec and pushing him away like somehow this movement will inflate my deprived lungs. Panic—pure panic. Everything becomes hazy again and . . .

"NO," I speak ruggedly at the growing darkness. "I'm. Strong. Er. Than. *This*." I fight for each syllable.

I audibly count to ten on my own in slow wobbly sounds. My vision is less cloudy and there is no longer a deafening roar in my ears. The picture in front of me comes back to focus, and I see Brec—standing too close—looking straight into my eyes.

"Yes, you are stronger than this." He agrees then adds one single nod before standing and affording me some personal space.

I reach out a shaky hand for the small black coffee in front of me that has considerably cooled off and choke on the shocking bitterness. I think about recovering and returning for another sip to save face but decide that today has been hard enough as it is, and I'm not drinking one more drop of this shitty excuse for coffee.

"Brec—" I say with my eyes darting away toward the wall to my right.

"Yes, Sage?" he replies, unable to hide his amusement.

"Get me a dirty chai—*please*."

"Of course."

"And don't be so goddamn amused by it," I call out to him as he begins walking away.

"Anything else, dear?" Brec intones in a loud, insipid voice.

"—Yes. Get me the fucking cranberry scone."

He turns to me and winks. The asshole winks at me and shrugs his shoulders.

"You can't break old habits, babe. It's good to see you back."

CHAPTER Three

Over the next few hours, Brec walks me through Gage's prognosis, which isn't exactly as hopeless as I thought. By all means, the outlook isn't good, but clinical trials and experimental drugs are still providing optimism to the bleak diagnosis. Gage is a fighter, and I think we are all banking on that. Brec continues to explain that the sedation is largely due to the amount of pain Gage is experiencing regarding the placement of the gliomas. Gliomas are apparently angry little sons-of-bitches that play on the nerve endings and sort of short-circuit the brain. Add that to my brother's pre-existing multiple sclerosis, and his pain is nearly unbearable. To get him through the aftershocks of chemo they decided to apply a doctor-directed and monitored sedation period. They plan on bringing Gage back to consciousness tomorrow morning.

The options to proceed seem endless, but Brec informs me that Gage and his wife, Olivia, have some strong opinions on which paths they are open to and which they are not. I may be bossy, and I may be older, but I realize, as Brec lays out the many possible avenues, that this isn't my decision to make or my path to control. My job here in the coming weeks and months is to trust my brother.

The conversation naturally segues into talk of my nieces. Clearly, Brec has spent a substantial amount of time with the girls. He drags his wiry little chair over to my side of the table and uses his phone to show me photo after photo of vacations and outings with my family. I have Skyped with Anna and Emery, but I don't really *know* them. It makes me laugh and breaks my heart at the same time to hear all these stories that I'm not a part of. Apparently, Emery is a spitfire and is often referred to as Sage II. I have to admit, I am strangely proud of this even though I clearly didn't directly influence any of it. Anna sounds just like her mother. She is most definitely the spitting image of Olivia and seems to be created from some sort of Disney animation storyboard complete with singing birds and all. Poor Emery, I know what her road holds. It's hard to be the less-than-perfect child living in the shadow of the praised sibling. Then again, most of the time, it's also a lot more fun too.

I notice that most of the photos Brec flips through seem to be destination shots. The girls getting piggyback rides at the beach [where Brec "accidently" zooms in on his abs], or everyone bundled in snowsuits ready to ride down the bunny slopes [where Brec purposely uses his thumb to cover the image of the person in the right part of the frame]. In fact, out of the entire album, not a single shot is taken from a location I can recognize. As we pause for refills, Brec sees my confusion and answers my silent question.

"Sage, I don't actually live here, you know. I stayed in California after college; I'm in Santa Cruz now. Gage and I get together a few times a year with the family for vacation," he says gently.

"Wow. So, you just went ahead and became his brother anyway? Nice. Remind me to beat Gage's ass just as soon as he reenters the world of the living. In fact, remind me to beat yours too just as soon as you save my brother. —Because I'm counting on it, you know?" I gulp in a lungful of air before continuing. "You have to save him, Brec."

My desperate plea enters us back into reality and breaks the truce we had somehow temporarily forged.

It's late. It's really late, and I haven't actually slept in about 36 hours. I stand and clear the table, signaling that I'm done for the night. I may have a few dirty chais running through my system, but I know the moment I find a place to lay my head, I will openly welcome the reprieve. I give Antonia a real hug this time and promise to stop by later in the week just to catch up. She wiggles her eyebrows at me when Brec turns to open the door, and I shake my head at her never-ending matchmaking.

> Nearly 20 years ago, a still very young girl went on her very first date with a scandalously older, and out of her league, high school senior. He offered to let her choose the location, and she confidently chose Posies, the least romantic or pretentious place she could think of. She ordered a dirty chai and a cranberry scone but couldn't eat or drink a thing in fear that she would literally vomit all over the table. She excused herself, went to the restroom and completely fell apart. In the middle of her panicked mania, it occurred to her she had actually walked into the kitchen instead of the ladies' room. Enter Antonia. She found the girl among some dirty dishes and told the girl to pick her head up and own the night. She waggled those same eyebrows and advised the young girl to enjoy a boy that cute, fawning all over her because you never know where things might go.

I shake my head firmly at her again in utter sincerity. That boy's charm no longer holds any power over me, and Antonia's wiggling brows cannot encourage me to forgive the past. With that, I turn and walk through the open door heading toward my car. As soon as Brec sees my slightly vintage vehicle he softly chuckles.

On his way across the parking lot, his voice cuts into the darkness. "God, Sage. Don't ever change. I want this version of you forever."

"Go home, Brec." I yell into the night somewhere near his direction.

"Right behind ya, babe. We're staying in the same hotel."

I stop in my tracks but don't fully turn around. "Seriously? Fuck me. —And stop calling me babe. It's weird and wrong, and I'll punch you if you try it again."

Brec tries desperately to cover his humor, but his eyes gleaming in the streetlight above give him away.

"What, Brec? What's so damn funny this time?"

I see his humor change and turn into internal struggle. I truly feel like I might have missed something. It sure as hell wouldn't be the first time, but I'm afraid that I'm suddenly out of my depths and desperately need to catch up. Brec slowly stalks toward me as I fumble with my keys. I look down and search the moment for clues. His shoes are directly in front of me, but I can't look up. The silence is creepy, and it's totally unlike me not to break the awkward tension with some sort of inappropriate quip. Brec doesn't touch me or force me to look up, but he leans one hand onto my car and turns to my right ear to say, "Sage, the next time you tell me to fuck you, you better mean it. I don't do well with taunts, and I've never backed down from a dare. Just so you know, I'm looking for an excuse to touch you, so choose those words wisely, *babe*." He taps the hood of the car with his long index finger on the last word just to add a little emphasis and to remind me that he will always have the upper hand where my heart is concerned.

The weather is unnaturally cold for this time of year, so I blame the blatant shiver that runs through me on my lack of appropriate winter wear. I hate myself for reacting. I hate myself for letting him get a foot in the door. And I hate myself for the small blossom of hope that was just born inside my broken chest.

Without another word, he turns and walks away while I release my pent-up breath. I need time to re-center myself and find the hate that, just earlier today, burned brightly inside of me. I get in my car, lay my head against the wheel and know one thing for certain; I am absolutely not going back to that fucking hotel.

Without a place to go, I sit in my car in the silence—and the dark. I don't really want to stay in the Posies parking lot all night. I can't go back to the hotel. —Knowing my luck, Brec would have the suite next door to my parents. I don't want to drive all the way back to my childhood home when I'm this exhausted. So, I sit—and process the shit storm of my day.

I definitely wasn't ready for the reality of Gage's diagnosis, but in a mere 12 hours I went from all hope lost to regaining a careful modicum of optimism. I was blindsided by the rest of it, and I seriously wasn't ready for Brec to be added in the mix. But really, I have to let that go. It's long over and regardless of his boyish flirting and empty threats, I know the chapters to our story were written and finished years ago. I remind myself he's the best solution to Gage's survival. Gage comes first now. I vow, right at this moment, to stuff my feelings—hope or hate— as far down as I possibly can. I find my phone, scroll through my iTunes library until I find some background music to fit the mood: Frightened Rabbit - *Painting of a Panic Attack*. It seems to sum up my day pretty well. I settle in, amp up my car's pathetic excuse for a heater and open a new browser tab. In the spirit of moving on, I break my 14-year diet, type in 'Brec Aldridge' and feast upon years of missing knowledge.

Brec is four years older than me; he was a senior when I was a freshman. He was, maybe he still is, the epitome of elite—born a doctor's son in a long line of medical professionals. Somehow my class schedule got screwed up and no one noticed, least of all me. I was placed in a photography 4 class with a bunch of upperclassmen. On the first day of school, it was made pretty clear that I was not welcomed or invited into this seemingly blow off class. I've always looked young for my age, which was made much more distinct by my small frame. The first semester was filled with unimaginative and endless taunting, but I was either able to hold my own or ignore the idiocy well enough. The teacher and I got along really well. He was a young hipster that hadn't quite acclimated to the south, and I was a girl who never felt like she belonged here and who was willing to learn a lot. I fell in love with photography, maybe in part because it was an escape from the assholes I had to spend an hour-and-a-half with every other day. The spring semester arrived and with it a natural transition of students. Enter Brec Aldridge. Honestly, I didn't think much of him at first. I lived among the peons and stayed away from the gossip, so I didn't have a clue who this very tall, slightly imposing and clearly charming new guy was. I felt him watching me though, day after day. I think he was impressed that I was the only kid in there that gave a shit about photography and worked my butt off in class. I think he was impressed with how unimpressed I was by him. He followed me into the darkroom for weeks where I would work in silence, completely ignoring him. As far as I knew, he was never developing photos; I think he was looking for a time out from being . . . well, him. I remember the first day he spoke to me in that darkroom. I was angry about overexposing a shot in the stop bath and ripped up the photo in a moment of heated frustration. He picked up the pieces, tried to lay them back together in a reasonable order and then he spoke.

"So, what's the story?"

"I fucked up. That's the story."

He softly chuckled and ran a hand through his hair. I had surprised him, and I found that I liked surprising him.

"No, I mean, what's your story."

I paused and looked into his eyes for the first time. Without any hint of irony, and in a very rare moment of complete honesty, I replied, "I'm fucked up. That's my story."

If I surprised him earlier, this comment must have come as a shock, but he didn't brush off my truth. Instead, he offered up some of his own. "That sounds a lot like my story. Maybe we should hang out sometime."

Dead silence.

"Or not."

Dead silence.

"Okay. I give up. Look, here's my number." He stopped to scrawl a phone number on the back of one of the corner pieces of the shredded photo. "Call me, Sage. I think we were maybe meant to be friends—at least something more than one random conversation in a darkroom."

He walked out, opened the door and another photo was ruined that day. That was the first picture I ever framed. It was horribly overexposed and completely perfect.

As he told me, Brec appears to be a neurologist in Santa Cruz, California. The town looks cookie-cutter and elite—basically everything Brec was raised to become. He finished his undergrad at Stanford, which I knew. He then went on to med school at the Stanford School of Medicine, which I didn't know. It makes sense seeing as he broke our young love and childhood promises for a different freshman during his senior year of college. He must have stayed around until she graduated where—yep, they married in 2012. He would have been 30. He waited eight years to marry her. Well, I guess he learned his lesson about rushed engagements and hurried love the first time around. He finished his residency at Stanford Children's Health/Lucile Packard Children's hospital Stanford— Pediatric Neurology where he was on a clinical trial team for ADEM or, essentially, early onset MS. *Of course, he's spent his career trying to cure multiple sclerosis. Well, shit.* Then he moved to Santa Cruz, in a seemingly poor career move, for his fellowship at Dominican Hospital - Santa Cruz. From what I can tell the hospital isn't at all prestigious nor does it even have great reviews. It isn't a specialty hospital, yet that's where he's stayed for the last four years. Something doesn't add up. There has to be a missing link. The photos from hospital benefits feature both of them—the bright-eyed boy and the girl he left me for, but he looks strangled; he looks like the boy in desperate need of a darkroom to hide out in. The hospital has him listed as "currently on leave of absence." I guess this makes sense since he's been here with Gage for who knows how long—but 'leave of absence' sounds like some sort of suspension rather than a sabbatical. And where is Amelia in all of this? That's her name. Amelia Anderson . . . or Aldridge, I suppose. Even her name is so much more sophisticated than mine. She looks like an Amelia—always coiffed. She's tall and leggy, blonde and has vibrant, blue eyes. She was California and I was New York. You just can't compete with something that's not inside you, and I could never be California with all of its sunny brightness. I was darkness and edges, and after she shattered my world, I became black.

It's maybe 3:00 am here. So even though I'm at my familiar Posies, I'm still on alert. I'm startled out of memory lane when a motion catches the corner of my vision. A lone, large man, maybe a trucker—I assume based on my quick perusal of the only other vehicle in the parking lot—enters the 24-hour coffee shop. I already have my hand to the door handle ready to move into action if needed, but I'm quickly rewarded with an altogether different sight. Antonia leaps at the man with full force. He catches her and embraces her gently with strong arms. It's clear that I am witnessing a reunion of some sort. On autopilot, I reach into the backseat and my fingers find my camera, not even placed back in its case. I try to frame the shot through my windshield, but quickly realize the angles are all wrong. I step out into the frigid night and head toward the edge of the darkened parking lot. Posies is the only thing lit up at this time, and the dingy curtain-covered glass windows help frame the moment. There, Antonia and this man I've never seen stand directly in front of the glassed entryway, perfectly centered. I narrow the lens, so the brightness will consume just them. I snap a few frames, but I know the first one is the best. The way her body completely relaxes against his—the way he closes his eyes so tightly. I don't know exactly who this man is to Antonia, and I can't recall her ever telling me about a husband—or lover—or brother. I'm not sure about the exact kind of love they share, but it's obvious, that's exactly what this is. Love. The photo may just look like a dusty, old diner, but if you look closely, you'll be rewarded by the details. These are my favorite photos—the ones that trick you.

I sit on the curb and wrap myself into my loose-knit sweater. This is the perfect moment captured at the perfect time and the perfect place. This is what Posies is to me—It's comfort. It's love.

Suddenly, I'm exhausted. The sort of tired you become when life totally spins you upside down. I head back to my car and lock the doors—manually, of course. I pull something soft out of my backseat, roll it into a loose ball and fit it under my head. My car, though now off, stays relatively warm from my heater earlier. I look one last time at Antonia and this man who are now drinking coffee and having an animated conversation. It seems like they will be there for a while catching up; I'm safe. I close my eyes and fall asleep outside in the parking lot of my favorite place in the world.

Home.

I wake up with a start, completely confused about where I am. In the last three days, I have been in and out of four airports, flying over most of Europe and some international waters. When I opened my eyes, I half expected to be back in the plane with its filtered, frigid air, but instead, I witness a much bleaker sight— my fucking beat up excuse for a car. With the realization of where I am, comes the last 12 hours—the knowledge of Gage and the reunion with Brec. The pain of it makes me physically wince, which is when I realize, son-of-a-bitch, my neck hurts. I have slept in a lot of very odd, really unsafe places, but I don't think I've ever hurt this badly—I'm getting fucking old. I must have slept hard. Minus the hunchback and my inability to raise my left arm past my waist, I feel surprisingly refreshed. I head back into Posies for another dirty chai and cranberry scone.

Antonia looks to be wrapping up her shift and eyes me cautiously.

"Well good morning to you. Sage, your momma would be horrified if she knew you were living out of your car."

"Good thing she doesn't have to know about it. I couldn't go back to the hotel and the house was simply too far away. My car was warm, and I think Posies is as close as it comes to what I'd call a home here anyway."

She begins to heat the milk for my chai and suggests I do something with my appearance in the meantime. I scrounge through my car for a toiletry case and do my best to clean up in the ladies' room. I awkwardly try to wash my face and brush my teeth in my disabled state then let my hair down and brush it. It's obvious there is no saving my slept on hair, so I tie my long locks back into bun and smooth it down with a little water from the sink. I find some off-brand, foreign deodorant among my things, apply it and call it a day.

As I exit the restroom, Antonia peruses my outfit and laughs.

"Sage, it looks like you just had a very sloppy one-night stand."

"I did, Antonia—with my car." I say completely monotone and unamused.

I grab the chai and inhale the cinnamon smell before I begin drinking. Antonia cleans the already spotless counters and waits me out.

"So, hotel did you say?"

"Yep, it's where my parents are staying—and, fun fact, Brec's there as well. Thus . . . " I trail off and point out the window to my rundown Altima.

"I see."

That's Antonia for you. She makes you crazy. She doesn't ask questions and rarely gives advice. She just waits you out until you spill your guts to her. This is why she was my unproclaimed life coach for so many years. I finish my entire breakfast before we speak again. I'm looking at the shiny, stainless-steel appliances and wondering how hard it would be to operate these semi-complicated looking machines when she breaks the silence.

"I'm sorry about Gage. He's the best of all of you, you know."

I didn't expect our conversation to take this turn, but it does put everything rightfully back into perspective—which may have been her intention all along.

"That he is, Antonia. And, if I have anything to say about it, he'll continue to be. Don't count him out. He's got a strong-willed, pain-in-the-ass sister to contend with in case he feels like calling it quits." I find I can talk about him today without crying and view this as an improvement.

I open my wallet to pay the bill, but she pushes the gesture away. I must owe this lady a couple grand, at least, because I cannot for the life of me remember one solitary time I've actually paid for my food or drinks here. I'm gathering my layers and toiletries when Antonia suddenly slams me with her vague, cryptic wisdom.

"Give him my love and a big hug."

I assume she means Gage, but her next comment completely confuses me.

"And don't forget, Sage, you don't give up on the ones you love."

"Yeah, I know," I say bewilderedly. "That's literally what I just said."

"Hmm . . . is it?"

Yes, it is, weird Italian Yoda lady, I think to myself, but by the time I'm buckled into my car and pulling back on to the highway toward the hospital, I get what she means. —Damn her and her never-ending matchmaking.

CHAPTER Four

I head straight for the hospital because, really, everything I need is already in my car. When I arrive, there is an arsenal of people in the waiting room. My mom takes one look at my appearance and sniffs. [This means I have once again secured the title, "Daughter of Shame".] My dad also seems concerned about my appearance but simply raises one eyebrow at me in question. I'm not sure if the question is, "Where did you sleep last night, oh daughter of mine?" or something more along the lines of, "Did you sleep with *him* last night, Sage? —Because, you know, he's married now." I try to tamp down my father's fears with a solitary shake of my head from left to right [which still hurts like a bitch]. The girls are there with Olivia. I make my way across the small room to them when Brec appears, looking every inch of the professional he is. His eyes immediately fall to me in my rerun outfit, and he sucks in a breath with a slight roll of his eyes. I realize now what this must look like to everyone. We publicly, in front of the nurses and medical staff—not to mention my parents—made plans to meet late last night, and then I return the next day obviously wearing some slept in looking pajamas. This doesn't look good for him. I make a mental note to apologize later and do a better job at . . . you know, being clean and stuff.

I close in on the girls, and they both sort of shimmy behind their mother. We speak—maybe not regularly—and I see them on at least one holiday a year, but in this weird space, where they are already so scared, I am little more than a stranger. Olivia leads by example and leans forward to hug me tightly. If it takes three miracles to make someone a saint, she became a saint decades ago. She's been in and out of hospitals with Gage and the girls for years and has never once faltered. Even now, she looks polished and ready for the day—come what may. In short, she's my mother's dream daughter. She's as beautiful as it gets and can somehow shoulder everyone's needs and emotions without ever cracking. Cynic that I am, I can't even mock her perfection because I'm just so glad Gage has her to rely on. I'm so thankful people like her exist in this world—even if their existence threatens my every insecurity. On my knees, I press a side hug into each of the girls and kiss the tops of their heads. They rigidly accept my affection but quickly return back to their mother's side. Taking in the moment, I realize this isn't something I ever want a picture of—my own life. It's so obvious among the family strung around the room that I am the outsider. Even Brec is a stronger part of the group than I am, and he lives in California. I inhale my guilt, truly feeling how ashamed and angry I am at myself. In all my 'living', I cut them out of my life somewhere along the way.

While we wait out whatever protocol the doctors are running through before they can take Gage out of sedation, I jump into a conversation with Olivia and my mom about the girls.

"Well, we have to be careful about how many days they miss. You would think they wouldn't have such strict rules for pre-K and 2nd grade, but apparently the world falls apart if the girls miss twice in one week."

"Olivia, homeschool or private tutoring could be an excellent option—you know, for the time being. Don't worry, we can help cover the expense if needed," my mother magnanimously offers while patting Olivia's knee.

I chew on my lip, formulating a plan. "You know, I could take them. Photography is mostly spec work, and I'll have most of my days free while I'm here."

I can tell everyone is stunned by my offer, and Olivia is looking for a way to politely decline me having free reign over her children every day. My mouth trembles as I realize I'm not even worthy to help out; I'm not trusted. In a last attempt, I lower my voice and look directly to Olivia.

"Please, let me do this. Let me get to know them. Let me help. I need to do this—for him."

I didn't realize Brec was still there with us, apparently this isn't his part of the horse and pony show, and he's waiting just like the rest of us. He nudges Olivia in a playful manner to lighten the mood.

"Come on, what would it hurt? Sage is like a walking cartoon character. The girls would love her if they got to spend some more time with her."

I'm already raw from the moment and being compared to someone like Cathy from the Sunday comics—by the man I once loved—does very little to boost my morale, but Olivia turns to me and hopefully asks if I'm qualified.

"Like a certified teacher? Hel—ck no. But I'm positive I can keep them alive and teach them something way cooler than they would learn in regular, boring school. It's just temporary." I can see that I'm losing her, so I add, "I can write up some curriculum, or whatever they call it, and run it by you beforehand if that makes this easier."

And just like that, I have talked myself into a job. The girls eye me suspiciously from their chairs, and I smile broadly at them like I just fucking won an award.

Gage is awake about an hour later without much fanfare or drama—which does instill a little hope that these jackasses know what they're doing. They will still only allow one person in the room at a time and insist on keeping him in ICU for the time being—which seems a little suspicious and like, perhaps, Brec was painting me a rosier picture than the one that's actually in front of me.

Olivia is the first through the door. We can all see into the window-paned room, and I lose a little confidence as I see Gage fight for a smile. It's apparent that he's in severe pain, but he also looks completely *unlike* my brother. He may be conscious again, but the life is drained out of him. Olivia is all smiles and nurturing sounds for the first several minutes. Then I see her take out a notebook and pen and get down to business. She's now speaking in a hushed tone that none of us can hear, and out of respect, most of us look away and begin picking up our own side conversations to pass the time. I sit on the floor with Emery who has managed to cover nearly every surface in the waiting room with her drawings. At four years old, her coloring skills leave a lot to be desired, but as she holds out the crumpled page in front of her and states that this is for her daddy, the scribbled mess turns into art. Love can do that, you know, turn a mess into art. I try my best to flatten out the many folds and rips along the page then turn to head toward the nurses' station. I kindly ask for a piece of tape, which the nurse begrudgingly hands over as she eyeballs me. [Apparently, she's heard the rumors about Doctor Aldridge and me.] I place the tape at the top of Emery's work of art and hand it back to her.

"Aunt Savge. What do I do wivf dis now?"

"Come here, princess."

I lift her to the window where she can peek into her daddy's room. She waves wildly at him and hits me in the face. Twice. She then roughly pats my noggin and states, "Awll bedder." As if we were the same person, she suddenly reads my mind and lights up then takes the somewhat less crumpled page and tapes it to the window. In case everyone didn't already understand, she yells through the ICU hall while animatedly pointing to the hanging artwork, "Dis for you, daddy. It make you good agaiwn." She pelts me once more in the head, this time pretty good, but doesn't even notice because her daddy, Gage, is looking right at her with the fiercest smile. He mouths to her, or to us both, "You're stunning." Tears pool in my eyes, and I blink rapidly as I try to get myself together. Of course, because I'm already weak and vulnerable, Brec takes this time to pop up and lean into my ear.

"See, I told you." He smirks.

"What? He wasn't in a coma? Yes, I can see that now dumb a—butt." I correct myself with a wince and look at the precious little girl blowing kisses to her daddy while still in my arms.

"No, mouthy—I told you she's your mini. I've thought a lot about what your kids would be like, but Emery here doesn't leave much to the imagination. She's all sass and fearlessness, and she loves with more loyalty than anyone deserves."

Right now, I'm done with these games. "Why are you here, Brec? Are you just trying to get on my nerves?"

Brec dons his flirtiest smile then swiftly wipes it away and changes gears. "I'm here to save my best friend."

Okay, I'm a bitch again, and I lose whatever battle we are fighting here. I release Emery, who runs to her mom as she exits the room, then I turn back to the waiting area. Brec grabs my elbow and runs his hand down my thin arm until he reaches my fingers—effectively stopping me. "And, Sage—I'm here to make it up to you."

"Make what up? Being a cheating douchebag?"

"No, Sage—letting you down when it counts. I'm trying to make sure life doesn't break you apart again."

I jerk my wrist free from his loose grasp and whisper with as much vitriol as I can muster, "Life didn't break me, Brec. You did. Stop rewriting history."

The line for Gage's attention is a long one, so I use the time to pop downstairs to regain some balance and find a freaking snack.

Late in the afternoon, after Gage has napped and the girls have gone home, I head back up to the ICU floor and knock on the outside of room 4. I can see the despair on his face in the moment before he tries to hide his fear behind his signature smile. *Gage—the best of all us.*

He waves me in, but then cradles his head in his hands and explains that he feels like his skull is about to break apart. For most of our conversation, Gage keeps his eyes tightly shut and makes small involuntary, moans. In truth, this totally freaks me out, but it also energizes our bond. Maybe it's that I am the last visitor of the day, or maybe we have a different sort of truth between us—he can show me the pain that he wouldn't let the others see. Either way, I take it as an opening.

"Serious talk?"

"Sure, serious talk."

"How bad is it?"

"The pain?" He asks while opening just one eye.

"Sure, the pain. Let's start there."

"Today, right now, it's bad. It's the kind of pain I would die before I let my girls experience."

"Gage?"

"Yes?"

"That's a *really* shitty choice of words."

He tries to laugh but ends up in a fetal position and self-administering another round of morphine.

"Ready for part II?"

"Have at it, sister."

"How bad is it?"

Silence.

"I don't want Brec's sugar-coated truth, and I don't want mom and dad's blame game. And God, I love Olivia, but I don't want her optimistic song and dance either. Gage, I'm asking you—how bad is it?"

"Okay, truth? I'm running out of options. This is my second clinical trial in under six months, but the tumors are bad. Brec won't confirm it, but I think they're spreading and duplicating—quickly. It's not common for someone with MS to get these sort of neurological tumors, and it seems like the medical cocktail for curing one sends the other spiraling out of control."

I can't tell if the words themselves hurt him or if three sentences are simply more talking than he can do. He is suddenly short of breath and white-knuckling the railing of his bed on either side.

I continue on in a much gentler tone. "Is surgery an option? Why not cut the shit out rather than radiate it to death?"

"So Brec really is sugar-coating it for you? Surgery isn't a viable option at this point." Gage has to take several short, ragged breaths before continuing. "It's a shot in dark—I guess it's all a shot in the dark—and in my current condition it's not expected that I would," breathe, "survive."

My tears make a comeback. As I clear my throat, I desperately try to control the wobbling in my voice.

"Okay." Nope. Try again. Inhale. Exhale. Inhale. Speak. "So, we need to come up with a cocktail of drugs that blasts those fuckers away while keeping your MS under control and the symptoms at bay?" I pause and think to myself for a moment —putting every hope and ounce of brain energy into a solution—any solution. "You know Brec worked on a clinical trial for curing early onset MS? Have you talked to him about his research? Maybe we can completely get rid of the MS then focus on the cancer."

"What, did you guys have a reunion or something? Of course, I know about his clinical trial." He finally opens both eyes and looks directly at me. "Why do you think I brought him out here?"

I try so hard to keep the anger out of my voice, but the words come out as an accusation regardless. "Because, apparently, he's your *best friend*, Gage."

"Shit—You know? God, I never meant for you to find out like this. I always swore that we would have a heart-to-heart about it. I thought that one day you two would figure it out, and, you know, the years in between wouldn't really be that big of a deal."

Silence.

"I'm sorry, Sage. Really. But he's . . . he's been here through it all." Which, of course, implies that I have not.

How do I argue with that? Basically, I deserve this because I've been a shitty sister. In fact, I was the last person Gage told about his diagnosis. Hell, he didn't actually even tell me—Mom called. A small voice from somewhere inside me tells me to shut up and get over it. This isn't about me, and this is my chance to be here—to regain some of the ground I've lost.

"Well, you're right about one thing—that shit isn't really a big deal in the grand scheme of things. And, I get it—I'm *sort of* hard to reason with. I wouldn't have wanted to be the one to tell me you'd become best friends with my asshole ex-fiancé behind my back either."

He laughs again, a little less painfully, and with that the Brec conversation is closed.

"Did you bring your gift with you?"

"The album? —Of course I did. My entire life is in the backseat of my car."

"Sage, please tell me you aren't living out of your car."

"No, baby brother, I'm not living in my car."

"What's your current address?"

Silence.

"Seriously? You don't even have an address, Sage?

"I mean . . . I'm between places. Give me a break—I was out of the country for months, Gage. It's not like most people keep paying rent when they are living off-the-grid in nowhere Europe."

"So where did you sleep last night?"

I guffaw at the loaded question. "Not fair. You've talked to Mom and Dad."

"Nope. But I've heard these nurses talking and there sure are some suggestions as to where you, uh, 'laid your head' last night." He waggles his nearly hairless brows at me suggestively.

"I slept in my car, asshole. Are you happy now? —Oh my God. I'm sorry. You're not an asshole. I'm just embarrassed that everyone thinks Brec is cheating—and with me at that. It's a weird position to be in, you know. The whole thing has me on edge." I say all quick and breathy.

"Yes."

"Wait, I'm lost. Yes, what? It's weird? I know—"

"Yes, I'm happy now. I'm happy because this story—you two—aren't over."

"NO!" I shout. "Not you too. You and Antonia should make a club or something. Gage, I seriously don't want to talk about Brec. It's an off-limits cover—"

"Last comment, so listen up, sis."

"What?" I grumble. "Now you're giving *me* a headache." I say mostly under my breath.

"He and Amelia split. It's not my place to tell you why, but that is a question you need to ask him when you're ready."

I am completely mute which, pretty much, never happens. He's still wearing a ring. Surely this must be a new separation we're talking about here, not a divorce. I literally have zero response. Nothing to say. Gage enjoys his upper hand for a minute longer before a nurse, clearly one who's heard the gossip, comes in to check his vitals and such. I know my time is up, and Gage likely needs his rest. I debate whether to hug him [I may crush him] or kiss him [which we never do], so instead, I go in for a weird handshake that feels totally lame, and at the last minute, I decide to add a kiss to the outside of his hand. I'm one second away from fucking curtseying at my little brother. God, I'm so weird. Gage laughs it all off good-naturedly and reminds me again to check out the gift.

"I didn't get you a present to let it rot in your car like the rest of your shit."

"I love you too, brother. Get some rest."

And then I leave him.

Downstairs, I find Olivia nursing a cup of tea and pouring over some documents. I can see the complete defeat in her eyes; apparently, she knows the version of the truth that Gage just shared with me. I take a seat next to her and pull out my MacBook from my cross-body bag and begin working. We sit in complete silence for almost two hours then she packs everything back up into an accordion style case and looks directly forward at . . . nothing. I watch her movement, but I don't know what to say and hope my presence here is enough.

"Sage—" she asks without looking toward me or even really acknowledging that she's speaking to me.

"Yeah?"

"Where did your name come from?"

Okay, today, it seems, is the day for weird, non sequitur conversations. I go back through the file of my memories and try to pull up the one that holds the answers to her question.

"Honestly, I don't know the full story. My mom had always wanted a daughter named Prudence. When she and my dad became pregnant with me and realized I was going to be a girl, my mother was overjoyed. Their first real fight is said to be over my name. Look at me, stirring up trouble since I was a fetus—I guess, my dad refused to give his kid a name that could be shortened to 'prude'."

She laughs at the irony.

"I know, right? I sometimes think that if my mom had named me Prudence, I would have ended up a lot more like her. Anyway, Mom explained to Dad that she wanted these noble names for her kids. She loved the idea of naming her kids after these really lofty attributes or whatever. Then my dad offered up Sage. I don't think Mom ever really liked it, but she's of the era and mindset that your husband has the last say."

"Huh. So, what your mom really wanted to name you was wisdom?" Olivia quietly voices.

"Yep. Though, I haven't really lived up to it. Then again, I sure as hell wouldn't have lived up to Prudence either."

I quickly get lost in the thought of what a 22-year-old, pregnant version of my mother would have been like. I bet she was one of those perfect pregnant women. I bet she was beautiful.

"And Gage? What deeper meaning does his name hold?" Olivia asks, still clearly trying to mull over something bigger.

"I think it means pledge or something like that. In truth, my mom won't ever admit it, but I'm pretty sure she just loved how cute the names sounded together. Nothing could be more perfect that having kids with rhyming names, right? —In actuality, it was a pain-in-the-ass. Half of the time we never knew who was yelling for whom. It was a mess. I also think the whole 'name them after these idealistic character traits' thing worked out so poorly with me that mom gave up the fight. Sorry about that—my wild child tendencies scared my mom out of deep, meaningful child names. I was a jinx."

The frown line between Olivia's eyes deepens and she focuses harder on the same sport directly in front of her—never wavering. I bite the bullet and reach out to grab her hand and hold it firmly.

"But you know what Gage will always mean to me? Gage means warrior and protector. He is strength. Olivia, he's spent a lifetime preparing for this—to survive this."

She looks at me for the first time and big, round tears spill from her eyes. I know I should be thinking something big and profound to say—some wisdom to lend, but all I can think is that she is the world's prettiest crier. —Yep, my name is totally lost on me.

I let her cry until she's ready to move on. I don't offer up anything else to say. I just sit there, hand in hand with her, thinking about how much her life is changing—how she's balancing on a precipice. It turns out no one is strong all of the time.

When she calms down, I offer to show her what I've been working on while we've been sitting there. I open my MacBook back up and show her a rough outline of a monthly calendar. It turns out it's pretty easy to look up kid's curriculum with a simple Google search. I found something called 'Five in a Row' that seems like it would have been right up my alley when I was younger. I've also work in weekly "field trips" to help get the girls out of the house. I've even order a couple point and shoot cameras for all of us, so we can document our homeschool experience—and I can teach these nieces of mine a little something about what I do for a living.

As I'm excitedly sharing my ideas, Olivia picks up my laptop and scrolls through what I have laid out. I'm nervous she'll fire me before we even really get started, but instead she starts making notes in the comment section and tagging boxes of events where she wants to join the girls and me. She adds her last few notes and details to the spreadsheet then shares the document with Gage. I promise myself to make a daily photo diary for both Gage and Olivia . . . and myself—to mark this experience. Maybe, now, it's my turn to make some color.

Olivia pulls out some neatly stacked papers from one of the many accordion tabs and lays out her plans to bring the girls to the city full time. Things are only getting more complicated with Gage's health, and she needs to have better proximity and access to the hospital. She called the hotel earlier today, reserved a suite a few floors above my parents and already let the school know she would be withdrawing the girls indefinitely. We make a plan to head to the house tonight and begin packing up the girls' things. I will stay the night and officially file the paperwork to remove Anna and Emery from their current educational institutes—otherwise known as the very subpar district

Gage and I were both products of. Then, I'll drive our things to the city and get everyone set up in the suite. I will officially begin my "teaching duties" next week after the girls have had some time to acclimate. This plan saves me from heading back to the hotel tonight, and I'm a little excited to be helping out with the girls full time. The suite only has two rooms, but it has a lounge area I decide I can convert into our "class-room". I silently wonder where I will fit in this very odd family compound situation we have set up at the Residence Inn. I'm sure my mother will perceive it as a slight if I choose not to take their spare bed-room; however, I am positive it's best for everyone if we keep some distance from each other. Olivia and the girls don't have extra space, and Brec is obviously not an option—at all. I decide to pull up the hotel's info and give them a call to secure my own single room on my drive over to Gage and Olivia's house.

I have to believe that Gage would be over-the-moon right now. It's never been an issue of Olivia and I not getting along, but when we did all find a chance to meet up, once or twice a year, I was in desperate need of Gage's time and attention. I didn't mean to monopolize him or ignore everyone else, but I can see now that's exactly what I did.

I start the car, but before I can pull out, I reach for my camera again. It's not that I want to take a picture of this architectural pile of crap, but I do want to capture the juxtaposition of this symbol of hopelessness against a sky so beautiful—so full of every color—such an obvious reminder of life. I quickly frame the shot through the lens and release the shutter. The moment I hear the click, a small dose of hope releases in me.

CHAPTER *Five*

The girls are exhausting. I don't know how parents do it. I started the day off so well. I got up early and made one last breakfast for everyone in the house—*their house*—with their Mom . . . and their Dad. Heaping piles of pancakes and bacon, as well as biscuits and gravy, cover the breakfast room table. I am full of pride at my first real accomplishment as the girls' caretaker.

Then they wake up.

It turns out the only breakfast eater in the house is Gage—thus the surplus of aging breakfast items. Emery very loudly complains that it smells gross and gags a couple [dozen] times. *Gosh, now I see how annoying all my "personality" must be.* Anna is much less harsh in her admonishment of my early morning work. She thanks me for the effort and offers to throw it all away for me. *How kind.*

After that, the day is a whirlwind. When we get to the school, they don't have me listed on the girl's check out card, so obviously, I must be a serial kidnapper. Never mind the fact that I went to the very same elementary school and the elderly lady in front of me was once, long ago, my school secretary as well. The office staff has to call every freaking person on the list to make sure I do, in fact, have authority to fill out the paperwork sitting out on the front desk. Once the girls are officially no longer products of "the system", we go back to the house and begin loading up my car—which poses a problem because, you know, it's already full of all my crap. Somehow, yesterday, in all of our amazing planning, Olivia and I forgot about that small detail. In a fantastic organizing effort, I quickly transfer everything from my front and back seats to the trunk. I plop both girls on top of the trunk to help me close it—then we begin loading the car with Olivia's pre-labeled boxes. [We could not be more different.]

The girls are incredibly excited to move into the hotel. They have told no less than six people about this today—two of them complete strangers who looked slightly worried that I was, actually, a kidnapper. It seems that, to kids, a hotel holds an appeal much like a theme park or Chuck E Cheese. These little munchkins are negative help as I unload the boxes. When my arms are full and my vision obstructed, they choose to dart away and hide among the lobby's shrubbery. I have dropped something like four boxes and broken both a dollhouse and some sort of kid's makeup kit—which effectively makes both girls cry. Needless to say, I am not winning the day.

By midafternoon, Emery really needs a nap. I try to settle her down with Octonauts in her new "bedroom" which turns out to be a really dumb move, and I suddenly understand why parents don't allow their kids to have TVs in their rooms. Emery is wide-awake and singing the Octonauts theme song while bouncing along on the bed. [I think we are now on the fourth episode?] Anna is very carefully trying to piece together her beloved makeup kit, and I'm the one nodding off with my feet propped up on a still unpacked box. Before I crash, I decide we all need a Starbucks run. I get the girls packed into their seats, and as soon as I am back on the interstate, Emery is asleep. What the hell? This demon, monster child refused to sleep in a bed, yet she's asleep in her awkward car seat in less than five minutes? Kids are weird.

After finally doing something right for the day, we are all feeling a little more reenergized. The girls actually enjoy unpacking the boxes and setting up their own space. I try my best to unbox Olivia's items and set them up in a very organized, neat [anal] way. I even space her hangers one inch apart like my mom used to do. I know she will likely take one look at it and change it all to whatever her system is, but if I can take away any small piece of her burden, then the effort's worth it.

The girls and I take a look at the now empty sitting area and envision what we want it to look like as their classroom. They both seem a little more agreeable with the thought that not only will I be their daycare system, but also their teacher as well. It's like they had to see for themselves that I wasn't completely incompetent. We make a list of general items we will need in order to get started. Anna, of course, is all reason and logic as she goes through a short list of school supplies and teaching materials. Emery is decidedly less helpful. She adds to our list: snacks, snacks and more snacks. I wonder to myself what they are doing over there at her preschool for food to be the only thing she equates with learning.

I pull up my Amazon app, and we have a blast spending Aunt Sage's money. We buy basic supplies like pencils, paper and crayons, but we also purchase these hella-large sticky notes that are, like, poster-sized. We buy a small easel chalkboard because I think it's just so freaking cute, but neither of the girls actually knows what a chalkboard is. They are each allowed to choose two books to add to the cart, and because I am a TOTAL pushover, we add some snacks. "For rewadds," Emery states matter-of-factly. I have to call down to the lobby to ask how one gets Amazon packages delivered to the hotel [which turns out to be incredibly easy] and then click the button that solidifies the beginning of something new—for all of us.

By late afternoon, the girls are becoming restless, and I still haven't heard from Olivia. I know within the recesses of me that this isn't a good sign, but I try to power through the worry for the girls. To keep everyone busy, we dress in our spy gear [black clothes] and scout the place—all 15 floors. *Lucky me.* We look at the exercise room and talk about what we can do for PE.

Truthfully, I don't know how to operate any of the machines except the treadmill, and even that appears to have way too many buttons and functions for me. We make it to the pool where both girls immediately become sullen because no one told them to pack their bathing suits. How was I supposed to know they would have an indoor pool? I can't stand to lose the footing I've gained with my nieces, so once again, I take out my phone, and before moving on to our next locale, the girls each choose a swimsuit to add to our Amazon delivery. As we roam the floors above our own, even Anna becomes intrigued by having snack and drink machines just a hall away. They love the rooftop, and both practice the Kate Winslet move from Titanic. *Seriously, how does a 4-year-old even know this stuff?* The dimming sky reminds me it's probably time to feed the girls. I pull up the hotel's restaurant menu on my phone and read out the night's specials. Anna turns a little green with the selections, and Emery is literally rolling around on the pebbled rooftop pretending to dry heave. So, I guess we can rule that option out.

The most practical solution at this time is to quickly grab some food, but I'm not sure what Olivia allows the girls to eat—and she's still MIA. We get in the car and head out to see what we can find. While Subway is likely the better option, I can't help myself when I see a Taco Bueno. This is exactly the sort of trash food my mom would never allow me to eat, and with my mouth watering, I suddenly remember how much I love those sweet, little party burritos.

Both girls are less than excited with my pick for dinner; however, when I tell them they can get anything with cheese on top they are decidedly more accepting. Anna and Emery have NO IDEA what they want. [For two very opinionated little girls, they sure can't make decisions.] After 10 minutes of holding up the line, I order them one of almost everything on the menu and two party burritos for me. We look absolutely ridiculous as we pile every-thing onto the Formica table and dig in. I am lost in the cheesy goodness—and my personal exhaustion—when I notice an older lady watching us eat. People have always been pretty impressed with how much I can eat, so I write off the interaction with ease. The girls are finally silent because they are savagely attacking some burritos, and I chalk it up as another win for the day. Suddenly, my metaphorical pat on the back is interrupted with a powerfully choking, floral aroma. I turn toward the smell as soon as she begins talking.

"Why, aren't they dolls? —How old?"

I feel impressed with myself that I know the answer, but before I can swallow and respond, both the girls have piped up and answered for themselves. Emery even held up her fingers to show the woman—in case we didn't all know what 'four' meant.

"Oh my, such big girls." She continues. "And what are you all dressed up for?"

I realize she's referring to our all black ensembles. This could easily be mistaken for funeral attire, and I am almost dragged to my dark place when Anna saves me.

"We were casing the joint. —Isn't that right Aunt Sage?"

Dear Lord, you can't tell kids anything. I literally cover her mouth with my hand and try to recover the moment. "She's just kidding. We were on a mission to search every floor of the hotel."

"Dat's what she swaid," Emery joins in. "We wiv in de hotel now." She adds with complete earnestness.

And just like that, my metaphorical pat on the back is revoked. The lady clears her throat and adds, "Well, ya'll look very cute. I thought that maybe you were doing matching family photos or something."

Huh, she must have thought I was their mom. I've never been mistaken for a mom before. At 32, I've certainly thought about the possibility but always with a type of foreboding fear—never with pride or a feeling of protectiveness.

The rest of the meal is relatively uneventful. We pack up our many leftovers and head toward the car. The quick conversation with the lady and her cloying perfume stays with me though, so before I get the girls all settled in the car, I dig through the trunk for my camera [still not in its case]. I line the girls up in front of the Taco Bueno sign and tell them to pose. I take several shots and between each click the girls instinctively change poses like they are in some sort of professional photo shoot. We are all giggling as we jump back in the car, but Emery suddenly cries out, "NO. We didn't get one wid you." My camera is back in the trunk, but I pull out my phone and select the selfie mode. We are all belted into our seats but lean our faces together for a quick shot. Just as the camera is about to click, Emery turns her head and licks me, because . . . well, she's four . . . while Anna makes a crazy face. *Oh, these girls.*

Back at the hotel, my fear is amped up by the fact that Olivia *still* isn't here, and the room doesn't show any signs of use since we left. Anna easily takes a bath when asked, but Emery is another story. She's tired—I'm tired. She's yelling—I'm yelling. Before the cops can be called, I give up. In truth, I'm not exactly sure that a 4-year-old is supposed to bathe by themselves, and I'm at my limit of experiencing "new" and "exciting" firsts for the day.

In silky princess pajamas, I put both the girls to bed and promise that mommy will be there when they wake up in the morning. Typically, the girls each have their own rooms, but I'm grateful they are all snuggled up together right now and have each other to lean on. *This* moment would make a great photo.

Once they're asleep, I'm scared to death to move—or breathe—and wake them up. I quietly pull out my laptop and hook up my iPhone. I scroll through my albums and choose something soothing to help me recover from the day: The Civil Wars - *Barton Hollow*. The only photo I have access to is our crazy car selfie. I quickly sign up for a blog site and add the photo with a quick caption of our day.

> Sage takes on day 1. The girls are moved in and are excited by all of the "neighbors". I may have accidentally insinuated that we were spies on a mission, note the black getups. They experienced their first ever party burrito [p.s. big parenting fail there, you two]. We are ready to rock and roll for school next week, and everyone is sound asleep . . . including me [almost].

I share the blog's link with Gage and Olivia and close up my laptop. I'm nodding off to *Poison and Wine* when Olivia knocks on the door. She looks about ten times worse than I feel—which says a lot. I help her get settled with a cup of tea and, in general, just sort of flounder around her. She sits and kicks off her shoes, so I take the opportunity to show her the day's blog. She smiles, but it doesn't reach her eyes. I'm at a loss for what to do or say right now, and I think that all *I* really want after my long day is some space and time alone. Maybe she's feeling the same. I gather my messenger bag and MacBook and head toward the door. I show her where I left the room keys and tell her that I'll be back at 8:00 tomorrow morning. She nods but remains quiet. She literally hasn't said a word since she walked in. Without anything else to fill the silence, I open the door and leave. Once in the hall, I have no idea where to go—where I'm heading. I remember that I reserved a room for myself, and at 9:50, I head to the front desk to finally check myself in.

The lobby is dead quiet, and I have to wait awhile before any-one emerges out of the office area. It's been over 24 hours since I last spoke with Mom or Dad, so naturally they are going to assume I'm dead. To ward off any potential search parties, I shoot a text to my mom and let her know I've been with the girls all day, I'm getting my own room and I will see both her and Dad in the morning for breakfast.

Still waiting, I scroll through the few photos on my phone. I rarely take photos for work on my phone, so most of what is on here are odds and ends of my life. The Turkish Market, Iraq's inexplicable blood-red lake right outside of Sadr, a ridiculously beautiful night on the beaches in Palau and more recent pictures from the Color Festival in Mumbai. From the outside looking in, this life looks charming, but I can't help but compare my photo reel to the one Brec showed me a few nights ago. Hand my phone off to any stranger and they can take over these pictures—my memories—because I'm not in a single one. They could simply be postcards anyone can claim. Then I hit the end of the line and see three slightly blurry little faces. It's probably the worst picture I've taken in at least a decade, but for the first time, I can see how much we all look alike and that makes me instantly cherish it. I quickly save the photo as my screen saver and make a promise to take more bad pictures with these girls.

Finally, I see a man walking through the lobby and flag him down. I get a quick lecture about calling ahead for late check-ins before he begins typing away, looking for my reservation. The phone rings several times, but apparently, customer service is not at the top of the list at 10:20 on a Thursday night at the Residence Inn. I try to make small talk with the employee, James, but after a few grunted responses, I give up and lay my head down on the marble counters while I wait to officially get my own key card and head up to bed. James slides the cards across to me and tucks them under my arms/makeshift pillow. I open one eye and attempt to muster the strength to make it to the elevator and then on to room 613—according to the pouch I am now holding. As I am turning and waving away James in thanks, I almost run into Brec. A very casual, much younger looking Brec. The boy Brec—the one I lost. His shirt is unbuttoned—revealing a plain white tee underneath. He's wearing jeans rather than slacks, and they are slung low on his hips like either a stylist has chosen them for him, or he's lost weight since he last bought a pair of jeans. His hair is a mess—sticking out in several directions. I like Brec more like this. I feel like this version of him could maybe be a kindred spirit. I immediately think back to what he said in the Posies parking lot a few nights ago, "I want this version of you forever," and I wonder if that was our problem all of those years ago. Maybe we only liked just one version of each other instead of loving the whole person. Suddenly, Brec grabs my shoulders and looks straight into my eyes, breaking off the memory.

"Sage? Seriously, you okay there? I'm talking to you."

"What? —Yeah, I'm fine. I just got checked into my room, so, uh, see you later."

"Wait there for just a second." He says slightly impatiently. "I need to get more towels and I'll go up with you."

"But I'm tired, Brec—really tired." Dear Lord, I'm whining at him. I'm way too old for this, but being bossed around by him just makes me . . . I don't know . . . it makes me . . . it makes me too many things.

"Suck it up. I'm sure you've been through worse, Ms. National Geographic Photographer." He teases.

I don't know why I can't just play along—just let this moment be. "You *sure* about that? Worse than waiting for my brother to die and realizing I lost my family or gave them up somewhere along the way? Is there a worse?" I don't fully cry, but my brown eyes are big and glassy with tears that are just waiting to be blinked into existence.

Brec gets his towels, but I'm already at the bank of elevators waiting for the next one to arrive. Of course, he's back by my side before the elevator doors even open. Obviously, we are both going up, but he pauses as if looking for my approval before riding in the same enclosed space with me. I wave my arm forward in a gesture that I hope reveals, 'just get on, ass-hat.' I push the '6' button—he pushes '4'. I give tiny, meta-phorical spirit fingers to fate for letting me have this one. The elevator is one of those that speaks to you. The doors open, and a soothing voice comes on to remind us that this is the "fourth floor". I'm leaning my weight against the back rail and give a half salute/half wave as Brec begins to walk away. Before my hand can return to my side, Brec grabs it and pulls me out of the door with him.

"What the fuck? I'm tired. Too tired for this—too tired for you. Please go find someone else to bully." I grumble.

"Is that what I'm doing? —bullying you?"

"I'm warning you, stop messing with me. I slept in a child-sized bed last night with a little kicking minion and in my car the night before. I just need a bed, and if you drag me any further, I'm going to lay down on this hideously-patterned hotel floor and call it good enough."

Brec produces his key card from his jeans' pockets but pauses before unlocking the door.

"Answer one question."

"One and then I get to go to sleep?" I say now leaning on the wall.

"Yes, one—and then I'll freaking carry you up to your room if necessary."

"Shoot."

More gently he asks, "Where are your clothes? Your things? You have a key, Sage, and literally nothing else. What are you going to sleep in?

Well shit. I'm currently kicking myself right now for not thinking of getting anything out of my car when I was waiting on James, the slow hotel employee, but I'm not going to give that information to Brec to use against me. So instead, I noncommittally shrug my shoulders.

"That's what I thought." And with that, he pushes me through the door and into the room.

The room smells like him. Walk me in here blindfolded with a 50-year absence from this man, and I could still immediately tell you this is Brec Aldridge's room. I don't know what I'm doing here, so I awkwardly stand in the entryway/kitchenette area. I can hear Brec rifling through his things in the other room, and I take the moment to make some quick observations.

1. It's clear that Amelia's not here. I know Gage told me they weren't on great terms, or whatever, but it's obvious that a woman hasn't been in this room—especially one as tightly wound as Amelia.
2. This space looks lived in—really lived in. Brec has boxes, lots of boxes, stacked along the walls and under the windows. He has legit plates in the sink and the sitting area has at least three different forms of personal tech-

nology sitting out on the table wide open. For the time being, this is his home.

He returns with what appears to be a t-shirt, a towel and a bag slung over one shoulder. I'm not actually sure what he's up to which is not good. With Brec, I always need to be on guard.

"Time to shower." He says as he hands off both the folded towel and t-shirt.

"Huh?" That's the best I can do with confusion and exhaustion swirling through my mind.

"Give me your key for tonight. Take my room and some clothes." He motions to the shirt that's now in my hands. "I have everything you'll need in the shower."

I look at the Stanford t-shirt and back to Brec.

"Yeah, I'm not wearing this." I say with a scowl.

"You bought it for me. Remember?"

"Yep—which is precisely why I'm not wearing it."

"Of course, you won't. Try the top drawer on the left. You'll find a bunch of t-shirts. I don't really give a shit which one you wear, Sage. They're all meaningless. They're just t-shirts."

I can't handle the whiplash. *Here, let me propose this really kind gesture. Just kidding, I'm going to punch you in the face instead.* He grabs the key card from my fist and leaves, the door closing harshly behind him. I don't know exactly what just happened, but I know I'm maxed out on my Brec allotment for the day.

In the shower, I'm briefly able to clear my head and focus on tomorrow—*what time I need to set my alarm for, texting my mom for their room number again and make sure I give them mine, what adventures I'll plan for the girls in the days ahead.* But my head keeps getting clouded by the supremely masculine smells of the shampoo and body wash. It *almost* makes me feel like I am showering with a man. God, I can't remember the last time I did that. My sex life has been on the rocks since, well, pretty much forever. Travel and just my general personality don't lend well to relationships. My conservative upbringing, added to my fear of intimacy, have kept me safe from one-night stands and the sort of self-loathing that accompanies such things, but at this moment my starved libido is seemingly a very dangerous thing.

I use the toothbrush by the sink, and I hope it's a spare—mostly because it feels like too personal an item to share with Brec. As promised, the top drawer is filled with t-shirts, most of them I don't recognize. I touch and turn over each one, but in the end, I still pull the Stanford shirt over my head. It's very worn and thin and feels like brushed cotton against my skin. I turn out the lights and pad to the bed leaving wet hair droplets in my wake. The bed smells like him. The pillows smell like him. I'm wearing his shirt. I could close my eyes and imagine it's 17 years ago at his apartment in Stanford. Rather than take another trip down memory lane, I flop onto my stomach, shut my eyes and enter the land of my subconscious.

I'm startled awake and on my feet before my vision can catch up with me. I reach for the closest, densest object, which happens to be an old generation laptop sitting on the bedside table. Standing on the bed, I wind the laptop back like a baseball bat and am ready to swing the moment my attacker comes within reach. Fucking Brec. He looks into my eyes first—crazed and fearful, I'm sure—then he drops his gaze down my body. There isn't a mirror in sight, but I turn on my senses to feel for what must be amusing him. I went to bed with wet hair and in a t-shirt—nothing more. No bra. No panties. The t-shirt has clearly crept up far past what is modest, and my small breasts aren't provided much coverage in the old, thinning shirt. I'm both angry and embarrassed.

"Get out, pervert," I squeal then plop down and smother myself into the covers. In a muffled screech, I continue, "Seriously, what are you doing here?"

All I get in response is laughter.

"This isn't okay." I yell over his laughter. Brec takes a minute to gather control over his obvious delight in my humiliation.

"I'm here because it's my room." He begins to go through his closet, selecting items.

"I'm here because I need to get dressed." He takes off the t-shirt he came in wearing.

"I'm here because I have a job I need to get to." He pulls off the pajama bottoms and is left in nothing but boxer briefs. Dear, sweet Jesus.

I look away and my cheeks flame with heat. Immediately, I rummage through the bedding to find my phone. What time is it? Have I already let the girls down by day two? I grasp the thin metal phone and am relieved to see it's only 6:00 am. Now that I have the time squared away, I don't know what to do or where to look.

Brec smirks at my inability to be an adult in these situations. He always found it hysterical that I could be such a badass until sex was brought up, and then I became the shy, scared teenager that I tried so hard to keep hidden from the rest of the world. In these moments, I can never quite keep my walls up or my facade in place—even now. My eyes tell too much truth.

"Sage, I'm just trying to make it even. I saw yours—you saw mine." He motions down the length of his body.

I shake my head back and forth to try to get through this moment—to push past the intimidated little girl.

"Sure. Of course. I get it. We're both adults. No. Big. Deal." I say in breathy puffs.

I feel like I'm in someone's bed after a one-night stand and begin to look desperately for my clothes, so I can get the hell out of here. Unfortunately, my clothes are still on the bathroom floor where I deposited them before my shower last night. Damn my dirtiness. I look to Brec and silently beg him to help me out of this. He raises one eyebrow and his hands in surrender. "Fine, I'm going. I'll be in the shower."

He hangs the clothes he selected on the outside of the door, which keeps it from closing all the way. I get up and look for pants, any pants. The closest ones to me are his discarded pj bottoms which will have to do for now. I stuff my feet back into my shoes and sling the messenger bag over my shoulder. Before I can quite walk away, I sneak a peek back toward the cracked door. I can hear the shower begin and see a sliver of Brec's ass cheek before he suddenly pops his head out of the door. BUSTED. I'm so busted.

He has a lazy smile on his face—happy to have caught me, no doubt. That southern drawl makes a rare appearance as he says, "And Sage, yours looks *really* good . . . *babe*."

"Whatever," I huff then fling myself out the door.

Not a great way to start my day.

CHAPTER Six

A week passes, and I haven't killed my nieces. Everyone still has ten fingers and ten toes, and Aunt Sage has some very whittled patience. I suddenly want to write apologies to every teacher I've ever had. Who knew this job would be so hard?

Emery is a little maniac that needs to be entertained every 5 minutes, but heaven forbid you actually help her or—you know, *teach* her how to do something. She is the most stubborn, most strong-willed child there has ever been. We practice shapes, and she cuts mine up. We write out the alphabet to practice our handwriting and letters; she roughly markers her letters over mine and mixes them all up—on purpose, I suspect. During naptime, she cries, and in "PE" she falls asleep on the weight benches. On her own though, when she feels like it, I see her perusing her picture books and making up stories to tell her dollies, so I am encouraged that I'm not failing this child altogether.

Anna is a different type of albatross. I quickly learn that I need to double the amount of curriculum I originally intended for her. She flies through concepts much faster than I can get new stuff ready, and her brain processes information at lightning speed. She asks upward of a million questions each day, and I can no longer play it off like I'm just teaching her how to use Google to find the answers to each of her bizarre questions. She's onto me and knows precisely what kind of dumbass I am. Needless to say, I am less encouraged with this child. Though, the silver lining is that she can pretty much teach herself.

The best moments of the week are our scheduled "field trips". Olivia has penciled in her attendance for Thursday's visit to the zoo, but at the last minute, she can't make it. I give each of the girls their cameras, and we spend an entire morning talking about the mechanics of a photo. Emery rolls her eyes the whole way through my impassioned lecture on how shapes, color and balance are all the qualities any amazing photo needs. I continue explaining that what most people misunderstand about photography is that a perfect photo isn't really about the image or object at all, it's about the structure within the picture. Anna soaks up everything I'm telling her like the little sponge she is and is rewarded with my unspoken "best student" of the day title. In truth, I'm just excited to finally be able to teach her something without the aid of Google.

At the zoo, we spend most of our day in "Africa" with the elephants and giraffes or visiting and revisiting the snack stands. The weather is crisp in a slightly unforgiving way, and I have the girls bundled in several layers, but Emery still insists that she's cold and needs hot cocoa to "wahm her up". This is my fault. I stupidly passed the first cocoa stand and offhandedly told the girls when they got too cold we could stop for an afternoon treat. We have since had *three* treats—three very sugary, very chocolatey treats. The girls each take nearly 100 shots of the same thing. —The giraffe with its tongue out. The giraffe eating the leaves. The giraffe looking at us. The giraffe walking away. In short, my genius camera idea falls flat. It seems even Anna can't really put my photography lessons into action. As a last-ditch effort, I create a contest to see which girl can take the best selfie with an animal—any animal. It's incredibly more difficult to frame a selfie through a one-way lens than with a two-way camera phone. I have to teach the girls to turn the camera around and note how to line up the lens with the subject [themselves]. Emery is already clicking away, no animals in sight, before I've even finished explaining the technique.

We visit the monkeys and find they are much too mobile to become good selfie subjects. Here we also discuss the evolution of these animals—why their tails are such an important part of their everyday lives and what would happen if monkeys suddenly lost their tails. Emery is obviously amused by the idea of chopping off all of the monkeys' tails, and I can see her mind twisting the possibility around—little hellion child.

Next, we head toward the brilliantly colored birds and find that the "Amazon" has awful lighting and the "subjects" are quite hard to photograph through the trees. Anna brings up how certain types of birds have naturally camouflaging abilities which can make it difficult to tell which part is the bird vs. which part is the tree. We talk about survival techniques and what other animals have natural, intentional characteristics that help them survive in the wild. Anna's wheels are obviously spinning as she chews through this new conversation.

"Aunt Sage? Do humans have survival traits?"

"For sure. Fight or flight is an obvious one that protects us from predators . . . or, you know, bad dates." I say in complete seriousness.

The girls clearly don't understand the idea of fight or flight because they both blink blankly back at me.

"Fight or flight? You've never heard of it? Okay, it's the idea that when something big is about to happen, your body releases a chemical called adrenaline. That adrenaline makes you superhuman for a little bit—long enough for you to either A) fight the predator, attacker or feeling or B) runaway away from it to find safety."

"What if the attacker is inside you? Can your adrenaline still turn on?" Anna asks despondently with her eyes cast down.

I see where this is going. I find a bench nearby and pull the girls toward it with me. I sit Emery in my lap but hold on to Anna's hand.

"Yeah. When the attacker is somewhere in you, you still get to choose whether to fight or runaway. And you know what I think your daddy is doing?"

Both girls look toward me with so much trust and so much hope in their eyes like somehow my next sentence will either save or sentence Gage.

"He's fighting. He. Is. A. Fighter. Your daddy isn't giving up on you two."

"Can wve help hem fidght?" Emery asks.

"Heck ya!" I respond with fake enthusiasm. "We will be his army."

The conversation quickly turns to ordering camo shirts and creating a training camp to help us prepare to 'fight for daddy'. And just like that, the heavy mood dissipates. I love that about kids—they don't wallow in the darkness. They feel it and touch it and choose the light instead.

We find that fish are actually the best subjects for our selfies due to their lazy nature and natural interest in the flash. My favorite photo of the day is one of Anna's selfies. She's nearly cut out of the shot and is so focused on getting everything lined up that she forgets to smile. The fish looks a little stunned but definitely adds a nice pop of color to the structure. The reflection of the tank reveals both Emery and me in the foreground. Emery seems to be 'busting a move', a phrase I'm sure she's coined from Gage, while I'm anxiously aiding Anna in her new-found photography skills. By all critical standards, it's an absolutely, awful mess, but we're all there—you just have to look at the details to find the beauty.

I've kept the photo journal up all week for Gage and Olivia to see, but this is by far my favorite entry. I choose Anna's selfie and add a short caption:

> Just a few zoo animals in their natural habitat.
> p.s. sorry about all of the hot chocolate.

While I love all of the time I've been afforded with the girls, our schooling schedule almost completely overlaps with Gage's ICU visiting hours. He's been good at responding to the blog posts or shooting off a quick text to me, but I haven't actually *seen* my brother in over a week. With Olivia's near complete absence, I'm guessing I need to get to the hospital sooner rather than later.

With that in mind, I ask my mom to watch the girls the second Tuesday of our new "home schooling" system. I get them through all of their morning classes but leave around lunch to avoid the typical afternoon meltdown. [Good luck, Mother.]

At the hospital, I quickly notice Gage has lost some weight and some more color since I saw him last. He's just tired he says—I don't buy it. We mostly talk about the girls. I know I light up when I tell him about each of our adventures. It's unlike me to show such a blatant display of animated emotion, but I really am amused by what these crazy kids come up with each day. We discuss our hatred for the upcoming holidays and make a plan to bust him out of this room, so he can gorge himself on all our Thanksgiving favorites. I even offer to bring back a holiday addition of 'hospital murder in the dark'. It's a great hour-and-a-half, but none of it is real. None of it is truth. We are both excellently avoiding admitting Gage's turn for the worse. His next Chemo treatment is late this week, and they're already planning on sedating. It's there, though it's not spoken, the possibility he won't wake up from sedation. It's possible my brother won't live to see another Thanksgiving or Christmas.

The reality is too much—it's a predator finally catching up with me. In a split decision of fight or flight, I run away. I tell Gage to get some rest and kiss his clammy forehead before, literally, running out the door. I can't go back to the girls in this state, so I choose my home away from home, Posies. I decide to recharge with a dirty chai and some space to think.

Posies is always relatively quiet—it's the south's best-kept secret. Antonia must be off today because a younger, thinner version of her is operating the counter. For the first time in my history of this place, I pay and tip well to help make up for so many freebies over the years.

I find a corner of the café to sit and think. To block out the noise and intermittent, hushed conversations, I pull out my ear buds and select one of my most well-worn albums - O by Damien Rice. This album has been there for all of my darkness and has seen me through it, so I hope it will work some magic once more.

Clearly Gage's current course of treatment isn't effective. Brec must have something more lined up. There has to be something *more* experimental in the works—and the only way I'm going to find the ace up his sleeve is to go find him. I pack up my scone, surprisingly not hungry for once, and discard the remnants of my empty chai cup. I don't have Brec's phone number anymore, but I'm willing to bet he's still at the hospital since it's only midafternoon. What I do have is his room number and the ability to manipulate just about anyone when I put my mind to it.

Back at the hotel, I scour the lobby for James, the very absent hotel employee from my first night. For my plan to work it has to be James because he's the only one that saw Brec and I together. I spy him chatting with other members of the staff. Of course, he's not actually working. I grab his attention across the room and point to a corner of the lobby in a gesture signaling I needed to talk to him away from his throng of subpar employees.

Rather than looking confused, he appears to be amused and maybe even interested in where this conversation might lead. Shit, he's flirting. That doesn't work well with the direction I plan on aiming this talk. I take a deep breath, plaster on a broad smile and go in for the kill.

"I'm sooo sorry for interrupting ya'll. It looks like you have some real nice friends over there. Look, I am sooo embarrassed to do this, but remember when I checked in the other night?"

"Yeah. I remember when you *checked in.*" Vomit. How can someone make the words 'checked in' suggestive? I'm not trying to flirt here. Pick up on the clues, dude.

"Well, there was this guy in the lobby with me. He's kinda an old friend and we sort of . . . " [big swallow] "Well, we sort of reunited. I know what you're thinking, but I promise you, I'm not that kind of a girl." I look as earnest as I can and widen my eyes to show my endearing innocence. "It's not like anything really happened, but I did leave a bag in his room. He clearly wanted to take our conversation further, but I just couldn't cheat on my boyfriend. I didn't know what to do, so I just left. I think maybe I made him mad because he won't return any of my phone calls, but I really do need my bag."

"What an asshole. So, he blew you off because you wouldn't sleep with him?" I'm really getting James worked up over here. God, this is too easy.

I nod my head vigorously and look like the saint that . . . well, I've never been. "James, I just need a way to get my bag back. My boyfriend will kill me if I have to explain why I lost my laptop and stuff. Nothing happened, but it looks soooo bad. I'm sooo stupid. Why do I always have to be so trusting?"

I'm internally rolling my eyes at myself. I sound like a pathetic excuse for a person, but James totally falls for it—hook, line and sinker.

"I'll take care of it ma'am. Would you like me to go up there, personally, and retrieve it? You shouldn't have to go back to the room."

Oh shit. I didn't plan for this little curveball.

"Um, no. That's okay. If I can just get the key? I'll be up and back in a jiff. I can see how busy ya'll are down here. I don't want to be any more of a pain-in-your-neck than I've already been."

He walks me to the counter, and I have the key in less than five minutes. I call out my thanks and promise to return in a matter of minutes. *Sucker.*

I run up to Brec's room on the fourth floor, open the door and almost close it all the way except for the small crack created by the pack of gum I strategically place in the doorway. I then realize I need to actually create a missing bag, so I head up to my room on the sixth floor and pack a fake bag to finish selling my story. I drop the key card back off with James, pat his hand in a "sincere" thank you and point to the bag. I mouth the words, "You're a lifesaver!" and head back toward the bank of eleva-tors. Man, I've missed being this devious.

The first thing I do when I get back to Brec's room is set an alarm. This isn't my first rodeo, and I don't want to be caught in here. I'm fairly certain he wouldn't press charges, but it also won't bode well for me with the family or hospital staff if I get caught in here—there's still some lingering question about my "infamous" missing night from a few weeks ago. I look for all of the technology that was haphazardly scattered about, but everything appears to be password protected. Shit. I try all of his high school passwords without much luck. I try his birthday, his wedding date [I may have done a little more internet invest-igation], his wife's name—plus the year they met, his favorite basketball team. I'm quickly getting nowhere with this line of searching. From his sitting area, I scan the room and look for anything that seems "doctory". The room mostly seems to be overcrowded with a ton of boxes—which become the next thing I dig into. The top several boxes are labeled by room. [Bedroom, Office, Garage] I'm fairly certain I'm looking at the remains of Brec's marriage and his life in Santa Cruz. I still haven't brought up the conversation Gage and I had regarding Brec and Amelia's split; however, the internet—knower of all things—pretty much confirms that they haven't been in touch for months. Her social media is littered with new men and fancy dinner parties, and his seems to have gone radio silent about eight months ago. The next layer of boxes may be heading in the right direction. They are labeled by what appears to be random numbers and dates. The first box has 'Stanford Children's Health' letterhead all throughout the box. The files make little to no sense at first, but I notice a common patient number repeated page after page. Ten minutes in, and I've hit the jack-pot. These must be Brec's notes from his case trial for ADEM. I feel certain that this is the answer I've been waiting for. If I can find what worked for the clinical trial patients, I might be able to give Gage some hope—or at least another fucking option other than endless chemo and routine sedation. Box one takes a while to get through and doesn't seem to result in any progress with ADEM. Box two doesn't take as long since I now know what I'm looking for, but by the time I flip through every page, it also seems like there was little to no positive reaction for this patient. By box three, I'm growing tired and frustrated. Same— no improvement. Every freaking box is the same story. Patients' symptoms would immediately decline before actually having a symptom surge brought with a host of new issues. Every single patient ended up worse than they were when they started.

Papers are scattered over every inch of the floor and tables, and I don't have the energy to give a shit. Looking at Brec's life's work, I realize I got an answer, but it wasn't the answer I was expecting or ready for. The answer is . . . there *isn't* an answer.

I curl up into a ball right where I sit and I cry myself to sleep. For weeks, I've been waiting for the super-secret big guns Brec carried with him from his fancy schooling and years of research. It's exhausting to have all of your hope drain out of you.

It's dark when Brec finds me. I guess my dumb alarm didn't help me after all. I can't find the right words to pretend like this is somehow all an accident, so I don't even try. Since Brec waltzed back into my life he has been quietly apologizing for the past and walking on eggshells around my many mood swings. I hope his vintage guilt will get me out of this too, but one look at his face tells a different story.

"WHAT THE HELL, SAGE? Have you completely lost your mind? These are medical documents, *sealed* medical documents. This is illegal."

He's loudly yelling at me but makes no move toward me or toward the many papers I have crumpled while I slept. I have no fight let—what's the point? This isn't going to be a happily ever after. Not for us. Not for Gage. I extract myself as carefully as I can from the research, smooth my clothes out, reach for my messenger bag and head for the door. The laptops are left out with their blue screens blinking, and the closer I get to the door, the more I realize just how bad this looks. Brec isn't mine to push around or manipulate anymore. This is *really* wrong. I'm embarrassed that I even attempted to use my same old tricks on him decades later.

I get to the door and he calls out to me once more in an icy warning.

"SAGE—"

I turn my head toward him steadying myself for whatever verbal lashing is coming my way, but Brec simply throws me the package of gum and says, "Don't forget the rest of your shit."

I have to do something to make this moment better, so I go for the most honest explanation I can give.

"Brec. I'm sorry. I needed hope. I needed answers. I just—"

"So, you thought you'd what? —break and enter into my room and con a solution out of me? Do you really think I had some better option or treatment that I was just holding out on? Do you think I'm not doing everything I can to save my friend? Don't you realize I hate myself because I don't have another answer?" Tears well up in his eyes.

I've only seen Brec cry a few times. His dad passed away his sophomore year of college—my junior year of high school. The funeral was one of those hopeless events that was devoid of any joy. Brec's dad was a strong, rich man, but he also destroyed a lot of the people that loved him. Brec told me in the limo that he refused to cry for such a cold-hearted bastard, but at the graveside one lone tear escaped. Months later, I asked about that, and he said his sadness wasn't over what he lost but what they never had.

When Brec left me, it wasn't premeditated. We got engaged the spring semester of my senior year. We were young, *really* young, but we were the sort of close most married couples can never quite achieve. In fact, we were downright dependent on each other. Brec was already in California, and I applied to Cal Art partially because I wanted to be close to him and partially because it felt like an obligation. I also applied to several places on the East Coast. I visited two and knew immediately that NYU was it for me. Obviously, it was going to be hard to have a transcontinental engagement, but we had done long distance for so long that I never expected this one choice to unravel us.

My art didn't initially blossom in New York. I really struggled my freshmen year. I was alone in a way I had never experienced before, and I shut down—shut everyone out. I needed Brec most then but didn't know the right way to ask. I spent most of the fall pushing him away and most of the following spring trying to win his attention back. In May, I flew out to Stanford on a whim. He hadn't answered my phone calls for days, and for the first time, I was really worried about us. That was the day I met Amelia. In his apartment. With his pajamas on. It's not like I caught them in some sort of compromising position, but I didn't really have to. Never, *ever* had it occurred to me that Brec would cheat. I knew we weren't in a good place, and honestly, I wouldn't have been surprised if he had said he wanted some space or we needed to take some time apart. But he had already moved on—without me. I had one lone carry-on with me and, after witnessing her in his apartment, abruptly turned it around and ran down the fire escape stairs of his apartment. I was in shock. You see, when life really knocks you down, you don't feel it all at once. It's not like one huge punch that bruises you and then allows you to heal. It's a big punch and then a few more smaller ones—then a huge one again followed by a series of intermittent, unexpected punches later on—never allowing you to heal, just constantly beating you up. For me, this was just the first punch. I think that moment was different for Brec. I still don't know how long Amelia had been in the picture, but I imagine his guilt had been punching him for a while. And that day he got completely knocked out. He caught up with me outside in the parking lot while I was waiting for a taxi to take me back to the airport. He had big, sloppy, fat tears running everywhere. I was all ice, and he was this broken boy. He wouldn't cry over his own father's death, but he completely fell apart over *his* choice to cheat on me—to break me. My last words to Brec were harsh and cruel and wounding.

"Shut the fuck up, Brec. You did this. You just lost the only family that actually cared about you. Have a nice life, asshole. I hope you enjoy turning into your dad. Just remember, no one cries for those cold-hearted bastards."

Then I left and didn't see him again until exactly two weeks ago.

Brec's shoulders shake, and I realize that he's known all along. He's carried the burden alone, that Gage's case was so incredibly hopeless. He cries for his friend and for his failures, and I stand there watching the man I once promised forever to, cry by himself. In the kitchenette, I find a bottle of whiskey and pour him a glass—and then me one as well. We sit on the hotel's hard, scratchy couch and drink in a silent salute to my brother—and to all the patients he couldn't cure. I lean my head on his shoulder and let him carry all of its weight. And just like that, right there on the hotel's couch, I spend the night with Brec Aldridge for the first time in 14 years.

CHAPTER *Seven*

Thanksgiving is upon us. No one discusses the idea of celebrating because there were complications after the last chemo treatment, and Gage still hasn't been woken up from sedation. Brec encourages the family that he is stable, but they still need to keep him sedated for the time being. I call bullshit.

The girls and I make a few Thanksgiving crafts to brighten up the ICU, but even they are pretty on edge at this point. I decide to give them Wednesday and Thursday off, but we are back at it by Friday because the girls and I actually do better with the distraction of school. Today is another scheduled field trip. This time we're off to the Science Place. Since I've begun my experiment as part-time nanny/part-time teacher, I've noticed that both of the girls really love science. Anna's little brain was made for mechanical and physical science. She loves to find out how things are made and what they do. Emery seems more motivated by the chemical and life sciences. I tried to create a science experiment for us one day last week; however, it was a huge failure. By the end, we had a shattered beaker, a crying kid and absolutely zero chemical reaction. I'm learning a lot about this job, but it appears, what I'm learning most is how much I suck at teaching.

I'm excited about today and hopeful that this could give the girls a chance to forget some of the tension that fills their hotel suite day in and day out. Olivia looks like she hasn't eaten in a couple of weeks, and the girls aren't oblivious to their mom's pain—no matter how much she resembles a Disney Princess.

This place is absolutely amazing. The girls are having a blast, and I don't even need to resort to fake competitions or sugary bribes. I bring my Nikon along and document this rare moment of pure joy. Emery is a complete mess of dish soap and sand within the first hour, and of course, I forgot to pack a change of clothes. Luckily, she's found a new favorite animal—dinosaurs, T-Rex to be specific—so I buy her t-shirt in the souvenir shop. She's stunned into absolute silence when we see the Tesla Coil, and because I so enjoy the momentary quiet, we visit it at least four times before leaving at the end of the day. Anna processes everything in a much softer way, but I can always see her thoughts turning nonstop. She rarely offers up what she thinks or feels, but I am incredibly honored when she gives me a sliver of her heart.

"Sage?"

"That's Aunt Sage to you, missy." I playfully say and tap her nose.

"Aunt Sage." She corrects with a slight eye roll. I smile in pride at her new-found sass. "What kind of dinosaur would you be?"

"Hmm . . . tough question, kiddo. You know, I think it's changed over time. When I was little, like Emery, I was all T-Rex. I was fierce and strong and loved to dominate and use my power over your daddy."

"But you're so small." she giggles.

"I am, but at one time, your daddy was even smaller." I gesture like I'm holding a baby to give her a picture of what I'm talking about. Just thinking about Gage as a baby slays me. As an older sibling, you have this innate feeling in you like it's your job, no matter what, to make sure that tiny little creature is okay. For as much as I was fiercely and strongly dominating, I was even more fiercely and strongly loving.

"So, you don't think you'd be a T-Rex now?" Anna asks.

"Nope. Not a T-Rex anymore. As I got older, I turned into . . ." I peruse the displays around us and decide, "a Stegosaurus."

Anna thinks through this for a moment but clearly doesn't come up with enough information on her own, so she prods a little deeper.

"Why a Stegosaurus? They're also really big."

"Well, that's true, but I wasn't really thinking about the size." I point across to the display in the far-right corner. "You see how the Stegosaurus has all of those spikes on its back? Aunt Sage is kind of like that; I can be prickly on the outside and sometimes I feel like I need to be meaner than I really am in order to protect myself. But you know what's pretty cool about the Stegosaurus?"

Anna shakes her head "no" and I am mildly impressed that I've stumped this kid for maybe the second time ever.

"The Stegosaurus is also known for being incredibly loyal and defensive of their family and friends. In fact, they're always willing to fight for the ones they love."

Anna graces me with one of her rare smiles.

"Then I want to be a Stegosaurus too," she says as she slips her slim hand into mine.

We go back to the gift shop where Anna and I get matching Stegosaurus tees. The three of us go pose as our dinosaur characters in front of the Tesla Coil where, thankfully, some kind bystander offers to take the picture for us. Emery is standing on top of a trashcan with her arms pinned to her side, hands flopping about and her mouth open in a predatory pose. Anna and I are on all fours [if elbows count] below her while making little heart signs with our index fingers and thumbs. We're a goofy little trio, and I wouldn't have it any other way.

The girls are exhausted after we leave, but we still need to pick up some groceries in order to make dinner. It's then I learn the horror of taking kids to the supermarket in a big, awful way. Emery has a complete meltdown and screams at me. Anna tries to help but ends up getting scolded and hit as well. The whole thing ends with Prego jars being smashed to the ground and Emery screaming, "I just want my momma," before crumbling on the floor in a flourish of messy, anguished tears. Sometimes, in life, you just need to know when to cut and run. This is the time to run. I apologetically hand off my partially-filled cart to a store employee, and we get in the car to head back home. *Real* home. The girls need some time in their own space—the space once occupied by their Mom *and* Dad. I quickly shoot off a voice memo to Olivia—since I'm driving and all—that I'm taking the girls to the house, and I think they sincerely need some time with her.

At the house, we have pizza delivered [I'm not sure that I trust anything in their fridge to be edible at this point] and curl up in Gage and Olivia's bed for a family movie. Olivia shows up about halfway through Beauty and the Beast, and all four of us fold into the moment of love and little girl giggles. Everyone is asleep by the end, including Olivia. I leave a note in the kitchen about locking up and seeing them later before I head back to my little hotel room an hour away.

I pull into the hotel well after midnight. I don't have to get up with the girls in the morning, so I'm in no real rush. In my room, I load up my MacBook and AirDrop all of today's photos into the cloud. Even though Gage still isn't conscious, I keep writing my daily blog, and I keep sending him the link. I find our dinosaur picture and laugh at the horrible execution. Emery's eyes are closed, and she looks like she may be falling off the trashcan rather than a fierce predator atop it. I am looking down at my fingers to make sure I made my heart correctly and I'm not throwing the camera some weird, accidental gang signs, and Anna is looking at me. None of us are actually looking at the lens, and the whole thing is skewed maybe 5 degrees from center. But this is the memory I want to hold onto from today. So, I select it and create a new blog entry.

> The Science Place was a win. I think the girls chose their spirit animals today. Much to everyone's surprise, Emery is now a T-Rex while Anna is a stunning Stegosaurus. Sending you our love.
>
> xoxo

Thinking about that Stegosaurus, I grab my keys and head to my car. The back and front seats have remained fairly clean in the last few weeks, but my trunk is another story. I remove every article of clothing, object, or memory one at a time. In the dark, I quickly make two piles—keep and throw away. The first pile gets stuffed into a couple duffels and reusable grocery bags. The second pile takes me two trips to the dumpster to get rid of. Closing my trunk, I feel a sense of satisfaction. I load my arms up with the bags and awkwardly stumble upstairs to my room. Fortunately, the Residence Inn has laundry machines on site, and for the first time in years I wash all of my clothes— literally everything I own is clean which is a damn big deal for me. I pack it all into the room's drawers and closet. Then take my precious few items out of the remaining bags. I have a set of lovely wine glasses from Venice that I display in the wet bar area. A pretty decent vinyl collection goes into the cupboard below the TV. I've kept two framed photos—one of Gage and me when he came to visit New York all those years ago and one of Brec and me on the day he proposed. I display Gage prominently on my nightstand while I tuck the other photo away in the drawer. I rifle through my camera bag and pull out some of the girl's artwork I have been graciously gifted. I don't have any tape, but I chew up tiny pieces of gum and use it as sticky tack to hang a few my few, precious pictures. I survey all I have accomplished in the last few hours and smile.

My watch tells me it's past 4:00 am, but I feel more energized than I have in a long time. For the first time in a decade, I have a home. I've unpacked all my things and officially moved in as if to say, "I'm here for the long haul." Which means, for the first time in weeks, I'm hopeful there is a long haul to stay around for. Into the quiet of my room I say a little prayer—to God—to Gage. *Brother, I'm fighting for you. Don't give up yet.*

CHAPTER *Eight*

It's two weeks before Christmas, and Gage is finally awake. I got the phone call today from my mom, and I can honestly say, I've never been happier to hear from her before. The girls and I are at the hospital in less than 20 minutes—though it's hours before they allow anyone in the room, and every blind is closing us out from what's going on behind the glass panes. My mom looks like she might be literally ill. I ask her if she's feeling okay, but she waves me off. I look to Dad for guidance and remind her, my dad, the entire room that if any of us are sick we don't need to be around Gage. A cold could *actually* kill him. This upsets my mom, and she walks away from the waiting room with a sniff and hurt feelings. *Even when I'm not trying to be a bitch, I manage to upset her.*

I leave the girls and quickly chase after Mom. I catch up with her at the nurses' station where it's becoming more obvious, as she leans her weight onto the counter, that she really is sick. I ask a nurse for a basic thermometer and a cool cloth. Luckily, the ICU nurses have either long forgotten the salacious gossip regarding good doctor Aldridge and me, or the holiday spirit has them feeling forgiving. I take my mom to a more open and vacant waiting room to check her out. I apply the cool compress and place the thermometer under her tongue. She's shivering, so I take off my wool sweater and lay it over her tiny body. Like this, my mom looks so small—so fragile. In the silence, we each blink back and forth, exchanging a silent conversation of trust. I've grown up incredibly in the last month or so and have had to take on the role of 'mother' quite a bit, so this picture isn't really all that surprising; however, it's always odd for the mother/ daughter roles to reverse—especially with my mom. We stay like that, studying each other, until the thermometer beeps. 102. Yep, Mom is definitely sick. I can only imagine how much this kills her—to be this close to Gage and unable to see him. I'm still captain of team positive as far as Gage is concerned, but I'm also smart enough to cherish each visit with him. Even I admit that every laugh, every hug, every visit may be our last.

I gather my things along with Mom's and let Dad know she's not well, so I'm taking her back to the hotel. Likely, this is just a bad cold, and a few rounds of whatever I can find at CVS will do the trick. But she still has no business hanging out in the ICU until she's fever free. As soon as we get up to her room, I send her to bed. She doesn't even argue, which is very unlike my mother. I put the kettle on for her tea and look through the medicine cabinet in the bathroom for anything that can help get her temperature down. On the sink, I see the freaking blue PM cream and smirk. I'll never understand how my mom operates or why she's wound so tightly about seemingly meaningless things, but I know that through all of this—the hell we're all experiencing—I can now appreciate her quirks rather than mock them . . . *mostly*.

She sleeps.

I badly want to go back up and see Gage. I'm itching to hug my baby brother and smother him in all of my excitement from . . . well, from him still being alive, but I stay put. I don't leave my mom's room once in the next 24 hours. I pick up my MacBook and settle into one of the sitting chairs near the bed. It's not necessarily that she needs me more, but Gage has everyone looking after him. Mom just has me. *Lucky her.*

For hours, I write. I write Gage's story. From the moment he entered this world and tried to steal my thunder to the devastating day we found out he was sick with MS. I write every kind of ridiculous childhood story. I write about some of the things we've successfully kept hidden from our parents like the pot stash in high school to all the times we got busted for being unruly teens. Through it all Gage was the light. He was, quite literally, the voice in my head telling me to make better choices. I write about Gage the husband and Gage the father. Gage the encourager and Gage the fighter. I'm stuck like that in my reverie when mom finally stirs.

"Sage—are you crying?" My mom's strangled throat asks into the dim room.

"Naw, just thinking, Mom."

"Are you thinking about Gage?"

"Yep."

Then my mom begins to weep. I mean openly and disturbingly weep. She cries so hard she begins to gag and loses her breath. She falls apart. I allow her the moment and move to the bed to massage small circles into her back. Her head falls to my lap and she wraps her entire body around my waist. She cries. And cries. And cries. I'm so worried I'll say the wrong thing, but I take a small breath and softly speak into the dark.

"It's time to be strong now, Mom."

She slowly looks up at me, blotchy and tear-stained.

"This isn't my fault. I don't know how to be strong, Sage. No one taught me how to lose my child," and she breaks out in a fresh batch of new tears.

A month ago, I would have been incredibly annoyed with this statement and blamed it on my mom's inability to see the bigger picture, but now I just feel sympathy and sadness for a woman who doesn't know how incredible she really is.

"Mom, I'm not sure that strength is something you learn. It's something you have to leap into. When there isn't another option, you choose strength."

I wipe the wetness from her face and continue.

"And all it is, Mom, is the acceptance of being broken. That's strength—the absence of fear over not being able to control the outcome. Accepting that life may end in tragedy—or defeat—and choosing to try anyway. That's. Strength."

I let the words settle into my heart and realize how weak I've been about so many things in my own life. About Brec. About work. About home. I grab her hand to help let her know she's not in this alone.

"It's time to be strong now. We can do this."

Mom nods her head, and for the first time in my life, she repeats my Dad's worn phrase. "Sage, you really are stunning."

I kiss my mom's head, and we lay there breathing out the fear and finding our strength. I can't access my laptop, but from memory, I tell my mom about what I've been writing. I start at the beginning—the day Gage was born.

We fall asleep like that for the rest of the night, two broken souls tangled in each other, and we wake up stronger together—each healing from a lifetime of hurts and disappointments. Disappointments in ourselves and in each other.

By lunchtime, I gather the girls and take them with me to the hospital because I can't wait any longer to see my brother. This is one of the many beauties of homeschooling—I'm allowed to prioritize what matters in the moment. And right now, Gage matters most. The girls are bouncing bubbles of energy when I tell them about taking a day off to visit their daddy, but we are all unprepared for the grizzly sight when we arrive.

Gage may be awake, but an array of machines still seem to be keeping him alive. Through the window, we can see that he's intubated through his trachea, which makes Emery absolutely hysterical. I leave the girls in the waiting room with Brec and suit up to visit the room. For now, we each have to wear masks and protective gear in order to see Gage. Immediately, the room feels colder, and Gage is more distant—less like my baby brother. He can't speak, so I talk for him. I pull up the blog on my phone and read him each entry from the days he's missed. I tell him all of the beautiful things—the moments filled with life and color—but leave out how the girls are beginning to crumble without their Dad. I tell him about the night I had with mom and what I'm learning from spending more time with the family. I even admit that I'm really enjoying my teaching gig and have looked at what I'd have to do to get a teaching certificate—you know, just in case. Though I do amend this comment by telling him there is no way in hell I'd ever teach anyone younger than high school. I may love my nieces, but I'm just not cut out for those small, germy minions. Gage falls asleep somewhere in the middle of my talking. I hold his hand for a minute, memorizing the feel—the image. I take an internal snapshot of our hands joined because my camera is too far away, and then burn the moment into my memory.

It takes me a couple minutes to de-suit, and apparently, Brec has called my dad to come pick up the girls during my visit. It seems wrong to force the girls, essentially my job, on my father, but Brec encourages me to leave it alone. Dad also needs his time with the girls.

Brec looks rough. For 'Work Brec' he's incredibly sloppy and, if I'm not mistaken, he looks a bit hungover. Drunk doctors don't bode well for any patient—but especially not for Gage—

because I know what this means. Brec's never been much of a drinker, so a hungover Brec is like big, red alarms blaring.

He's folded into one of the hard waiting room chairs looking over documents when he notices me watching him.

"Don't you have anywhere else to be today?" I ask, testing the waters.

"No, Sage. I just have the one patient here, and as you can see, I'm doing a pretty shitty job at—" he gives an awkward half laugh that has no humor behind it, "well . . . my job."

I'm not good at emotions, not the real ones where, you know, you have to say the right thing or you can send someone spiraling out of control, but I can't leave Brec like this. I aim to lighten the mood, which is odd because he's usually the one doing emotional gymnastics around my mood swings.

"So, what's the story, morning glory?" [God, who am I?]

My very out-of-character question gets Brec's full attention.

"Who are you right now? And what have you done with Sage?" Brec asks with a very small smirk.

Weird. It's really weird how after all this time we can still be so in sync.

"Stop deflecting, Brec. What's the story?" I ask more formally—now embarrassed at my awkwardness.

He pushes the papers around in front of him, crosses one ankle over the opposite knee and leans his head heavily on his propped up hand.

"What do you remember from the night I told you about Gage's condition?"

"Everything," I say without missing a bit.

Brec waggles his eyebrows and repeats, "Everything?"

"STOP DEFLECTING."

"Do you remember the difference between the glioma and the lymphoma?"

"Yeah. One of the tumors is on the retinas and one is close to the ventricles."

"No. Well, yes . . . kind of . . . but no."

God, I hope he's not this confusing with all his patients.

"The gliomas are sitting on the retinas and the lymphoma starts adjacent to the ventricles, but the difference in the types of tumors is much more of the issue right now."

I wait him out because I assume he is going to continue with my education on cancerous tumors, but instead Brec begins shuffling the papers around again in an uncharacteristically manic manner. I place my hands on top of his to still the movement and tell him to rip off the Band-Aid.

"The gliomas on Gage's retinas are specifically called optic nerve gliomas. They are annoying fuckers and are triggering a large amount of pain as well as quickly deteriorating any eyesight Gage has left."

Okay, I think to myself. If that's the worry, then we can deal with it. Living on pain meds isn't ideal, obviously, it's just a matter of time before Gage is completely blind. But blind and in pain are much better than the other option we are facing.

If only Brec finished there.

"Lymphoma is a totally different breed. These are aggressive, metastasizing tumors."

"Metastasizing?" I ask trying the word out for size. "Meaning, they can spread?"

"Meaning, they already have."

This makes more sense. This is why Brec is drinking. This is why Gage looks like shit. We aren't talking about one organ anymore. We're talking about . . . God, we could be talking about his entire nervous system—his very compromised nervous system from years of MS.

"Where?" I ask, afraid to know the answer.

Brec wanders into thought and begins rambling. "We were so lucky that we caught the lymphoma early. You can't possibly understand how fortunate it was that we were looking at one tumor and not lesions all throughout his CNS. The gliomas were actually a blessing much more than a curse. They're why Gage got the scans done in the first place. I immediately knew I had to get here and that the first course of treatment was to get rid of the lymphoma which is almost always . . . *fatal.*" He says the last word in a small breath. It's the word we've all been tiptoeing around for weeks . . . months. "We couldn't wake him up after chemo because his newest scans showed a rapid growth in the number and variety of lesions—tumors."

Once Brec gets to the end of his speech, he looks empty—like holding onto this information was the only thing keeping him going, and now that he has shared the burden with someone else, he'll just collapse.

"So, are we looking at just the brain still? Have the tumors . . . spread beyond that?" I ask in whispered anticipation.

"No. It's *not* just the brain."

It's never one punch. They. Just. Keep. Coming.

Brec organizes the papers on the table in front of him and slides them into a large manila folder labeled, "Gilbert, Gage".

"So far, I've mostly been working with a team of medical and radiation oncologists. I made a call a few days ago to a friend of mine from Med School to come out and join us. He's a hematologist/oncologist. Maybe it was a mistake not to bring him on from the beginning. It seemed mostly neural from the onset. —I thought I could control it." He's mumbling and looks so lost. He continues in a staccato monotone voice. "I'm sending him Gage's information, so when he gets here later this week we'll have a plan of action . . . for . . . keeping Gage alive."

There it is. That's the truth. The knockout.

I fold inside myself and sit in the darkness. It's cold here. It's silent. Pain hurts less in the dark because the darkness is pain. When everything hurts, it's like nothing hurts at all.

Out loud, into our combined darkness, I find some strength and begin counting.

One.
Two.
Three.
Four.

By five we're counting together, in unison.

Six.
Seven.

On eight he grabs my hand.

Nine.

Last breath.

Ten.

Then I choose hope. I touched the dark and came back to the light for the first time in my life. Thank you, Anna and Emery, for showing me how to find happy in the middle of hell.

I start my line of questioning firmly, "Brec. Today, is there anything we can do? Can you change any of this right here, right now?"

"I don't think so," he whispers in defeat.

"How long has it been since you took a day off?" I ask looking at his completely disheveled appearance.

"Sage, I don't get days off—not until I can fix this."

"Today you do."

Hands still locked, I stand up and pull him up with me.

"Come on. *We're* taking the day off."

I pack Brec up in my beat-up Altima and decide on our first destination, Posies. He needs coffee, and I desperately need a cranberry scone.

It feels awkwardly nostalgic to walk into Posies with Brec. I can't decide if I wish for it to be all those years ago when life was simpler—with fewer troubles and fewer hurts—or if I'd do it all over again to wind up here as the person I am—the softer version I'm becoming.

We intentionally choose a different table—new beginnings and all that. We both decompress with the caffeine, and I see Brec coming back to life little by little. He looks around and voices my thoughts from earlier.

"Would you do it all again?"

Because I suck at sincerity and relationships and just, you know, general speaking with other humans, I can't directly answer his question.

"The cranberry scone? Hell, ya. In fact, watch out, I may do it again in about 20 minutes."

"Would you do it *all* again?" he says slower and without breaking eye contact. He's being patient with me now.

"How can I know the answer to that question? How can I know . . ." I trail off before looking back at him, "what I don't know? What we are, whatever this is, I can't change it. It just is. We don't get take-backs in life, Brec."

"Fair enough. You're right. We can't rewind the past, but we can," he drags a hand through his hair—he's nervous, he's hopeful. "We can begin again."

"I'm not up for this game, Brec." I say shaking my head back and forth.

"No game—just a first date."

"You mean *another* first date?"

He shrugs his shoulders and reaches across for my last bite of scone. "Sure. Let's go with that. Another first date."

I think for a second before responding—toying with him and giving into this game of cat and mouse. "Fine, but just so you know, you've already blown the date—you ate my last bite, and I don't play around where food is concerned."

The next hour is fun—simple fun—what a first date should be. We take turns asking questions as a way to absorb the person we've each become rather than the versions we left behind in college.

Brec's turn, "Favorite movie?"

"Easy. Amelie," I say and pop a new cranberry-filled bite into my mouth. [He got me a new scone. He's learning.]

"Still? I never did understand what you saw in that movie. It's a freaking *foreign* film."

"Leave it alone," I say in warning. "That little French sprite is my spirit animal, and I love her."

My turn, "Favorite meal?"

Brec blows out a long puff of air. "Whew. Gosh, that's hard. Does it have to be a meal, like an experience, or can it just be my favorite food?"

"Fine," I amend, "Favorite food."

"Much easier, thank you. Mexican—then, now and forever. Queso runs through these veins, baby."

"Boo. Boring. Everyone says Mexican."

"I don't think this game is called 'Sage, please judge my answers from your high, hipster horse', I'm pretty sure it's just called 20 questions. Now it's my turn. Favorite Album?"

Oh, we're pulling out the big guns here. Queso may run through Brec's veins, but music runs through mine. Brec begins humming the jeopardy countdown to rush me, but real answers take time. After thinking through my entire internal music library, I come up with a brief list of my all-time favorites.

"Can I give you a top 5 instead?"

"Sure, as long as you tell me why you chose each one."

Damn, he just got the upper hand. Music is an extremely personal reflection of yourself. I don't know that I can candidly explain to this man what I so desperately love about each of these lyrics—about how they each found a home in my heart. But I guess I have to try.

"Deal."

Brec raises his pointer finger to signal number 1.

"*Jagged Little Pill* by Alanis Morissette. She understood my teenage angst and was the only real friend I had for some of my more formative years. For that, I will always be thankful."

He nods his head as if he accepts this response and gestures for number 2.

"Ben Folds - *Rockin' the Suburbs*. This is the all-time best mix of sentimental, angry and angsty. No matter what mood you're in, this album is perfect. Road tripping? —*Rockin' the Suburbs*. Bad break up? —*Rockin' the Suburbs*. New Job? — *Rockin' the Suburbs*."

Brec rolls his eyes at my explanation but holds his third finger up.

"*Agaetis Byrjun* by Sigur Ros which literally means, 'a good beginning'. It feels like heaven—or maybe—more like happiness. This could be the soundtrack for every one of life's 'bests'. Best day. Best choice. Best meal. Best sex.

I am rewarded by slightly shocking Brec. I hate that I still love doing this so much. He raises his eyebrow but dips his head forward for me to continue.

"Number 4: Damien Rice - O. It's touched all of my dark places. Every one of my fears and hurts and sins are etched into that album. It knows every scar. There's something comforting about the idea that someone has seen all of your ugliness and is still there for you in the end.

Brec looks away, and I'm sure we're both recalling our darkest days together—and apart. Words said that I desperately wish I could take back. Words that no one deserves. He looks back to me with glassy eyes but slowly raises his thumb as he mouths, '5'.

"*The Bends* - Radiohead. This has been my anthem album through, well, everything. Every place I've been—every picture I've taken—every day I've lived."

Looking down, Brec shifts the empty cup in front of him as he mumbles, *"High and dry."*

I know what he's thinking, but it's more than just that one song—that one moment. Did a part of me feel and understand those lyrics? Absolutely. Did a part of me attribute them to that day, long ago, in Stanford? Certainly. But it's more than that.

"Not just that one. *Bullet Proof, Street Spirit, Fake Plastic Trees*. They were all songs I needed to find strength. They were what I needed to help me understand what was going on inside me, and it pushed me to peel myself away from the darkness."

"So, music did what I couldn't? A fucking album saved what all of my effort—all of my love—couldn't fix?"

The heaviness threatens to creep back on us, but I ward it off with the truest statement I can think of. "Nothing was going to save me until I was ready to be saved, Brec."

Brec clears his throat and grabs our trash. He takes a step away from me—away from the moment—as he cleans the table. When he comes back to me, I realize I'm holding my breath—waiting to see what happens next after opening this little crack of myself.

"Come on. I get to choose where we're going next."

Brec grabs my keys from the table and jogs quickly out to the door to my car. I'm already huffy and looking for a fight as I trail behind him until I see his 6-foot frame trying to smash himself into my driver's seat—arranged perfectly for my 4'11" body. That's what he gets.

I completely trust Brec with my car and wherever he's taking me, so I recline in the seat, crank up the music and decide it's time for a nap. I sleep dreamlessly and finally get what it is about the car that lulls Emery into to her naps. I wake up startled with the feeling that something is awry. The car is stopped, and I open my eyes cautiously, unsure of what to expect.

I should have kept my eyes closed.

Above me, Brec is leaning dangerously close—watching me. That's what's awry—Brec's cologne, Brec's breath, Brec's proximity to my mouth.

Warning! Warning! Warning! I panic and reach for the lever to release my seat back to its upright position. The catapult forward knocks my forehead into Brec's nose, and we're both left cradling our heads in the end.

I'm shit at romance. Seriously, I'm like a walking, talking rendition of the Three Stooges. Fan-fucking-tastic.

Brec has taken me for drinks part II—the alcoholic version. It's been weeks since I've had anything to drink, mostly because I'm too exhausted at the end of every day with the girls to do much more than pass out while watching made-for-TV movies.

This is a new brewery in the city that I've never seen before. Most of the bar has outside seating. There are picnic tables and metal chairs of every possible variety scattered about. I find the tackiness of the place absolutely charming. White lights are strung above the entire patio illuminating the dusk. Luckily, there are heaters and literal fires going to keep the customers warm. This place is perfectly me—gaudy in an endearing way.

Brec orders a flight of beers for us to try before we officially decide what to order. Everything is local or made onsite. We grab some typical bar food because I haven't eaten in nearly an hour, which is a bit of a travesty, and Brec is still trying to earn back those points he lost from eating my scone.

Some of the beers are amazing, others I sip and immediately pass on to Brec. The brewery has live music tonight, some sort of a fiddle-type band. The group around us is filled with contagious energy and happiness.

Brec and I order another round and reminisce about all of the mischief we got into in our early years. He blames the spray paint debacle of 2001 on me, and I can't even argue with him. We talk about skipping school to make out in his car and the first [and only] time his parents caught me in his bed. —I wore turtlenecks and jeans to his house for the rest of the summer to help ease my embarrassment.

It's the perfect ending to a perfect day—the part of the day I want to remember, anyway.

I'm feeling a bit tipsy when we get up to leave, so I willingly hand my keys over this time. Brec steers us back to the hotel, and before I know it, it's all over. We walk to the elevators in a new-found silence—both of us recognizing that our moment has expired. Tomorrow, Gage will be sick again and Brec will be the boy who broke my heart. I take my phone out of my purse and snap a photo. The picture is simple—two pairs of feet in an elevator the moment before we step back into reality. "Fourth floor," the overly articulate voice reminds us. Instead of stepping out, Brec turns around to me and pushes against the elevator doors to keep them open. It's an invitation, but he's waiting for me to make the move. Cat meet mouse. I cross my arms over my chest and lean my head to the side. He has clearly forgotten how stubborn I am—because I will wait him out, and I will win.

He's on me in one quick flash of movement. It isn't a soft, teasing first date kiss. It's a repressed and bruising reunion. My hands involuntarily move to his hair, and, with his hands around my waist, he lifts me up to meet his mouth. My body responds completely on its own. I'm climbing his torso, looking for a way to somehow push closer to him. We break for air, and the elevator slows once again "—sixth floor." God, I hate this elevator bitch.

Then it's over. He sets me down, and my mind begins swimming. What. The. Hell. Just. Happened?

The doors open, and I prepare for my escape—but he still has my waist. He looks back and forth between my eyes and in the worst possible Icelandic accent ever he says, "Agaetis Byrjun." I can't help it. I double over in laughter and I'm literally crying before I come back up for air. Out of everything that's happened today, I'm the most pleased by the realization that I'm clearly not the only one who is total shit at this dating stuff.

I finally stop laughing long enough for Brec to kiss my forehead and whisper to me, "A good beginning, *babe*."

"Cheesy. Oh my God, you're so cheesy," and I break into a new fit of giggles. Then I'm pushed roughly out of the elevator, maybe rightfully so, but either way I wouldn't take it back. This man is such a fucking nerd.

Alone in the hallway, my giggles shift into girlish angst. A good beginning? It's tempting, but can I get two good beginnings with the same person in one lifetime?

CHAPTER *Nine*

I'm spending some time tonight getting holiday curriculum together for our last few days of "school" before Christmas break. The girls refuse to focus right now, so I'm gonna have to reconfigure these lesson plans and make things a little more engaging. Anna and Emery are all excited energy as we prepare for our altered Christmas celebration, and we are all pumped because Gage has taken a turn for the better. Dr. Russell, the hematologist/oncologist, has become my new, very favorite person on this planet. He's wasted no time changing treatment plans, and Gage already seems like a better, brighter version of himself. Finally, it's beginning to look a *little* like Christmas around here.

Brec's come up to my room a couple nights this week for 'date night'. It's weird to date someone you were once engaged to. I want to believe I already know everything there is to know about this man, but in truth, he surprises me constantly. There are certain truths that never wavered, for sure, but in a way, he didn't turn out to be quite what I predicted all those years ago. Typically, we just watch a movie and make a drink. Last night we ordered in Thai food and played heads up—the ''90s music' deck. Mostly we laugh. We ugly laugh and we cry laugh, and my abs always hurt by the time he leaves. Since our 'good beginning part II', I've thought about this a lot. I don't think we used to laugh like this before. Our love was more of the serious variety and this, whatever this is, is something lighter. This isn't a desperate need, this isn't someone fulfilling my identity—this is fun, this is easy and at the bottom of all of that, I wonder if this is also just a really good distraction and nothing more.

I text mom to see if she wants to join us later this week on our 'field trip'. I'm attempting Holiday in the Park at Six Flags. The girls have never been, and since we aren't decorating the suite with a tree, I thought it would be something a little magical for them. I drum on my keyboard stumped on how to fill the remaining two days of our school week, so I turn to my email inbox, which hasn't been opened in weeks.

Most of it is random shit. Sales for holiday gifting or notifications for bills. Luckily, I have a decent savings, but my depleting funds are there, floating around, with the many other worries I'm trying to ignore. One email sticks out—time stamped 6:41 today. It's from my, well, about as close to a boss/manager as you get in my line of work. I pause for a minute, not sure if I want to read the contents or save it for later. After about 30 seconds, I click on it.

> Hey, Sage. I heard about your brother—that's a tough break.
>
> Look, it's the holidays, so it's always hard to find spec photographers. I have a job in Israel. The Palestinian/Jerusalem feud is ramping up now that Trump has recognized Jerusalem as the capital, and I need to get someone in there to shoot for the upcoming cabinet meeting. I know you don't usually go political, but we're talking relative safe, easy shots, and a big payout.
>
> You know how to reach me.
>
> Take Care,
> Ty

Obviously, I can't take the job. Can I? I mean Gage *is* doing better, and I'm pretty sure my mom could handle the girls for just Thursday and Friday. Heck, I can't think of anything to teach them this week anyway. I open a browser to check the cost of airfare, but before I can even look at flights, my phone beeps.

> Would love to spend some time with you and the girls. Are you thinking about going tomorrow? Friday may be really crowded because it's Christmas weekend. Anyway, thanks for thinking of me, Sage. Oh, and sweetie, make sure to put a little makeup on tomorrow before we go out. You looked a little like a dead fish today. —But a pretty, dead fish, your father says. See you in the morning, dear.

I've spent so much of my life disappointing my mother—partially because I enjoyed being the asshole that let her down and partially because of her ridiculous standards. But now, I don't want to be the thing that continues to hurt her. I make a mental note to write Ty back just as soon as I'm done with these effing lesson plans that are now the bane of my existence.

An hour later, I've finally finished laying out two whole days of curriculum for a 2nd grader and a 4-year-old. Good Lord, how do teachers do it? It's still relatively early in the evening, but I'm snuggled under numerous blankets, and the allure of sleep gets to me. That beautiful bitch.

There's knocking on my door. Every light is on, but I'm passed out and completely out of sorts. I stumble to the door in my sleepy stupor, and Brec is there with a bottle of wine in hand. I didn't realize we had something planned for tonight. He invites himself in and plops down in the middle of my bed because, unlike the rest of my family, I don't have a suite, and the bed is pretty much all I've got as far as sitting room goes. I know if I get back in that bed right now, I'll inevitably be doing more than sleeping. Nothing beyond kissing has happened with us this time around. We're trying to take it slow, and it really does feel like the beginning of something new. But, with Brec, the temptation is always there.

With that in mind—and the fact that I obviously now have an early morning with the girls, my mom and Holiday in the Park—I tell Brec to open the wine anyway, and I turn to take a quick shower. In the middle of lathering and rinsing my hair, I'm assaulted with the hope that Brec will charge into my steamy bathroom and keep his promise from my first night home at Posies. Taking it slow sucks, so I formulate a new plan. I quickly shave and moisturize. I comb through my wet hair, brush my teeth and, even though I clearly brought pajamas in here with me, I head out into the bedroom wearing nothing more than one of the hotel's plush white towels. I've never been overly modest, nor have I ever had a ton of confidence in my own sexual prowess. I definitely know I'm not built like a Sport's illustrated model, but I guess I still expect some sort of reaction from Brec when I walk out of the steamy bathroom. Instead, his head stays stuck on my computer screen and he doesn't witness any of my grand entrance. Men.

Before I even make it over to him on the bed, he's slamming the laptop closed and standing to leave. Well, that went way worse than anticipated.

"Things get too real, Sage, so you've got to run away? We can't be in the same place for more than a month before you want to leave—again?"

I've missed something here. Like, seriously, missed a step. I'm looking around the room for clues to Brec's sudden shift in demeanor. Brec won't look at me, but I follow his gaze. My laptop? Oh, shit. Now it all makes sense. Fucking, Ty.

"Brec, I'm not going anywhere. It was an offer for a job, nothing more."

"And you *weren't* looking at flights?" He accuses.

"Actually, no I wasn't. I was going to but decided I didn't want to let my mom down." I bite back.

"Dammit, Sage, you have to tell me about stuff like this."

"No, asshole, I really don't. —Look, it's my job. It's not like a rendezvous with an old lover. And beyond that, I only considered it for a matter of minutes."

"So, this Ty guy—he's *just* your boss?"

Gage and his freaking big mouth.

"Yes. Now, he is just my boss."

"Which means he was more than your boss before that . . . " Brec huffs under his breath.

"Yes. It means at one time, I was lonely and sad enough to settle for someone who liked my work more than they liked me. Happy? It's not like we ever asked about exes, Brec. You can't blame me for this."

"Fine, but now I'm asking about exes. Is there anyone else I need to know about?"

"Not really. I didn't spend a lot of my time throwing my heart around. I learned long ago that didn't work out very well for me. And while we're on the subject—why don't we talk about your exes? Care to share? Oh, that's right, there's just me and the woman you left me for."

The bubble bursts. This is why you don't get two good beginnings—because the second one is littered with everything left over from the past. Brec stands there, motionless, staring at me. He started this, but I guess I just ended it. He looks at me and says, "I'm sorry," before leaving. I'm so fucking tired of hearing that man say he's sorry. And now I'm left angry and disappointed—and standing in the middle of my room in nothing but a towel.

Holiday in the Park was a much better idea in theory than actuality. It's freezing, and while Emery is game for every ride, even the ones she is much too short for, Anna is terrified of heights. I wish I knew that *before* I took the girls to an amusement park. In the end, we decide to split up. Mom goes with Anna to watch some shows, while Emery and I attack the mini mine train again and again—*what joy*.

Christmas is literally just a few days away, and I have yet to get anyone anything. I figure while I have Emery's undivided attention, now would be a good time to ask about what she wants from Santa. She thinks this over for a while—chewing on her bottom lip—smiles and says, "I want daddy to live and a Fur-Real Friends."

Punch.

Sometimes kids really do say the damndest things.

The four of us meet up for hot cocoa and a train ride through the park at night before we head out. The girls want to sit beside each other, which forces mom and I to team up. Once, not so long ago, I would have had a volatile physical reaction to being forced to sit next to my mom for 30 minutes in below freezing weather, but I actually find myself relieved to be near another adult for the first time today. I don't have to blow noses, speak in funny voices, sing random songs from Frozen or deal with tantrums. In short, my very picky mother is actually the least amount of work. The park is beautiful like this. The girls 'ohh and ahh' over the lights and snow scenes. They're giggling with their heads bent together, and I quickly pull out my phone to snap a photo of two little blonde heads shimmering in the holiday lights. I imagine Gage and me at this age. I wonder if we would have fought to sit together, or if I would have shoved him out of my seat and off the moving train. Over a lifetime, there are so many moments taken for granted. I've always loved my little brother, but I know there were definitely times I didn't appreciate him like I should—and there's no way I can take any of that back.

I feel tired and depleted now that I don't have to constantly entertain my nieces. I barely slept last night after Brec left. How in the world did I screw that up so quickly? I keep replaying what I said—how I went straight for the jugular. We were both unfair, but I wasn't ready for the laughter—the fun—to end so suddenly.

"Sage. What are you thinking about?"

"How freaking tired I am. Parenting and teaching is one hell of a job."

I'm aiming for humor, but I immediately realize what I've said and try to back track. "Sorry. I don't mean *really* parenting. I was joking. I'm sorry. Gage and Olivia will always be their parents."

"Don't apologize, sweetie. You're basically being a parent right now. In fact, you're mostly taking the place of two parents, and you're doing rather well."

"Oh yes, I'm like 'parent of the year'. You do know I've taken them to Taco Bueno at least once a week since I've been back? Olivia is the rock star. I'm just the backup—filling in where I can."

"I see, and how many nights have you spent with the girls in the last week?"

"Four? Maybe five? It doesn't matter. I'm just glad I can do it."

"Well, I'm proud of you—I want you to know that. Annnd . . . " The way she draws out the word immediately makes me wary. "How is Brec doing? I've noticed you two getting closer."

It's not like Brec and I made some big announcement to everyone and said, 'Look ya'll—we're trying this dating non-sense again.' But, my sudden lack of hateful diatribes and his sudden appearance by my side at all times kind of did the telling for us.

"Brec . . . is Brec. He'll always be a beautiful idea, Mom, but the reality is, we just don't work."

"And you're okay with that, sugar?"

Do I even get a choice? I don't think life asks us if we mind before ripping our hopes and dreams away. It sure as hell isn't giving any of us a choice with Gage. This is a slippery slope with mom, but I choose honesty.

"Nope. No. I'm not okay with it—but I'm trying to accept it this time around. Really, we were ruined before we even started this thing. We have the black hole of our past looming around us, and it was always going to consume us." My mom nods along like she understands that boys filled with brightness and girls who loom in the shadows can never work out.

"What happened in Stanford, Sage?" My mom quietly demands.

I've never shared this story with anyone. Not a friend. Not a boyfriend. Not my brother. Not even a stinking diary. The hurt was so deep that I always had to apply pressure, or I'd bleed out. To protect myself, I had to keep it close—I had to keep it covered. A few months after I returned to New York, I sent the ring to my brother and told him to do whatever he wanted with it. Send it back to Brec. Throw it in a fire. Melt it down. Turn it into a bullet and murder my ex-fiancé—all were acceptable solutions. All they knew is it was over, and I guess, that's really all that was important at the time.

"He left me, Mom."

"So, you went all the way across the continent for Brec to tell you it was over? Why didn't you give the ring back then? Why wait two months and send it to your brother?"

"He left me for someone else. I didn't tell him I was coming." I take in a strangled gulp and try desperately not to weep. When that doesn't work, I lock my jaw and count to ten. "I just showed up. When he opened the door, she was right there —cooking breakfast in his kitchen—wearing his t-shirt. She had sleep hair . . . and she was . . . *perfect*," I end in a whisper.

The tears fall, and I use both hands to cover my face. But I continue.

"He stopped loving me, and I never even saw it coming. I always put him on a pedestal, and in the matter of 10 seconds he fell off this perfect perch and threw the pedestal at me—

crushing me to smithereens." I stop to catch my breath and get my bearings. I look to my mom with a tear-soaked face.

"He just . . . I guess, I wasn't loveable anymore." I try to shrug off the memory. "I left, and we never talked again."

My mom, heaven help her, is trying so hard to keep her mouth shut. I can literally see her smashing her lips together to keep her judgments to herself, but in the end, the words win out—they always do.

"So, you never *knew* the nature of their relationship. You never asked? What if you read it all wrong? Sage, I swear you're so stubborn. If you only would have talked to him maybe this could have been resolved decades ago."

"Mom, I didn't even know Brec decades ago—don't exaggerate, and I didn't need to ask. His face . . . it said it all. He was so tortured. You know that was the hardest part. He destroyed me that day—it was the worst day of my entire life—and when he came after me weeping, all I wanted to do was comfort *him*. I wanted to somehow take away *his* pain. How messed up am I? What is that, Mom?"

I'm nothing but a puddle of tears and hiccups at this point. I give up. This man was made to keep my heart shattered. My mom lifts my head to cradle it in her hands. She wipes under my eyes with one gloved hand and forcefully says each word.

"Sage, that is love."

CHAPTER Ten

I'm raw from re-living two break-ups with Brec, so I throw myself full force into Christmas. The girls and I get through Thursday's lessons, but we take off Friday to go shopping. I silently apologize to the teaching gods and swear to make up for this with extra time and homework when we get back at it after the New Year. I give each of the girls $50 to spend, but they seem to have zero concept of money. Emery wants to spend all of her money on a Build-A-Bear [for herself, of course] while Anna has her eye on a rather pricey superman costume from a party store for her dad. In the end, we go with a joint gift for each of their parents. We get Gage a Build-A-Bear in a superman outfit that has a voice recording of the girls saying, "I love you, Daddy." The voice recording catches a moment of Emery's giggle right after the final word, and it's absolute perfection. We opt for a manicure/pedicure package for Olivia and go to pick out a few Lush products to round out her "spa" gift. I desperately try to get the rest of my shopping done, but Emery—though she's already out of money—wants to stop at every store to buy things for herself. [I'm not too sure she gets the whole 'spirit of giving' thing that goes with Christmas just yet.] By noon, I realize the girls are only slowing this whole expedition down.

We meet dad for lunch at Taco Bueno—the girl's choice. I choke back my maniacal laughter, but admit, I could not be more pleased with myself. Afterward, Dad takes the girls for a playdate for the afternoon, and I return to the mall for round two.

I bounce back and forth on a spa day for my mom and maybe some nice cigars for dad. I wander in and out of stores looking for something that just screams Gage or Olivia, but in the end, I only buy a couple more items. I get Emery a FurReal Friends 'Torch My Blazin' Dragon' because I assume a Dragon is about as close as I can get to a Dinosaur. Anna is a little harder to shop for, but I decide on a legit looking doctor's kit—leather bag and all. She's hurting more than she shows, and I hope this will give her a little control over her fear of the situation. Though I spend a good amount of time looking all over this hellish mall three days before Christmas, there seems to be a whole lot of nothing everywhere. So many gifts with so little true value. Feeling frustrated, I decide to head back to my car. On my way out, I pass the ever-noisy Build-A-Bear. On a whim, I rush back into the store among the masses of pint-sized, squealing children. I speak with the slightly overly animated employee stuffing the bears and purchase three heart recorders before leaving. I have an idea.

Friday night I kick back with some merlot and my very favorite holiday compilation by Bing Crosby. I text Gage and tell him about my plan. I have to get to the hospital relatively early tomorrow morning for us to pull off our super-secret mission. For a little bit, as we text back and forth, this feels like Sage and Gage the early years—always trying to pull some sort of coup. Gage's numbers have continued to rise after Dr. Russell came on board. I still don't know exactly what this means, but I know it has to do with his blood and the lymphoma, and that overall, it's a really good sign. Gage was even up to FaceTiming with me a couple nights this week. He's strong enough and steady enough to hold the phone. He can nearly open both eyes, and his speech is much less slurred. He's still not the brother who taught me how to surf just yet, but there is such remarkable improvement in such a short amount of time that we all begin holding our breath for a miracle. He has to go to bed, and I flip back to my Amazon app to finish my shopping. I've never been a great gift-giver, but this year seems to be so much harder. I am so over this corporate-run Christmas and high-priced plastic shit. I chug the last of my merlot and look through my new, updated photo reel.

When I started with the girls, my photos lacked personality and meaning. They were beautifully executed and perfectly filtered, but they weren't me. Now my camera is full of horribly amazing pictures. Some of them—selfies of just the girls—must have been taken without my knowledge because I've never even seen them before. This is why I love photography. Our brains—our memories—so easily get altered by emotion, aging or life, but photos stand the test of time. They capture every detail accurately when our brains forget what's real. Suddenly, I know exactly what I want to do for Christmas. I just need to set aside some time tomorrow to run a few quick errands.

I look out the window before I go to bed. This is, by no means, the first Christmas I've spent in a hotel, but this is the first Christmas I've spent happy in a hotel. Brec aside, everyone I love the most in the world is here, and though it's untraditional, it's still a day—a place—filled with love and hope.

Christmas day arrives, and the girls are an animated flash of squeaky enthusiasm. Their voices register at a decibel only dogs can decipher. We are celebrating today at the hospital, though we first had to get permission from ALL of Gage's doctors. We are still only allowed in the waiting room while Gage stays in his own room, but one at a time we can enter and give him our gifts. We decide to each exchange gifts with Gage first and then with each other while Gage naps. When he's awake we will do a hospital friendly meal [shoot me] and watch some home movies that Mom and Dad have put together [shoot me twice].

I go first because my gift to Gage is actually his gifts to everyone else. I walk in and see that someone has decorated his bed for Christmas. He has little twinkle lights around the headboard and some fun garland running up his IV pole. More importantly, my brother looks happy—his color is back. This is all I've wished for weeks—for Gage to make it to this day, and now that we're here, it looks like I get to keep wishing for more days. We discretely try out each of the gifts to make sure they work, and then stuff them neatly back into their bags. He gives me a hug—a good hug, a sturdy hug—and we sit there like that appreciating every moment, every quirk, every memory we been blessed to have together. One tear escapes my eyes, and Gage frowns at me.

"Don't Mom out on me."

"Shut up. I swear I won't combust into an explosion of bodily fluids. I'm not crying because I'm sad. I'm crying because I'm thankful for you—for a lifetime of you. I love you, baby brother, and I'm so sorry I haven't taken the time to say that more."

"I love you too, Sage. I love who you're becoming—it's amazing to see you open up a little. You've never put up a wall between us, but I'm glad you're allowing others to see some vulnerability. You deserve to be loved, Sage, but you have to allow people to love you."

I know he's right, but I don't know the right words to say in response. Besides, the kids are getting restless for their turn. I kiss Gage's cheek as I get up to leave. He understands that I need to lighten the moment, so he acts like he's choking on my rare moment of physical affection. Right before I walk out, he calls for me.

"Sage?"

"Yes, brother dearest? How may I serve you?" I mock.

"Listen to that album, okay?"

"Sure thing."

Emery and Anna go in next so very proud to give their daddy the Build-A-Bear that they, or at least Emery, not-so-secretly wanted for herself. Gage looks at me through the glass when he opens the gift. I shrug my shoulders. [I mean I had to get the idea from somewhere. Grown women don't just think of Build-A-Bear all on their own.]

Emery opens hers first. It's a stuffed toy T-Rex that's half her size. She loves it immediately and hugs it with all her little might. Unexpectedly, the toy talks to her, "I love you, baby girl. Be fierce and remember—you're stunning." Emery looks scared at first, like she doesn't know what to do with this toy that sounds just like her Daddy. When she figures it out, she gets the biggest smile on her face and continues to squeeze the poor thing so the recording plays again and again on a loop. Anna gets a Stegosaurus with a slightly altered message. "My strong girl, I'll always love you. Be brave. Love, Daddy". I look across to Olivia watching the scene unfold through the glass-paned walls. She has tears rolling down her cheeks, and I know I've done well.

The rest of the gift giving seems to wear Gage out, and he barely makes it to my parents. Once he's resting, we open gifts with the family . . . and Brec . . . because, like it or not, he's somehow an honorary member of my family. Mom and Dad give Olivia and me a spa day, which makes me really glad I didn't get her the same gift back. That could have been awkward, and I'm desperately trying to ignore the obvious meaning behind my mother and I giving the same gifts. [Oh God, I *am* my mother's daughter.] Olivia and the girls give us all matching t-shirts. They are camo baseball-style tees that say #TeamGage on the front and have each of our names on the back. I love the gift, but I'm nearly moved to tears by the thought that I was a part of the creation of this idea. For me, this isn't just a gift, it's a cherished memory.

I'm nervous about my gifts and almost scrap the whole thing at the last minute. It's vulnerable and sentimental—pretty much everything that absolutely scares me to death. I hand out each wrapped rectangle and step away for them to open their gifts. My mom opens hers first because the girls are struggling with the scotch tape. She hugs the frame and bursts into tears. My dad gets his open and kisses Mom's head as they sit with heads bent looking at the frames. Olivia gets the paper off hers, looks at it once and then abruptly turns it over. I'm worried I've utterly screwed up, but she comes to give me a big hug that eases my fears a little. The girls are the last to wiggle the paper off. Emery hugs the frame and says, "Daddy, Daddy," while Anna looks at hers and turns hers over like her mother. She looks up to me with a trembling little lip and says thank you.

Brec saves his gift; he doesn't even attempt to open it. I wasn't sure if I should give him one, but as I looked through the photos, there were just too many of the two of them to leave him out. For Brec I chose an oldie—some truly vintage Gage and Brec. This is the moment I should have known these two were going to end up best friends. Brec and I had been dating for about five or six months, and he went with our family to Maui on summer vacation. Brec abandoned me and spent the entire day with Gage boogie boarding. I was just learning about photography back then. I remember taking shot after shot of strangers in the ocean—enjoying vacation. The photo is framed in front of the late afternoon sun and the gorgeous ocean. Both boys are sunburned and disheveled as they're looking out at the water. The older, bigger of the boys has his arm hung loosely around the smaller boy's shoulders. When I took the photo, I didn't even realize it was them. I just knew it looked like family. I think, maybe, that's really when their brotherhood was forged.

My mom's was an easy one, and really what sparked the whole idea. It's always been one of my favorite photos in the albums.

Gage can't even be a year old in the picture. My mom is holding him in her arms, and they are touching noses while looking into each other's eyes. Mom has a rare smirk on her face, and Gage is all lit up with laughter. It's a completely beautiful moment.

Dad's photo is of the two of them at the lake when Gage was maybe six. Dad's helping Gage tie his fishing line. He's on his knees in front of Gage and looking up into his eyes. Gage's face is pure trust and admiration, and that is exactly how Gage has felt about Dad ever since. Dad has always been Gage's hero, and he always will be.

The girls have almost identical photos. They are from years ago when we all met in Aspen for Christmas. Anna is all bundled up for the slopes, and Gage is walking her down the hill hand in hand. It's snowing and they each have their tongues out to catch the flakes.

I took Emery's the same day. I remember that she was pretty little for the snow and the cold, and she could barely toddle through the uneven drifts. Gage has her in his arms—she wanted to fly like the snowflakes. In the photo she's in the air, "flying" fearlessly, and looking at her daddy with pure trust. Gage is laughing with his hands up ready to catch her. There's just something poetic about the whole shot.

Olivia's was the hardest one for me. Before they got married, Gage and Olivia had a miscarriage their senior year of college. I thought only I knew about it, but I now have a sneaking suspicion that Brec was told too. They were young, yet excited to start their family, but incredibly worried about all of the details you never think about when these things are unplanned. When Olivia had the miscarriage, I thought it would break Gage. I remember flying down to meet them. It was the most heart-wrenching weekend, but the love between them was so obvious —so real. The photo is a private moment when Gage has his hand protectively over her nearly flat belly. They are looking at each other, and her eyes are wide and glassy—in fact, I think that is probably the only other time I've seen Olivia cry. To anyone else, this may just look like a sweet photo, but I know, for them, it was the beginning of their family that no one else knew about—it was the beginning of their forever.

We celebrate with a decent meal, you know for shitty hospital food, and watch a nostalgically sentimental compilation of home movies from over the years that my dad put together. It's hard to reconcile my version of the memories with the film in front of me. We see the buck-toothed Gage and awkward teenager Gage. My braces and tween years make their way into the film as well, and I immediately throw my napkin at my dad. Gage's many hairdos make the cut, and as we get to high school, Brec is in more and more of the movie. It's hard to watch them—those kids who had no idea how much life would hurt. Back then, I always felt like I was head-over-heels with Brec—the aloof, unobtainable cool kid—I felt like I was always one step away from losing him. Though watching these home movies tells a completely different story. My body language is standoff-ish, and he is all PDA. I'm the biting remarks to his sweet quips. I look at him across the waiting room, and he mouths, "I miss her," as he nods to the screen. The girls quickly pick up on the fact that their "uncle" Brec and Aunt Sage used to be together, and Emery asks if we are going to have babies. Gage loves seeing me squirm and adds, "Yeah, you two gonna have some babies or what?" I love my brother, but he sure can be an ass-hole.

Emery is like the walking dead by the time we head back to the hotel. Christmas just has a way of wearing everyone out. We've all been living off of adrenaline and excitement from finally seeing Gage well for the first time in a month, and that com-pounded with the typical after-the-holidays kind of tired, makes for pure exhaustion.

Before heading up to my room, I make a pit stop on the third floor to see Mom and Dad. Dad has always been a man of few words, but I know how much time he spent putting the video together for today and how hard it must have been going through all of that footage. Footage of a childhood Gage—before MS, before cancer. Dad and I each have a few fingers of Scotch while he watches some sort of sporting thing. I curl up beside him and put my feet under his legs to keep them warm. When I was little, this was the one annoyance Dad couldn't deal with. He would always push my tiny toes away and tell me to get some socks on. Today he just allows it. He warms my little popsicle feet without complaint. Mom comes in to join us and, surprisingly, pours herself a glass of Scotch instead of opting for her typical, nightly tea. We sit there in comfortable silence watching the game. When my drink is gone, I rinse out my glass and go to leave. My dad calls for me before I'm out the door.

"Sage—"

I smile knowing what comes next. I look to him before the words come out of his mouth.

"—you're stunning, sweetheart."

I gaze back at them both and smile. I fiercely love these two people who were tasked with having to raise me.

"Goodnight, guys." I have my hand on the doorknob but turn back around. "Today . . . today was a good day." I'm so incredibly happy, but somewhere in the back of my mind, I wonder how many more good days we'll get. I can't fully let my mind wander there, so I leave.

Outside of my room, I have a wrapped package sitting beside my door. At first, I'm a little worried it's from the ever-creepy hotel employee, James, who still goes out of his way to find me every time I'm in the lobby.

I've changed into my yoga pants and Brec's Stanford shirt—which I never gave back—before I even look at who the gift is from. I open the card and glance at the sender. Brec, of course it's freaking Brec. I'm worried about what's inside this box. Whatever it is, he didn't want to give it to me in front of the family, and he didn't even want to give it to me in person. This calls for wine.

I look at my limited alcohol selection. I only have some vodka left sitting out on the wet bar. I had some Scotch with dad, and I'm not great about mixing my liquors. I decide I better pass on a drink.

I take the card off and read it.

For the girl who has all the vinyls and no way to play them.

Merry Christmas, babe.

Xoxo,

Brec

Shit. I need the alcohol after all. I pour myself a vodka cranberry and dig into the gift.

It's beautiful. This thing had to be expensive. Brec has given me a vintage tabletop record player in perfect condition. I don't know how he knew that I no longer had one. In college, Gage and I always listened to everything on vinyl—I am a music purest; however, by the time I took my first assignment overseas, I sold off most of my possessions—the record player included. I had a pretty decent selection on my own, but Gage has continued to stock my vinyl library for nearly every holiday since. I didn't have the heart to tell him the truth, and I liked the idea of him carefully choosing each album for the lyrics—the words—he wanted to tell me.

I excitedly put on some of my older albums that I haven't listened to in forever. Music from my childhood and music from my youth. I spend hours in my hotel room drinking and dancing around to Waylon Jennings and Mazzy Star. David Bazan and Bon Iver. Ryan Adams and Amy Grant. I get lost in the music and am feeling maybe a couple steps past tipsy when I rifle through my selection for something new. Ah, yes, my birthday present from Gage. He keeps bugging me about listening to it, but I obviously missed the deadline to tell him about my missing record player years ago. Now, I can honestly say, I've listened to it—you know, only about six months later than intended. I quickly unwrap the cellophane and finish off my drink.

My God, I've missed Death Cab. Their early years will always be the best. After Brec, I used to play *Someday You Will Be Loved* on repeat all day long. I've always felt like Ben Gibbard and I were best friends in a former life. He is my heart in lyric form. Each song from the album unlocks old memories. Some that make me laugh. Some that make me teary. Some that make me embarrassed for the dumb girl I once was. I'm at the bar deciding yay or nay on drink number 5 when the next song clicks on—*What Sarah Said*.

The instrumental opening already hurts me before the words even begin—before I can quite recall the song.

I'm hyperventilating before the song gets to its closing. I know this song. I remember Gage and I talking about it once a long time ago—it was the most melancholically beautiful tribute to death—the darkest of all Death Cab's songs. He sent this to me in June. In FUCKING June.

I was the first person he told.

I'm suddenly running through the room looking for the card that went with it. What exactly did Gage say? Please tell me this is coincidental. I tear apart my camera bag and my small stash of saved letters and postcards. Nothing. I grab my keys and run, barefoot, to my car. Surely, it must still be in my car. I opened the gift in here months ago for Christ's sake. I tear through the glove box and every nook and cranny of the vehicle and come up empty-handed. This is why I don't clean shit.

There is no way Gage sent this to me on purpose. My birthday was long before he was even in the hospital. He wouldn't do that. He wouldn't . . . *tell me* . . . in an album. My mind keeps going back to how many times he's asked me to listen to this. How many times he's asked me about *this* gift and never a single one before it.

This is just a coincidence. "A FUCKING COINCIDENCE," I scream at the top of my lungs into the dark, starry night. And then I fall to my knees in a pile of anguish on the cement lot below me.

This isn't an accident. This is Gage's warning. He's telling me—goodbye. I wasn't the last person he told—I was the first.

I'm all inconsolable sobs. I'm darkness. I'm hell. And I lay right there and fall apart all over again.

Brec finds me at some point. My eyes can barely open, and I don't even resist when he bends down and picks me up. He carries me, sobbing, the whole way to his room. He keeps me away from the song—away from my room—almost like he knows what hurt me. He pulls back the covers and puts me to bed, turns out the light and gets in right behind me. We stay like that, his tall body wrapped around my tiny frame, for hours. I nod off a couple times but wake myself up twice crying.

My mind is a jumble of noise and pain. Gage told me so many months before I came. He gave me the opportunity for so many more memories with him, and I just didn't listen. In this moment, I know I'll never be able to forgive myself.

And then behind all of my blame is the unbelievable realization that he's already given up. It hits me like a semitruck that Gage has known all along—this is the end of his road. Here I was foolishly hoping and fighting, when he's already resigned to letting go. How do I tell the girls, how do we watch him stop fighting for us—for life—for all his beautiful color?

I turn into Brec's chest, still crying. He kisses my head, and I think of how I wish I had stayed and fought for him in Stanford. I wish that this was my reality—this comfort, this love, this man—I wish it were mine.

I'm almost back into a fitful sleep when it dawns on me that Brec found me. I was in the parking lot, alone, way past midnight. Why in the world would he have been looking for me there? I sleepily ask him what made him go out to the parking lot so late at night.

"You."

"What? You were looking for me, so you immediately thought, 'let's go outside in the freezing cold during the middle of night?'"

"No." That's all he offers, but he tightens his grip around me.

Quickly, I'm much more awake. "Wait. Seriously, Brec. Why the hell were you outside?"

"I was waiting for you, Sage."

"So, you telepathically knew that I was going to go outside and fall to pieces on the concrete?"

"Sort of."

"You're not making sense. How did you *sort of* know what was going to happen?"

Then my sluggish mind puts all the pieces together. *He* got me the record player. That wasn't a coincidence either. That wasn't just because he saw my unused vinyl library. He knew. He knew what would happen to me, and he gave me the gift anyway.

I'm still encased in his arms and stuck to his side, but my tiny hands have turned into fists, and I begin using every ounce of energy I have to hit him. To hit all of the pain as far away from me as I can get it. To make him as broken as he's made me.

"Why?" I shrill. "Why would you destroy me again?"

His hold stays tight around me. He doesn't even turn away or flinch with my abuse. He just takes it.

"Say something! Answer me!" My voice grows an octave with every word.

But he doesn't. I hit him over and over again with more strength than I knew I possessed. I want to bruise him. I want to see him shatter. My darkness absorbs everything around me.

"Why would you do it, Brec? How could you?" I gasp out in strangled yells. "I loved you, you asshole, and you broke it all."

Everything. Stops. My fists, his hold. It's like we free-fall, together, for a second. Now able to get away, I scurry off the bed toward the doorway. I'm panting—from exertion, from pain. We both continue to register my question—as if I've asked it again and again. Somewhere along the way this stopped being about his betrayal with Gage—it became his betrayal to me.

My tears are gone, but my breathing is erratic. If I ask it again, he'll answer. If I don't ask, I'll never know. In my head I begin to count.

One.
Two.
Three.

My lips tremble.

Four.
Five.

"I didn't cheat on you." Brec says the words like they are being ripped out of him.

My brain can't immediately process what I've heard. I have imagined the possibility of this moment for a decade and *NEVER* were those the words I expected to hear.

"You what?" I ask, unsure that I heard him correctly.

Brec takes a deep breath and says, more articulately, "I never cheated on you, Sage."

"But . . . I was there. She was right in front of me. I saw—"

"—You saw what you wanted to see."

"What?" I splutter. "How can you even begin to believe that I wanted to see you with her? That's got to be the stupidest shit I've ever heard."

He shrugs his shoulders, and with the action, I watch him sink further into himself. Completely closing off—completely shutting down.

"Hell no. You don't get to act all wounded again. I let you get away with that shit the first time. I let you fall apart while I had to hold it together. I let you go—"

"Yes, Sage," he suddenly roars to life. "Finally, something we FUCKING agree on! *You*. Let. *Me*. Go."

He's shaking his head like he's disgusted with the memory—or with me.

I don't understand. I take a few seconds to quickly rewind my memory to see if I missed any glaring details.

I rode the elevator up to his floor. I remember checking my lip gloss in the reflection of the door. I shakily stepped off, unsure what the weekend would hold—unsure if we would still be us by the time I left. I went for the doorknob first, but it was locked, so I knocked. It was cold in the hallway even though it was spring. I shivered. Brec answered the door on the third, or maybe it was the fourth knock. He looked all wrong. He looked shocked and scared that I was at his door. My heart dropped to my stomach. He glanced away from me to look at the back of the beautiful girl in his kitchen—cooking over his stove, wearing his t-shirt. His eyes were wide, terrified, when he looked back at me. He opened his mouth to speak, and I ran.

"I didn't even know her."

"I'm pretty sure a one-night stand is still called cheating, Brec."

"I didn't cheat on you." He says once again with more authority. He struggles in silence for a moment before he blows out one long breath and starts. "I came home late that night from studying for a chem test. I lived in the library that semester to make up for my slipping GPA. I was tired. I was always tired. It was my senior year of college, and I was buried under a pile of work."

He stops for a minute to run his hand through his hair and pop his neck. It hurts to hear him talk about this—this lost year of us—this year that we were both essentially in love with the ghosts of each other.

"Ryan was having a party—mostly underage kids that I didn't really want to hang out with. I was in a bad mood from studying. I was in a bad mood because my space was invaded. I was in a bad mood because you were never, *ever*, around. She was just . . . there—someone who looked as unimpressed with the nonsense as I was. I got a beer and went out to the patio—just to escape the noise, but she followed me out there. I had no intentions of making conversation—I didn't intend on any of it."

One.
Two.

"She was nice—she was simple. She laughed—not because she was cynical, but because life amused her. We sat there making small talk through our drinks. It was just a distraction—a momentary time out from everything I was doing wrong . . . everything I couldn't fix."

"God, just say it. Say you fucked her, and she was everything I wasn't. Say something real, Brec."

Brec shakes his head in a motion I can't quite decipher. It's not an earnest, 'I'm so sorry I fucked up', but it's also not quite a, 'Why of course not, Sage' type of gesture.

"We went for round two . . . then three . . . and four. She asked about my story and I sloughed it off—the truth. I knew I should have explained you—explained us, but I just needed . . ." He bites the inside of his cheek and his jaw tics in unison. "She saw me as this amazing pre-med guy who had the world at his fingertips, and I just didn't want to be me for a little while. She was all hopeful energy, and it felt amazing to be able to make someone happy for just a little piece of time. When we finally got up to go inside, I realized she was pretty tipsy. She stumbled on her way in the door. I caught her around her waist—purely out of reflex."

Immediately, I can see flashes of what the rest of their night turned into. Her in his arms. How he kissed that spot on her neck that was once meant for me. How she looked naked. I can physically feel my shoulders folding in on me as I wrap my arms around my waist to hold in everything that threatens to bleed out of me.

"It was an accident, but it was enough. Enough to make me know whatever this girl was—distraction or flirtation or seduction—she'd never be you. I could bury it, and I could cover it up, but her admiration still wasn't the same as your love.

I sat her back up forcefully—maybe too aggressively—her hand slipped, and her drink spilled down her dress. It sounds cliché, but it happened. She laughed it off like nothing in the world bothered her, but I offered her whatever she needed from my closet. She chose your t-shirt, the one you bought me when I got accepted to Stanford. I warned her she could choose anything but that. Then, she directly asked if there was someone—she asked about you, and this dam finally broke inside me. She was all questions. She wanted to know your name—what you were like—how we met—where you were. I told her about the darkroom—about Posies and Antonia's never-ending opinions. I told her about when my dad died and the ache of leaving you every time I had to go back to school. I told her how I proposed. She immediately liked you and wanted to meet the girl who never gave a shit about what anyone else thought. I told her about NYU and how everything changed after that. We stayed up nearly all night, long after everyone was trashed or passed out or left, talking about you—about every time I disappointed you, about your silence and your distance, and about how to get you back. I ran her through our entire history needing someone to see it, to hear it and help me find out where I went wrong."

"But she stayed the night . . . I . . . "

"I slept on the couch. Nothing, *absolutely nothing*, happened, Sage."

He finally looks at me with such fierce sincerity as he sounds out each of the next words.

"I. *Never.* Cheated."

"But . . . but . . . " My mind can't find the words. I sag my weight against the doorframe behind me. I attempt to speak again. "But . . . I know what I saw . . . "

"What you saw were two sleepy, hungry and slightly hung-over people making breakfast. It wasn't guilt written on my face—it was worry that you were there to end us in person."

He pauses to look away out the open window. "And you did."

This has to be bullshit. I force the memory back to the forefront again. Replay. Stop. Rewind. Replay. *—There it is.* The island in the center of the kitchen was littered with dozens of beer bottles. The couch in the background was clearly recently used. He— *never*—cheated?

My voice is so small. I've lost years of self-righteous anger all at once. "But . . . but . . . but you married her." I release on a small gasp.

Brec's eyes gloss until they blink out a few lonely tears that roll down his cheek. With a single nod he agrees. "I married her."

"How does that even happen? How did you go from just meeting her one night—telling her our whole story—to marrying her eight years later? How am I supposed to believe that?"

"Because it's the truth—when you left. When you told me goodbye, the bottom dropped out for me. I . . . I didn't have a plan for my life that didn't include you. I was holding on to you by a thread, but when that string snapped, it cut me in half. She was there. She was my friend. She became my best friend. She was the one who listened to me night after night tell and retell our story trying to find some answers."

"Gage is your friend too, and you didn't fucking marry him."

He gives an effortless laugh—really more of a humorless puff of air. "It was six years before we went on a date. Six years of complete friendship before *anything* ever happened, and I remember still feeling like I was cheating on you. Nothing felt right. She was never you."

"But then you married her anyway?

"I only proposed after I knew you'd moved on. Gage told me about Ty. —He told me it was time for me to let it go and move on." We hold silent eye contact. "I married her, *anyway*, once I knew I could never have you."

I'm lost in my head. This is, well, it's all Gage's fault. —But it's not really. Gage may have given shitty advice, but clearly, we were already so very broken. Broken enough for me to believe the worst about the person I loved the most. Finally, I sink to the floor because my body just can't hold itself up anymore.

"Why didn't you tell me? You waited for six years—but you never came after me. You just let me believe you were a horrible piece of shit."

Brec tugs at the end of his hair and sits down on the bed, showing me his profile. We wait like that for minutes before he answers my question.

"Sage, do you remember us before that day? Do you remember that year?"

Of course I did, it was the worst year of my life made infinitely more bleak by that day in Stanford.

"Yes."

"I remember how hard that year was. I called you every day that fall. You returned two phone calls . . . *two*, Sage. I failed my first class that semester. I was paralyzed with fear: fear that we'd be over, fear that I'd failed you, fear that you would give into your fears—into your darkness."

I nod my head—I remember the darkness.

"I applied to one medical school. Just *one*. My academic advisor was livid with me, but I knew there was only one place I belonged—with you."

"You were going to move to New York?"

"Yes. I got into NYU School of Medicine. I thought that if I could love you hard enough. If I could fix you then you could love yourself. *Then* you could be happy."

"Brec, you always made me happy."

"Happier than the idea of being nothing? Of never hurting? Of never being scared or insecure or broken?"

"Brec, I loved you with every piece of me. I always loved you—even in the depression."

We both have slow tears trickling down our faces. Brec's tears are illuminated by the moon streaming through the window. I see each of them roll to his jaw and then fall away.

"I couldn't love you well enough, Sage. No matter how much love I had, it wasn't enough to make you better, and I couldn't spend the rest of my life failing you. I can't. Every time I hope. Every time I begin to believe in our happy ending, I'm completely smashed by you—by reality."

My breath is wobbly because it feels like I am losing him in a way I've never experienced before—not even when I thought he left me.

"I waited for you for years—for you to come back to me, to believe in us as much as I did—and you never showed up. You saw what you wanted to see that day." Brec releases a shaky breath before he finishes. "I've thought about this for a really, really long time. I think you were looking for an out. I think you were so ready for us to crumble, that you needed to knock it all down—to control the fall. You've been the victim for 14 years, Sage, and I let you be—but now, I need you to know, that day, *you* broke *me*."

I repeat his worn-out phrase—one that maybe wasn't ever even necessary, or his to say.

"I'm so sorry . . . "

I am sorry for allowing the world to break me and for allowing me to break us. I'm sorry for not fighting for him or at least for the truth. I'm sorry for wallowing in my indignation and animosity instead of noticing how hurt he was. I'm sorry for being weak. I'm sorry for being selfish. I'm sorry for all my destruction.

But the only words I add are, " . . . for . . . all of it . . . "

Then I get up, gather my keys and leave—shutting the door on Brec, on us. I'm releasing him to a new beginning with someone that deserves the boy who loves too fiercely and the man who forgives too willingly.

CHAPTER *Eleven*

The world turns bleak. The weather has finally snapped from crisp to cold to artic. Brec moved out of the hotel this week—quietly and without much fanfare. I guess it was his turn to runaway—that only seems fair. The girls can feel my shifting mood. I try to hold it together for them, but I've always been complete shit at hiding my feelings. I'm smiling [okay, more like grimacing] and going through the motions, but my heart just isn't open for anything or anyone right now. I'm shut down until I can find a way off this roller coaster.

My new record player stays on the coffee table for over a week as a reminder of my every disappointment, in life and in myself, and goes unused before I eventually move it to my trunk. I never thought anything could come between me and my love for music, but I now prefer complete silence to anything else. The notes feel sad and the lyrics feel empty, but the silence swallows me up and makes me feel a beautiful sort of numb.

I spend most of my days after Christmas in my room. The walls are very white and unmarked—like they're bragging about the hotel's newness. Lucky bastard, it hasn't had time to get a-bused. I can't find the strength to revisit Posies yet, so I try a mom and pop place downtown. Their dirty chai's suck and they sell bagels, not scones. It's not the same. Bagels feel so New York, and for the first time in my life, that doesn't sound appealing—it doesn't feel like home anymore.

The girls have spent most of their "break" with Olivia. I think they all need a little dose of normal, and I need some time away from chalkboards and chart paper and those little tiny boxes for lesson plans. They show up on Thursday night for an impromptu sleepover, which consequently reminds me how exhausting they are and that a full-sized bed was never meant for three people. I don't care if we're all pint-sized—*small* kicking legs still hurt. Olivia tries to talk to me briefly about Brec. I know that she must have forged a friendship with him too through all of my absent years, but I can't even begin to know how to process this new version of my past—the true version? I'm still teetering on the edge between belief and suspect. One strong gust in the right direction, and I could easily doubt every word he told me. I have 14 years of sordid assumptions to support me—14 years of imagining how a fictional night went down. My mind is warring with who I know Brec is—who he's always been—and my need to not be the one who broke us. In the empty moments, I think a lot about the conversation I had with Mom about strength. In many ways, that day in Stanford was my first leap. It was the first time I had to let go of my control and accept that life may destroy me. And it didn't happen immediately—it didn't happen for years—but eventually, I chose to try again. *Strength.* I may not ever know the true ending to our story, but I know Brec gifted me with so many of the best pieces of who I am today, and that's enough. I don't have to be happy right now, but I also know that I won't stay splintered forever.

The weather seems to have the power to change all our courses. Gage is talking less—much less, scary less. In fact, when the girls and I go to see him on Friday, his speech is so slurred that Anna asks if he is hurt. His lids are droopy, and he looks not so unlike a stroke victim. Emery is also alarmed by the sudden change over the last nine days and asks if we broke Daddy. I think to myself, silently, life broke Daddy—life breaks all of us—because life's a bitch. I want to reach out to Brec. I need to know what's really going on—why Gage's breathing is so erratic. We all hold our breaths while waiting to see if he'll take his next one. But I don't know how or what to say to him, so I'm silent—a new trait for me. I'm evolving and what not. Growing up is total bullshit.

Dr. Russell asks to talk to us—all of us—at the hospital today. New Year's Eve. The hospital is all anticipation and energy for the holiday—it's like no one told them it got cold and sad as fuck in the last week. They've missed the memo that the illusion of my recovering brother has been shattered. We walk into the waiting room, together—a unified front. I'm holding my mom's hand. She's holding my dad's. Olivia is walking slightly in front of us with both girls flanking her on either side. Whatever the news is, we are here to fight it as a family. I want to pull some sort of hope from my reserves, but it feels like all my strength runs dry the moment we cross into the ICU.

Brec's already there, sitting with Dr. Russell, and the waiting room is completely cleared. I look between each of their faces trying to read the moment, but they are each looking at the ground preparing to speak—to break whatever solace we've found in the last months. Unwelcome Death Cab lyrics rush into my head as I remember Gage's warning—*What Sarah Said*—and I'm hit with the impact of knowing how this all ends before anyone has a chance to say it.

Dr. Russell clears his throat and begins.

"As you know, we've seen a rapid decline in Gage's functions and motor skills. His most recent scans and labs show bad news, I'm afraid."

Olivia is stoic beauty as this typhoon threatens to blow her life—everything she loves—away from her in swirling, dark, stormy skies. With complete control she speaks for us all.

"What are our options?"

Even when you know things are bad. Even when you know they'll hurt, you're never quite prepared for the power of the punch. We all look to Dr. Russell, but he defers to Brec—who is, after all, his official doctor of record. Brec looks up, and his boyish face has aged ten years. He's just angles and shadows now.

"At this point, our best option is end-of-life care."

—and all of our hopes flatline—

My mom, who has done an incredible job holding herself together in the most recent weeks, takes the girls' hands and abruptly walks away. I'm not sure if she felt it wasn't helpful for Anna and Emery to hear the specifics of how their dad will die or if she needs an excuse not to know herself.

Brec lays it out for us. What we can expect—what comes next. Gage will lose his remaining vision, motor skills and neurological functions before he will likely go into multisystem organ failure. His immune system is beyond fragile, and we are basically, indirectly, discouraged from visiting him. We are suddenly faced with the conundrum of whether to continue any course of treatment or to give up. Chemo may slow down the rapidly spreading lymphoma, but Gage's body is so weak it may also immediately kill him.

Olivia, Dad and I process this information in complete silence. Dad swallows a loud, painful sob, and I know if I look at him we will both become puddles of defeat. Hearing my dad crack adds a new layer of pain to what I formerly believed already to be my broken heart.

Dad is the first to speak into the grief.

"I'd like to see my son."

Dr. Russell ushers him through the new protocol to enter Gage's room before opening the door to my brother and giving him a moment of space alone with his son—*his dying son*.

Brec loosely grips Olivia's elbow and they slip to the corner chairs for a more private conversation, and I'm left standing, rooted to this spot. Alone. I look down at the toe of my boots—scuffed and without much color. Brown. This faded sepia fucking world. I take a mental picture with that fucking faulty camera we call memory. I think about adjusting the ISO to create a distorted shot full of shadows and bursts of light. The sort of photo that you can look at all day and never know exactly what the object is. I love those photos. There is beauty in people, but there is art in allowing people to interpret a picture however they want—or need to.

The hushed whispers from the corner behind me shake me from the moment with my fictional photo—the one that, to me, will always be called 'the end'. I gather my strength, focus my vision and look up—through the glass. My dad is a bundle of 'protective wear' as he stands by Gage's side—his back facing me and obscuring my view of my brother. I see his shoulders' quiet movement—their silent rise and fall. Without seeing his face, I know that I'm watching my father cry for the first time in my life. I turn on more of my senses and reach out for pieces of Brec's muffled conversation with Olivia.

"Homecare may allow for the best outcome. For you. For Gage. For the girls."

"As in, Hospice?"

"As in Hospice. He would be back in your home—back with your memories. Studies show that this can actually have beneficial results with some patients. It gets him out of the ICU.

Olivia, it gets you all out of the ICU and away from living in a hotel."

"But what about his immune system? Won't we kill him faster if we put him back in the house with us—near our germs?"

"There are preventative measures that you can take. Hospice is there to help you through that. Remember, you'll have a nurse on hand nearly every step of the way."

"And you'll be there."

I hear Brec blow out a breath that he's been holding in. I am familiar with these breaths. When we were together, I used to memorize them. They always meant there was some partial truth he was holding back. They always told me to worry. They always fractured the trust.

"Olivia, in these situations . . . I'm a neurologist. In hospice care they won't continue with scans or CTs or labs. This is good for Gage. He won't be poked or prodded . . . "

I'm so proud that Olivia doesn't leave it there—that she's the sort of ballsy princess to push for more information.

"So what does that mean, Brec? You're leaving him? You're giving up?"

"No. But it does mean my ability to be of any help to Gage—as a doctor—has expired."

What he's really saying is death isn't his part of this three-ring circus. He's always been so much better at being the Savior than the Grim Reaper. He never did know how to fail.

Neither of them talks or clarifies anything for a minute, and I get a weird premonition that they're looking toward me—still standing in the middle of the waiting room. It's then I realize, with some pride, that I'm. Still. Standing.

"I need to have a job, Olivia, but you know I'm done with Santa Cruz. I officially gave them my resignation right before Christmas. It was really just a formality by this point, but it still needed to be done. The hospital, here, offered me a full-time position. God, I never thought I'd move back home, but it keeps me close to Gage—it keeps me . . . here."

Olivia goes on to offer him the guest bedroom at the house, but Brec tells her he's already looking at houses with a realtor. He's moving back. How can he move back here and pretend to pick up where he left off? He encourages her to officially leave her job, take some time off and allow the next few months to happen as a family. I didn't realize Olivia hadn't left her job. All this time I just assumed that Mom and Dad were covering the bills for them, but Olivia must have been editing all through the night and handling the endless hospital visits and doctor's meetings with Gage during the day. Olivia's a freelance editor and has always been able to make her own hours. It never occurred to me that she was still working through all of this.

I know, right then, I'll do whatever I can to help Gage's family enjoy their ending with him—whatever amount of time he has left. I shift my weight to move toward their conversation and offer my help, but Dad turns toward the glass pane first and seeing him wipes me of any former thought or movement.

Dad exits and de-robes from the mask and booties and paperish, cloth coverings. Dr. Russell suddenly appears and asks if any of us would like a moment with Gage. It's amazing how someone can go from being your favorite person in the world to an absolute asshole in such a short amount of time. Do we want a moment with Gage? No—*we want a lifetime.*

I turn toward Olivia, finally looking behind me, and lock eyes with Brec. I know we're both hurting in ways we've never known —and for once it isn't damage that we've caused each other. It's new to hurt with him and not because of him. Somehow this message passes silently through us—through eyes that have been momentarily stripped of life. From the corner of my vision, I see Olivia, beside him, nodding me toward Gage's room. I guess, it's my turn.

Dr. Russell runs me through the motions of suiting up, but I'm only half-listening to him. He has to correct me twice on how to tie my mask. Then he takes me in to the last visit I'll have in this stagnant ICU room.

Gage was blocked from my view when Dad was in here, and I'm silently grateful that I couldn't see his condition. His eyelids lift slightly, but behind them it's obvious, Gage can't see. His once bright blue eyes have a sort of dead, unmoving look. The right side of his mouth is slack, and I can see where he has drooled on the pillow. While perusing all of his physical changes, my eyes well up and my jaw begins to clench and unclench.

"So, I guess you've heard? —We're busting you out of here."

Gage doesn't try to talk, but I get a slight 'thumbs up' from him— just a barely-there movement. It's obvious this is going to be a one-sided conversation, and I'm worried that it's going to be our last, so with trembling lips, I continue.

"I got the album."

Gage's eyes scan the room 'looking' for my voice.

"I mean, I *got* the album."

I can see the left side of his lips tip up and his dimple faintly appears.

"You told me a really long time ago, and I just wasn't listening. I'm so—" I break for tears, and my mouth trembles before I can calm myself enough to speak. "—I'm so sorry. I wasn't here for you. I was never here."

I watch his reaction. I don't know how I can tell, but I can see it in the way he blinks. He's forgiving me. Forgiving me for only ever scheduling his needs and his life into my open time slots. Forgiving me for always hurting but never noticing who I hurt.

Gage opens the palm of his hand up, facing the ceiling, in a sort of 'what now' gesture. I continue and tell him everything. I tell him about Brec—about learning the truth and now dealing with my guilt and hate. I tell him about growing up and learning—noticing—how to be a better version of me. I tell him about Ty—how much it hurt me that he was never Brec, and how Ty didn't want me with an ounce of the same love. I tell him how much I admire Olivia. Antonia told me—God that seems like forever ago—that Gage was the best of us all, and now I'm telling Gage how Olivia is the strongest of us all. I tell him about Brec's gift and finally admit that I didn't actually have a record player [with that one I get another flash of his dimple]. I talk all about my drunken dance party and how much that night felt like us—post Brec and pre Olivia—that weird sliver of life where we were at the same place at the same time. I tell him all of my favorite memories from our childhood and list the things that I've always admired about him. I tell him that I will take care of his girls—who have now somehow become a piece of me—like they were always my own. I promise to make Olivia laugh again and to be the sister to her I should have been all along.

He's tired, and I can tell that my time is up but I have to make one last promise.

"I promise they will know you—through me, through all of us. I will tell them every story. I will show them every picture. They will know their dad, Gage. I promise."

His eyes leak a slim stream of tears, and for a moment, I'm mesmerized. His sight may be gone, but his eyes are still telling his story. The story of a beautiful man who lives with such *life*— who loves with such *color*. I lay my head and masked mouth right next to his. Without sound, he wobbly tries to mouth the words, "You're stunning".

"So are you, Gage. So are you."

I lift myself and kiss his forehead before walking out.

If I allow myself, I could immediately crumble right here in the hallway. I know we still have some time left with Gage, but our conversation was flavored with goodbye. Instead, I tear away the protective paper and head toward my dad, the only one left sitting in the waiting room.

I intend to curl up beside him and borrow some of his love—his strength, his calm—but the moment I take the seat beside him, he lays his head on *my* shoulder. It's a beautiful sort of role reversal. Even though I'm emptier than I've ever been, I'm glad to have something to offer my breaking father. And I have to remember, I've spent so much of my life broken—and this may be the first time my dad has ever felt this helpless, this devastated by life.

We wait for Olivia to visit with Gage before we say our goodbyes to the ICU staff and the cold, sterile waiting room that now holds so many memories. Together, we load up and head back to the hotel.

I don't know what to do with myself once I'm back among my four, barren walls. Just earlier this week, I was thankful for this sanctuary that is now feeling increasingly like an asylum. This isn't the longest I've stayed somewhere in the last decade, but it has felt the most like a home. I have various photos and colored pages littering the cabinets. I've regularly done laundry and put it away in the hotel drawers. I have my family close—close enough to know they are there when I need them, but not too close as to judge my daily wardrobe. I'm not sure what Olivia will decide to do, but from the conversation I eavesdropped on, it sounds like we are all packing it up and heading home.

Home.

I'm not sure where home is for me. I can't possibly imagine staying with my mom and dad, but I also feel like it may be important to give Olivia and the girls some time and space with just their family. I pull out my packed away duffle and reusable grocery bags in preparation to close out this hotel chapter. Before I can clean out a full bathroom drawer there is a knock at the door. I know Brec's gone—from the hotel and from my life— but my first hope is that he is here for me, so we can process today together; however, when I get to the door and open it, Olivia is the one waiting for me in the plush carpet hallway.

"Can I come in?"

"Yes, of course. Come in. —Can I get you a drink? I think I have vodka."

When I say vodka her brows shoot up.

"Don't toy with me, Sage."

"Right? Vodka is no joking matter. Let me rephrase—I'm sure I have some if you'd like a drink—or maybe eight. Grey Goose okay?"

"Are you kidding? I would take anything right now. Give me a glass of McCormicks, and I won't complain."

I pour us both a glass and then decide to add a twist and splash of tonic.

"So. What's up?" I break the ice. Clearly, she's here to talk, but I'm not sure what direction the conversation will go. I'm not sure if this is a crying conversation or a tactical one, so I try to be ready for whatever.

"Brec and I talked today about how to proceed with Gage's treatment. I talked to Gage afterward and, *I think*, we decided it's best for all of us to go home."

She winces as she says, 'I think'. I guess I never realized how hard it would be to make all of these choices solo. I'm not sure that she and Gage made contingency plans together in case he didn't get better.

"Yeah, I kind of caught that earlier."

"I wanted to see if I could maybe get your help packing up the girls and taking them back tomorrow while I'm overseeing the discharge and hospice stuff."

"Yes, absolutely. Olivia, whatever you need. I'm here for you."

She takes a few long pulls on her glass before she begins again.

"I'm not going to put them back in school."

" . . . For how long?"

"For . . . however long." I follow her unspoken meaning.

"I get that. I think the system we have works well, and I'm not in any rush to get back to the city."

"Good. Don't leave. But . . . Sage, I'm not going to put the girls back in school—at all."

"Oh."

"It's not you. I am so thankful for all you've done, and you are great with the girls. But, it's my turn to be their mom—we just need to practice being a family again. I selfishly need some time with them . . . before . . . "

I get it. I mean, I would absorb whatever time I had left too. I would wallow and roll around in it and make every second count.

"You know, I think that's smart. I think that's what Gage would want."

Her eyes glisten as she looks up at me.

"You think so?"

"Yes. I really think so. Take it from someone who never made time for anyone else. The best gift you can give him right now is . . . well—you, all of you."

We talk through some of the details, and she answers my questions about Hospice. When she leaves, I send her with the bottle of vodka and promise to be down in their room in about an hour to get the girls packed.

After Olivia leaves, I call down to the front desk. Just my fucking luck, James answers.

"Reception, James speaking."

"Oh, hey. This is Sage in room 613. I just wanted to let you know that I'll be checking out in the morning. I'll pay my bill then, or you can charge the card on file—whichever is easiest."

In a completely unexpected moment of humanity, James responds, "I heard about your brother. That's . . . well, I'm sorry. I will charge the card after check-out. Would you like your invoice delivered in the morning, or would you like to pick it up on your way out?"

"I'll have two emotional leeches with me in the morning, so I'd like to do whatever I can tonight to get things squared away. Can you just give me the balance right now?"

"Sure. It looks like your total is $5,593. Which card would you like to put this on?"

"The only one I gave you." I swear this man is the absolute worst at his job.

"Hmm... I see there are two cards on file. One under a Sage Gilbert and the other under a Brec Aldridge."

"What the fuck? Why is his name on my room? He checked out a week ago. So help me, if I get stuck paying for his freaking suite . . . "

"No, ma'am. The night you checked in, I gave you the key before I officially ran your card. There was not enough available credit for an indefinite stay—we require a $5000 balance. You had already walked away, but your friend said that you were both with the same party and he would make sure your room was covered."

Well, fuck me. I'm tempted to run the bill on Brec's card—and thank him for his altruism later, but I decide that we would both be better off letting the tension and drama lay low between us from now on.

"Fine. Whatever. Okay. Just run it on my card. So, what do I need to do in order to check-out?"

"Just leave your key card in the room. Check-out is at 11:00."

It's weird. It feels like any other hotel check-out—like suddenly this room doesn't harbor the growth and the hurt and the truth of the last few months. It's just a hotel room again.

Then I realize, I'm homeless for the second time since I've been back.

CHAPTER Twelve

It's got to be 1:00 am. My entire car is packed up. All my shit is stuffed into the trunk, and the girls have some boxes in the front passenger seat and on the floorboards. There is even a stack of boxes between Emery's car seat and Anna's booster. [I'm very proud that I have learned the correct terminology of such things over the last few months. When I got here I thought they were both just called baby carriages.] My room already feels so distant. I'm packed and ready to move on, so instead of heading back upstairs, I get in my car and head toward my favorite late-night spot, Posies.

I'm hoping Antonia will be here tonight. I've stopped in a couple times since our encounter on my first night [and morning] back without running into her. I pull into the ever familiar 'Daycare, Donuts and Guns' parking lot. I'm not 100% sure why I'm here. I mean, I'm never opposed to a dirty chai, but I know, at this moment, that's not really what I need. I can't put anything else on Olivia or Dad or even Mom who has asked several questions as of late about the whereabouts of Brec. We are all pressure cookers about to explode, so I need to find a different place to decompress. I scrounge through my camera bag for my ear buds, which I find in nearly record time and head into my happy place.

Antonia already has my dirty chai waiting as I walk in.

"Saw you out in that car. Wondered if you'd ever come in."

"You're a saint, lady—a saint." I smile at her, sincerely thankful, but my lips feel like they're trying too hard, and I know she can sense that something's off.

I grab the chai and find a seat in one of the few upholstered armchairs. I set my phone and the ear buds down on the table in front of me but curl up in the silence looking out the window instead of turning on iTunes.

"Need to talk about it?" Antonia calls over the whirr of the dishwasher.

"What's there to talk about?"

"Well, I don't know, but I imagine there's something goin' on if you *and* that tall boy who drools after you all the time come in here on the same night both as silent as mice."

"Brec was here?"

"Yep." She says, right beside me now.

For the first time in the history of me and Posies, Antonia takes off her apron, hangs it over the back of a chair and sits down with me.

"How bad, Sage?"

"Past bad. When I came, we were at bad. Now we're so far past that, I wish we could find our way back to just 'bad'."

I realize, for maybe the millionth time, that Antonia and I could be talking about Gage or we could be talking about Brec—or maybe I'm talking about both of them. I know better than to expect answers or straightforward advice from her, so during the silence I try to dig into my own shallow pool of wisdom. — Blank. I've got absolutely nothing. I'm totally screwed.

"What can you do?"

Her question startles me. I can't even decipher what's in my control and what's out of it anymore. Maybe I should make a list of all the shit going down in my life.

"I mean it depends on what problem I want to attack first. My dying brother? My broken heart and broken engagement? Both my fault, by the way. My housing situation? My financial situation? My sudden lack of employment?"

"Which one can you fix today?"

"I don't think I can fix any of it today."

"Then why are you here?"

"Honestly, I don't know. I was literally just thinking about that outside in my car. Maybe I'm here because this is a place that makes me feel good. It can't solve my problems, but when I'm here, it makes the problems hurt less."

"Could be."

Ah—typical Antonia and her obscure responses. I wait her out this time. I have a full chai to drink and have become much less mouthy over the passing months. I slowly take sips and think about each problem. The first, biggest need that I *can* fix is finding a place to live. I'm sure I can find an apartment available somewhere in my hometown, but I need to check my bank account first. I've mostly done Craigslist roommate stuff or rented a room from a friend of a friend. I can't remember the last time I actually signed a lease. I don't often commit myself to much for any length of time. I'm worried that my inability to pay for a deposit, plus first and last month's rent along with zero viable references, will be a hindrance in my search. My car clearly isn't a long-term option—it's fucking winter outside.

Before I know it, I've reached the bottom of my chai and my list of potential living arrangement options. I look up from the table to see Antonia still perched in her chair with an eyebrow raised. I've impressed her. She gives one silent nod, and I know she can see it like a badge of honor pinned to my chest. *Growth*.

"Want to know why I think you're here?"

"Nah—I'm good. I'm just gonna get back to trying to resolve my homeless situation."

Antonia laughs with every ounce of oxygen she has in her. Her laughs are real and come out in big bellows.

"There you are. I was afraid your momma turned you into one of those robot Stepford ladies."

"Me? A *lady*? Antonia, I'm offended."

I smile for the first time all day. Maybe that's all Antonia was looking for. I never really know what she's up to. She's either the wisest person I know, or she's totally full of shit. And I have no idea which it is.

"So, you staying in your car again tonight?"

"I have the hotel for tonight, but . . . it . . . " I stop and smash my lips together for a few seconds unwilling to cry anymore [for today at least]. "I can't go back. There are too many hurts there. I'm ready to move on. I need to move forward."

"Come here."

I follow after Antonia as she winds around the counter toward the back of the building where the restrooms reside. If you take a right you walk into the kitchen—the one I know all too well from the first, first date here with Brec. Antonia takes a left, and we enter a staircase I've never seen before. The steps are tiny and short like they were made for someone from the lollipop guild. The space suddenly opens up, but it's too dark to see what is up here. I have to silence a small part of me that worries this would be an awesome opening for some sort of horror movie. I stop walking, trying to adjust to the dark, but Antonia knows her way around the space. She walks over to a lamp and illuminates the room.

It's the most darling, little cabin-styled efficiency apartment. Everywhere you look there is oak—the bed, the dresser, the exposed beams above. I feel like I'm in the world's tiniest log cabin. The quilt on the bed looks homemade from actual pieces of someone's past. Everything in here feels like nostalgia and memories—like it took a lifetime of living to get it just like this. There are pops of color on everything. I'm immediately in love and run to hug Antonia who is still positioned by the light.

"This is perfect. I'm in love. I want it. I want it." I clap my hands wildly in front of her after I let her go.

"Oh, this wasn't for you, girl, I was just gonna show you something I have stored up here."

Oh my God, this is embarrassing. Here I thought she was my saving grace by offering me this adorable, cozy space. Of course, someone already lives here—didn't I just think how worn in this place looked? Oh. Dear. Lord. This is probably Antonia's house, and I am such an incredibly insensitive ass-hole.

Antonia must see the dreadful look on my face and puts me out of my misery. "God girl, I'm just sassing you. Of course, this is for you."

She runs me through the quirks of the place in one long breath. The heat works-ish if you bang on the pipes to the left of the bed. The lamp on the dresser works, but the lights in the bathroom are on the fritz and the pulsating rhythm makes you feel a little bit like you're at a rave. Add to that the fun house mirror in the bathroom, and it's a straight circus in there. The water runs hot then cold no matter which faucet you turn on. All the drawers in the dresser open except the last one on the right, which was apparently kicked some time ago and has never opened since. There isn't a closet, but there is a rolling clothes rack in one corner for hanging items. In the end, I only move 15 steps for the entire tour of the place.

It's pint-size, like me, and I'm in love with the first good thing that's happened to me in a long time.

Antonia tells me to set up whatever I need to, but she needs to go back downstairs and run her business. I move around her for the next 30 minutes—coming and going and unloading my car. On my last trek through the coffee shop, I stop by the counter once more to thank her, but the same gentlemen from my first night home walks in. Antonia lights up and dismisses me all at once.

"Good night, Sage."

Ah, so this *is* a boyfriend of sorts. I figure we can always settle the rent in the morning. In my room, I take all of my clothes out of the grocery bags and neatly place them in the drawers. I have a few nicer items that I hang up, and my duffel is filled with bathroom products that I easily stock in the carnival-styled bathroom. Gage's picture takes its position on my nightstand once again, and by the time the whole room is set up, I'm still smiling in awe of how this all worked out.

I set my alarm for 6:00 am to make sure I get to the girls on time. The minute my head hits the down pillow, I sleep easily with the ambient sounds of espresso machines and Antonia's laughter filtering through.

6:00 am is a son-of-a-bitch. This is not an hour my body knows well. I make it to the girls by 7:00, and we're belted and buckled and on our way by 8:00. We pull through a Starbucks to grab a quick coffee and two hot chocolates. The girls now think of me as the hot chocolate lady, and I'm okay with that. I'm pretty sure that's what aunts are supposed to do, so I feel like I am doing something right in the middle of so much going wrong.

Hospice arrives shortly after we get to the house to help us prepare for Gage's move back. The girls, Mom and I clean all day. We scrub every surface and wipe every germ away. By dusk, I've learned two things: 1) their house is much bigger than I had realized before I had to clean it and 2) I was an awful cleaner before today. Mom checks my work over and over again to make sure I haven't screwed something up. I re-clean the same bathtub three times before it passes her inspection. Even Anna is better at this than I am, and Mom doesn't scold Emery nearly as much as me. Being so bad at something is truly tiring. We are all exhausted by dinnertime when Olivia, Dad, Gage and a fleet of medical professionals arrive. Mom and Dad stay around long enough to converse with the Hospice nurse who seems to be pretty legit and instills some confidence in us. Then, following their cue, we all leave the house around 8:00.

My first thought after getting in my car and relaxing in my seat is that I've cleaned for 12 hours straight, and I don't even have a bathtub to go soak these sore muscles in. My second thought is more along the lines of holy shit, when I did I become the girl who complains about first world problems?

Posies is a 24-hour café, so I'm not too stressed about getting in at 9:00 on a Sunday night; however, as I head up to my little oasis, I wonder if I should, in fact, get a key for—I don't know, emergencies? I add that to my mental list of things to talk to Antonia about along with rent and a possible job. Now that Olivia doesn't need me, I really need to think about a way to pay for bills and basic living expenses. I'm not sure how much longer I'll be around, so I need a pretty flexible job that won't require a two weeks' notice or calling in to get shifts covered and that sort of bullshit. I know next to nothing about making coffee, but I'm a pro at drinking it, so I'm hoping that will bode well for me when I sit down to talk with Antonia.

Once upstairs, I stop, still impressed with how freaking adorable my new digs are, and smile in appreciation of this gift—this moment. I take off my shoes and flop on my bed which hurts so badly I think I bruised a couple ribs—it turns out these oaky frames, while quaint, are hard as a rock. I don't have a TV up here, so HGTV and made for TV movies are no longer able to keep me company. I don't really feel like reading either because that takes too much effort. Instead, I roll to my stomach and reach into the camera bag at the foot of the bed. I pull out an old work notebook and my ear buds then begin a list.

Shit Going Down in My Life

Apartment — Long term? Ask Antonia about rent

Money — Check account? — ~~Make a budget.~~
    Figure out how to make a budget.

Job — Find one. — Maybe email Ty

Brec — What do I want?

Gage ......

I stop when I get to the last item. Obviously, I don't have a solution, and I don't even think I believe there is one anymore. But I can't quite write down the real words—like writing it down somehow puts this truth into the universe—and I can't be responsible for that. So, instead of writing down what my heart is screaming, I return to the list and scratch in an alternate message.

Shit Going Down in My Life

Apartment — Long term? Ask Antonia about rent

Money — Check account? — ~~Make a budget.~~
   Figure out how to make a budget.

Job — Find one. — Maybe email Ty

Brec — What do I want?

Gage ...... Ask Olivia what she needs help with

The noise downstairs is unusually loud for a Sunday night. I put in my ear buds and scroll through my Spotify playlists until I find Kate Nash. The first song that comes on has me chewing my lip and tapping my pencil. I've heard this song a million times and I know nearly every lyric, but I never really applied the words to anyone—it was always just a pretty song—*The Nicest Thing*. As I listen to it, Brec floods my thoughts. Not high school Brec or college Brec. Not even recent memories. Somehow, I'm envisioning future Brec—and he's mine. Well shit, where did that come from? I look over my list one more time and make one last amendment.

Shit Going Down in My Life

Apartment — Long term? Ask Antonia about rent

Money — Check account? — ~~Make a budget.~~
Figure out how to make a budget.
Job — Find one. — Maybe email Ty
Brec — ~~What do I want?~~ Get over your freaking
self and go talk to him.
Gage ...... Ask Olivia what she needs help with

Even *Merry Happy* turned up to full volume can't drown out the roar of laughter from below. My curiosity and growing hunger lead me downstairs to an overly crowded café. I'm stunned. I've never seen Posies like this before. It's like every high school kid in a 30-mile radius decided to come grab coffee on a random Sunday night. Antonia is flying about the place, and I can see beads of sweat gathering on her forehead regardless of the night's chilly temperatures. I don't think I'm hungry enough to brave the crowd, so I turn down the hallway to head back to my hobbit hole.

"Oh no you don't."

Antonia grabs me by the elbow and hurriedly throws what appears to be a tablecloth at me.

"Go wash up then check on one, three and nine"

Huh? I stare at her bewilderedly, still busily buzzing around me, with the freaking tablecloth in hand. A snack definitely isn't worth all this.

"Do I need to spell it out, girl? I need help. Wash your hands, put on that apron and help me take some orders."

Okay, now that all makes a lot more sense. I thought she was trying to tell me to take a freaking shower—which I do actually need to do after a day of 'elbow grease' as my mother says. Sadly, I think I've just become accustomed to people interfering with my lack of cleanliness and telling me I need to shower. I've just come to expect it.

I wash my hands first then put on the apron, which fits a little more like a tablecloth or a tent—it's sort of comical. The pockets fit closer to my butt than in the front. I look under and around the counter for something to take orders on. Luckily, there is some sort of puzzle-looking, numbers book that I grab along with a purple marker and head toward a table of annoyed looking teens.

"Hey. What do you guys want?"

I've never been in any service type job, and I'm realizing, right at this moment, that I am not cut out for the customer service industry. The group of teens has various reactions to my unwelcomed, half-hearted greeting. The girls roll their eyes at me, two boys keep animatedly arguing about something sports-related and one acne-prone teen stares at my tits. I'm built like a 13-year-old girl up there, so the jokes on him.

"Is that, like, a crossword?"

"What?" I follow the girl's eyes to my 'notepad' for orders and realize what she's referencing. "No. I think it's Sudoku. Hey guys, I'm sure you've realized it's pretty busy in here, so if you could just let me know what you want, I can get that shi— stuff for you and go help another table."

They're still talking. Over me—over each other. Hell no, this isn't working for me.

"Okay, let me rephrase. You've got to the count of 5 to give me your fucking orders before I move on to another table— and just so you know, I don't plan on coming back."

Suddenly I get the whole table's attention. The arguing boys are notably less pimply and appear to be amused by my direct no-nonsense approach to waitressing, but the group is just star- ing at me—still silent.

"One."

Finally, they are all talking over each other in a rush, even though I stopped counting, so I could write down their orders. I think I gather from the cacophony of voices that the group wants a blueberry muffin, two Americanos, a ham and cheese crois- sant, two cokes, a slice of quiche and something else I didn't catch. Oh well, they can get a cranberry scone. Should have told me what they wanted the first time I asked.

I drop the order off in the kitchen and head to the next table of annoyed, hungry-looking teens.

"So, you guys need me to count for you too, or you going to tell me what you want the first time I fucking ask?"

The rest of the night runs pretty smoothly after that. I get a few orders wrong and tell them to suck it up. Mostly, the kids deal with me, and I with them, in a sort of amicable dislike. The place finally clears out around 3:00 am, and I am absolutely beat. The all-day cleaning plus impromptu waitressing is the most I've been on my feet in months. I flop over on the counter and lay down.

"Not easy, is it?"

"Not when the entire high school population comes in to wreak havoc. I've never seen it like this—that was crazy."

"New Years. The kids are all off on break and are gossiping about who did what last night."

I had forgotten that today—well, yesterday now—was New Years. A new year, a new beginning. Antonia hands me a cranberry scone. It's a little harder and more crumbly than it should be—it *has* been sitting in a case for hours now—but I accept it willingly.

"Figured that's what you came down here for."

"Yep." I say around big bites.

"How much you make in tips?"

I pull out the wad of cash from my jean's back pocket and count it—$74. All that work, and I made 74 freaking dollars. I don't know how people deal with minimum wage. I hold the money out toward Antonia, not really sure who it belongs to.

"Nope, that's all yours."

"Well, I actually still owe you rent. Take it," and I slide the crumpled bills across the counter to her. "Speaking of, we need to talk about rent and stuff."

"What stuff?"

"How long can I stay? Do I need to rent month to month? Should I give you a deposit in case I manage to trash the place?"

Antonia laughs.

"You think you're strong enough to trash the place? That oak will hurt you before you can hurt it."

That's probably true judging from my earlier encounter with the bed and my still sore ribs.

"Okay, no deposit. What about the rest?"

"You done taking pictures?"

Huh, I didn't even know that Antonia had an idea what I did for a living. Her question makes me think back to my list from earlier and reminds me of my need to email Ty to make sure I have a job to go back to after . . . well, when it's time to leave here.

"For now. Most of what I'm contracted to do is overseas, and I'm needed here. I'll go back to it one day, but for the foreseeable future, my career is on hold."

"No need for rent."

I have whiplash talking to this lady. I can never follow her train of thought.

"Antonia, I have to pay you something. I mean, honestly, I probably already owe like $1,200 in scones and chais alone."

"Oh, you'll pay me."

"But you just said I don't need to worry about rent. What am I missing here?"

"I'm giving you a job. I need you to work here 25 hours a week—you can decide what hours are best for you. Your hours will pay for your rent, and you can keep the tips."

I'm trying to work through the money in my head, but I immediately begin to get a headache—I've never been good with math. I need a calculator before I hurt myself. I pull out my cell phone and begin crunching the numbers. I worked about 5 hours tonight and made 74 bucks. That's what . . . $14.80 an hour? Well shit. $14.80 x 25 is $370 a week. It's not great, but it's doable.

Antonia peeps over to the numbers I'm crunching on the calculator on my phone and begins laughing before walking away to clean some tables.

"Stop cussing out the customers, and I bet you'll earn yourself a little bit of a raise."

Damn. I didn't realize she'd heard that. I'm pretty sure Posies isn't the sort of establishment people come to get their asses handed to them. I'll have to monitor my vocabulary and learn to be nice . . . well, maybe pleasant is more of a reachable goal for me.

"I got it down here. In the morning, let me know what hours you want this week."

I reach into the case to grab one more scone . . . I mean . . . it's sort of like my dinner *and* my breakfast at this point.

Even though Antonia's back is to me she must hear the case opening. "I'm taking that out of your tips from now on, girl." I smile because I really expect nothing less from her. "And Sage, good work tonight. You catch on fast."

Upstairs while munching on my scone, I pull out my laptop and go to my email. Ty wrote me weeks ago, and I never responded.

I figure it's probably not a good idea to ignore my boss indefinitely. I find his email and hit reply.

> Ty —
>
> Sorry it's taken so long for me to get back to you — I'm sure you've filled the Israel slot by now.
>
> Thanks for your kind words. It looks like I'm going to need to stick around here for a little while longer — hopefully a good while longer, depending on Gage.
>
> I know it's unlikely that there's any contract work around here, but I could use the money — and the distraction. Anything would be appreciated, Ty.
>
> Keep me in the loop. — I mean, I'd like to have a job to come back to.
>
> Sage

I hit send and lay back on the pillows. I love photography, but in a weird way, I haven't missed my job at all. I mean I didn't even think about writing Ty until tonight when I realized how badly I'll need some income to support my extended stay down here. I remember when I used to love this job so much that I would hunt down and fight people for assignments. Maybe I just liked, or needed, to be good at something.

It's after 4:00 am, and I feel like I could sleep for days. As I get up to turn off the one working lamp in the room, I notice my notepad from earlier. Feeling proud of my new employment, I make a few more adjustments before going to bed.

Shit Going Down in My Life

~~Apartment — Long term? Ask Antonia about rent~~
Money — Check account? — ~~Make a budget.~~
   Figure out how to make a budget.
         → $370 a week + whatever is in my
account
         → Bills?
~~Job — Find one. — Maybe email Ty~~
Brec — ~~What do I want?~~ Get over yourself and go
talk to him.
Gage ...... Ask Olivia what she needs help with —
tomorrow

As I lay back and snuggle into the colorful quilt, I'm humbled from my recent high when I realize I *still* haven't showered today.

CHAPTER Thirteen

I've finally hit a new rhythm—a new normal. Gage seems to be at his best in the mornings, so I make a point of dropping in on him in the hospice hell every day. As predicted, his vision and speech are completely gone, along with any gross motor skills. His fine motor skills are barely holding on, but he can still loosely grasp my index finger when I come in to talk to him. It's not lost on me how he seems to be growing backwards, and these moments, in a way, remind me of when he was barely more than an infant. As I talk to him and look at our hands, it's a beautiful reminder that I'll always be his big sister, and he will always be the little brother I fiercely promised to protect. I leave, most days, with a lump in my throat.

Olivia still allows me to help out and spend time with the girls in lots of little ways. I grocery shop on Fridays and help her clean the house afterward. [I am getting better at this cleaning stuff week by week.] I typically add a couple bottles of wine to the grocery list, and we spend Friday nights catching up on life. I realize after our second Friday that I may be the only friend she has to talk to, so I let her unload whatever she needs to talk about, and I just listen—you know and drink a ton of wine. It's eye-opening to see Olivia like this. She's still the most put together, organized adult I know. But it's good to listen to her hurts and her fears—it's good to see her humanity. These Fridays link us together in a true bond of trust and friendship. In truth, I think she may be the first female best friend I've ever had. I don't want to lose Gage, and I would do anything—ANYTHING—to stop what's coming, but, in a weird way, losing him is bringing me closer to having a real sister.

Mom abhors the fact that I've moved into a coffee shop and taken on a job better suited for a 16-year-old. No matter how much strength she builds, she can never get past the need to be seen as successful and important, and thus, I will always be her embarrassment child. I figure that this job, with its awful tips and socializing with ridiculous people, is helping her grow as much as it's helping me. I can also see how mom and I are so alike in this way—we both really hate growth. We eat brunch together a few times a week at the house. At first, it feels rigid and uncomfortable—being in that space and being such different versions of ourselves. With time, we've oiled the joints of awkwardness, and I'm now okay telling them about 60% of what's really going on in my life. Mom asks endlessly about Brec, who I still haven't seen since leaving the hotel. I promise myself daily that today is going to be the day I reach out to him, but every time I open my phone to message him, nothing comes out. And the days of silence just keep adding up. Dad asks about my photography, and we discuss some of my favorite pictures and locations. I tell them stories while showing them my portfolio, and we even spend some time together taking pictures after I give them a crash course in photojournalism. In truth, they're both decent students. We laugh some, and we argue some more, and we spend many mornings together brunching. But the one thing we never do is talk about Gage. It's this taboo, off the table, topic. We are each handling the reality in our own way, but, together, the best we can do is silently relearn how to be a family—of three.

In the afternoon, I shoot. I take my camera to the dilapidated barns and frame them against the midday sun. I visit the graffiti-filled walls of downtown. I go to the park and photograph the kids who are pure joy in action—all light and color. Anna, Emery and I still have our standing field trips every Wednesday. Sometimes I bring them to the park, so I can see that joy on their faces. I know Anna is itching to get back to school, especially since she's home now. She misses her friends and talks about them endlessly. Emery misses school as well but for a very different reason—snacks. I asked Olivia about her plan to get them back in classes, but I think she needs them home with her. It's not necessarily about the girls at all, I realize. *Olivia* needs *them*, so I keep my mouth shut on that topic moving forward. The weather is getting warmer day by day, but the girls still demand hot chocolate, which I bring them from Posies—but only on our field trip days. [Lucky me, I'm the one who gets to deal with the sugar rush.] During our outings, I've run into numerous old classmates. Some whom I remember. Some whom I don't. Some who think the girls are mine. Some who never knew I left. Some who are still exactly the same, and some who are drastically different. I'm figuring out how to navigate this place and all the stories and memories it harbors a little bit at a time.

In the evenings, I work at Posies from 5:00 to 10:00 on Monday through Thursday and 7:00 to midnight on Saturdays. During the week, I work by myself now—Antonia finally trusts me to work the cash register without screwing up the night's till. My math skills haven't improved, but I've gotten better at taking the time to painfully count back change to make sure I've done it right. My screw-ups stopped being funny once Antonia started taking the missing money out of my tips. Saturdays are busier, and I'm always scheduled with someone else. Sometimes it's Antonia and sometimes it's her look alike, Sophia, who I assume is her daughter, but I still haven't found the courage to ask for clarification. The shiny metal contraptions behind me that I once found incredibly complex now feel like rote memory. And though I will always love these cranberry scones, I would be happy not to eat another one for a year—too much of a good thing is most definitely a real thing. My favorite part of my job is that Antonia lets me DJ the music selection during my shift. I'm introducing all sorts of indie music to this small, southern town. In fact, I've created daily Spotify playlists that I link to the Posies website. Antonia is silently impressed with my technology skills, and I'm glad to be stretching my creative muscles a little bit as I play with the site's graphic design.

It's a slow Thursday night, and I have my laptop opened up on the barren counter re-imaging the Posies web page. I asked Antonia if I could use the picture I took in the parking lot many months ago as the site's main page, but she noisily refused. I did, however, get the photo framed for her, and she had far fewer complaints on that front. She still hasn't explained the man or the nature of their relationship. Watching her shut down every time the subject is brought up reminds me of what Gage said about me—that it was nice to see me open up. I hope he'd be proud of who I'm becoming. I'm still a fairly private, fairly bitchy person, but slowly I'm beginning to like and trust the people around me a little bit more.

I'm playing around with some pictures when the door sounds— alerting me of new customers. I finish cropping the photo I'm working on to fit at the bottom of the page when I hear a familiar voice—unfortunately, it's accompanied by an unfamiliar one. When I look up, Brec's standing 10 feet away from me, both of us frozen to our spots, and with him, is *another* beautiful blonde. This can't be happening. He sees my shoulders slump as my eyes fall to her—then he raises a single eyebrow. Is he taunting me? Asshole. Brec is a 35-year-old man—he should be past these stupid games. Hell, I should be past these games, yet I'm about two seconds away from decking this chick who literally hasn't stopped talking since entering the café. Finally, she catches on to the quiet and looks back and forth several times between our silent showdown.

"Oh. My. God! —I *totally* forgot. You're Sage, right?"

Shit, it's worse than I thought. Apparently, Brec is now dating someone who knows me—who knew *us,* and he brought her *here*? That douchebag, son-of-a-bitch, asshole. Well, two can play at this not at all fun game. I plaster on my best smile and try to filter all of the bitch out of my voice, "Welcome to Posies.

How may I help you?" I've literally never said that to a single customer, but I refuse to let him know how much this fucking bothers me.

"Seriously—You're Sage Gilbert, yeah?" She has this dopey smile that I'd really like to punch off her face as she points to me offhandedly.

I look at Brec once more trying to read his emotion in this moment. Is he being for real right now? I feel like this is a test— a test I failed so miserably the first time around. Every muscle in me is humming with adrenaline—ready to flee, but I look down long enough to ground myself and muster some strength before looking back at him. My smile only tilts on one side, but it's enough to show him that I'll win this game even if it kills me.

"Yep. Yes—I'm Sage," I say as I turn my attention back to the busty blonde. "I'm sorry, I can't quite place you. Remind me, what's your name?"

"Jennifer. Jen Nianouris," She says proudly as she extends her hand.

I'm always wary of anyone who feels the need to introduce themselves with both their first and last name, but I reach out and begrudgingly shake her hand regardless.

"Well, Jen, what can I get you guys?" I ask turning directly toward her and ignoring Brec.

Jennifer immediately breaks out into maniacal laughter. I'm beginning to see a pattern here with Brec and his attraction to crazy women.

"Oh" [loud breathy laugh] "My" [loud breathy laugh] "Gosh. —We're not here together. Man, oh man, on a date with

Brec Aldridge? What I wouldn't have given for that half a lifetime ago."

She *innocently* rests her manicured hand on Brec's arm, and I see red. I instantly look at Brec who gives a small smirk. It wasn't a test—it was just a fucking coincidence. This is worse than if it was a date. They're both assholes.

"Whatever," I huff out. I'm out of patience or pleasantries for this lady as I ask a bit too aggressively, "What do you want?"

"Hmm . . . well, what's good here? I haven't been back to this place in forever, but some of the students were talking about it the other day, so I thought I'd check it out."

"The dirty chai is good but the Misto and Americano are also popular items." I answer in monotone.

Jen looks at me with blank eyes like she's never had a cup of coffee in her life.

"Based on your complete lack of reaction, I'm going to assume you aren't much of a coffee drinker. Why don't you go with a regular chai tea? —It's sort of like a pumpkin spice latte."

"Those are my very favorite—a complete guilty pleasure. That's perfect."

"Why am I not surprised it's the only drink you've heard of?"

"Pardon?" She asks as if she had not heard me.

"Never mind. Why don't you take a seat, and I'll bring it to you when it's ready."

Taking Brec's order feels surreal. I don't have to ask him to know exactly what he'll order, but it feels wrong to assume anything about him—or us—at this point. I don't have the right to make his choices. I repeat his order back and ask if he'd like anything else.

"Yes. —Can you make that to go?"

My eyes immediately whip over to him, and my hands falter. So he isn't here for me? Coincidence number two, I guess.

"Yes. Of course. I'm on it."

I begin the loud espresso machine for his Americano as he leans his weight sideways on the counter and crosses one ankle in front of his weight bearing leg. He looks so casual like this— so unruffled by the moment or life in general. So, unlike a guy whose heart was broken and whose best friend is dying. Brec's always been the vulnerable one, but here I am completely floundering while he's cool, calm and collected.

"I didn't know you worked here." He says softly but just loud enough I hear him over the machines.

I nod my head to acknowledge that I heard him, but I don't know what to say in response. In three minutes, I've gone from jealous to angry to hopeful and then hurt. I'm having a bit of a difficult time sorting through all of this, and I'm unable to fake any of my typically self-assured comments at the moment.

"How long have you been here?" Brec pushes to open the conversation.

"Um, almost two months. Antonia and I have found our rhythm finally—I don't drive her nearly as crazy as I did when I first moved in."

"Moved in?"

"Yep. I live upstairs. Who would've thought, right? I mean I knew Posies was special, but I can honestly say, I never thought I'd call it home."

The chai is ready, but I'm waiting on Brec's Americano before I walk away from this moment—from the small amount of attention I can lap up from this man.

"How are you?"

"Working and living in a coffee shop? —I'm living the dream!" I can see Brec's disappointment when I opt for an old Sage response, so I try again. "It's hard. It's really fucking hard, Brec. But I wake up each day and tell myself that it's one more day I get with my brother."

Brec's Americano is ready, and I have two opened raw sugar packets in my hand before I stop myself. He looks down to the sugar and then back to me. How someone takes their coffee may seem so insignificant but being on the same page right now with this man feels huge.

"Go 'head." He nods toward my hands accepting this moment—that we'll forever be linked together in a way we can't undo.

I dump the sugar into his cup and use a stirrer before putting on the lid and handing it to him. Brec reaches for his wallet, but I stop him.

"On the house. You've bought me more than enough coffees here. This one's my treat."

"Hey, guys, not to interrupt, but is my chai thingy ready?"

Anytime someone has to preface their comment with 'not to interrupt' it means they fucking know they're interrupting. I swallow all of my sass and carefully hand over her hot latte. Jen stays at the counter, hovering around my moment with Brec, drinking her chai.

"Oh man, this is so good." She takes another sip. "So, so good," she says again—a bit too breathy.

Lord, I think she's trying to have sex with this drink. I begin cleaning the espresso machine to ease the awkwardly sexual moment, but Brec replies, "Chais have always been Sage's favorite." Then he adds a suggestive wink.

The moment surprises me so completely that while cleaning up, I accidently press on the steam wand and scare us all to death.

"Fuck me."

Oh shit. My mind immediately races to the night in the parking lot —and the night spent in a towel in the hotel room—and a million nights before when Brec did just that.

He reads my thoughts, and I can hear his threat in my ear. Posies suddenly becomes 200 degrees. I'm literally sweating and clammy in less than a minute. I pour myself an ice water and count to ten. Calm down, Sage, I reprimand. I think this maybe the first time I've ever had to count out my *sexual* frustration.

"Hey, what is this? It looks pretty cool."

Jen's flipping through my laptop, looking at the Posies website. Usually it pisses me off when people touch my stuff, but I guess she's forgiven since it was wrapped in a compliment.

"Just some stuff I'm messing with for the website. I'm trying to get some recent photos on there and update the site a little bit. Change the vibe, I guess."

"That's right—you used to play with cameras."

Just like that, I want to punch her again. Brec can see how hard I'm trying to hide my annoyance.

"Yep, something like that." I say between tight lips.

"Actually, Sage became a big-time photojournalist. How many pieces do you have printed between National Geographic and Life?" Brec chimes in from his corner of the counter.

"Uh, 27?" I squeak out.

"No. Freaking. Way." Jen says as she sloshes her chai onto the Formica bar top. "This is perfect."

"Is it?" I ask carefully.

She claps her hands with so much enthusiasm I'm worried I may have put a shot of espresso in her chai after all.

"Yes. Mr. Willmers just took a job midyear somewhere in the New England area."

"Mr. Willmers? As in my old photography teacher from senior year? —That Mr. Willmers?" Brec asks dropping his drink on the counter and officially moving over to join the conversation.

"Yep—that old weirdo finally left," Jen says with a conspiratorial roll of her eyes.

I'm a bit offended at her blatant dismissal of my all-time favorite teacher.

"Hey, I liked him. He was a hipster before hipster existed. Man, I can't believe he stayed around here for that long though."

"Well he left us high and dry at semester, and we haven't been able to keep a sub in that position since."

"We? Are you a teacher as well?" I ask, assuming it's an innocent enough question.

"NO! I'm the sophomore principal. I haven't been a teacher in at least 6 years," she huffs out.

"Oh. Well, good job. I mean, congratulations?"

"We are looking for someone to fill the spot for the rest of the year. Would you be interested? I mean . . . " She looks around at the dingy atmosphere in Posies, "as long as you pass the background check."

Brec looks at me, and he can't hide the hope in his eyes. He fought so hard for us to be in the same place at the same time, and now, here we are, both back where we started, and the prospect of staying for him—for Gage—is alluring. I chew on the inside of my mouth and think of what staying here—really staying—would mean. Can I really walk away from my career? All of the amazing people I've met along the way? All of the stories out there that are waiting to be told?

"I don't know . . . just for the rest of the year?" I ask noncommittally—avoiding Brec's glare. In panic I add, "You know, I can't make any promises."

"I understand. You have a lot going on with your brother. We miss him. Why don't you stop by this week—anytime. I will walk you through the job, and maybe, you can go visit one of Gage's classes."

That idea actually sounds amazing. Why hadn't I thought about going to see Gage's work? It was such a huge part of him—his passion. I like the idea more and more as I think about it.

"That would be perfect. I'd love to see Gage's classroom."

Brec stays until his to-go cup is empty, and I feel a small sense of victory. He may not have come here for me, but he did stay for me. Maybe reaching out to him now that the ice has been broken won't be so difficult.

Jen doesn't finish the rest of her chai, which is a mortal sin in my book. She gives Brec a lingering hug that I do my best to ignore, and then they both leave just like they came in. It's 10:00 on Thursday night. Antonia comes in to take over. I close out my drawer and count my tips—remembering to pay for Brec's drink. Everything feels so normal, but nothing feels the same.

It's Friday, and I'm excited to go see Gage and spend the day with Olivia and my two favorite little gremlins. Olivia and I don't talk about Brec, we don't talk about the past, and we DON'T talk about Amelia. In the months of helping around the house, I've seen photos of the four of them [Brec, Amelia, Gage and Olivia], and I've never been naïve enough to think that she wasn't a big part of their lives. However, I woke up on edge this morning, trying to sort through the Brec that was in front of me last night.

The calm, slightly aloof and just a little bit flirty Brec. Whatever spark we have hasn't died. Our hearts may be crumpled, but we just can't kill that damn spark. On my way to their house, I decide that today I am going to talk to Olivia about all of it. I'm going to get it all out and get her perspective. She's been there through most of our roller coaster. She's seen both sides. She's literally the last person I have to talk it through with.

When I get to the house, however, cleaning and Brec and groceries all become a distant memory. The house is all wrong from the moment I walk in. The girls don't come running to me, in fact, no one is in sight. There is just a hum of tension and the foreboding feeling that something incredibly bad is waiting for me somewhere in this nervous friction. I find the quiet chaos in the back, guest room—Gage's headquarters. Hospice is barricading the door and Gage's little family of small women are huddled together, on the floor, completely silent. I've learned that there are always tears. Crying has become a second language. We have tears for grief and tears for frustration. Tears of anger and tears for laughter. And amazingly enough, the crying no longer scares me; however, this silence does. The silence exists when you're paralyzed—when the tears freeze, and nothing comes out. Silently, I think we've all been ticking off each of Gage's milestones that take him one step closer to the end. We were given a timeline, we were given warnings, but we still aren't ready. I shut down everything in my nearly 5-foot frame screaming for answers and bend to the ground, noise-lessly, to hold my family. If we're falling apart, at least we're falling apart together.

It feels like I spend an hour hunching on the hardwood floor, drawing circles onto Emery's back since she has fallen asleep across my lap. Olivia and I never look at each other, but she grasps my hand as the door begins to open. Dr. Russell, who I haven't seen in weeks, emerges, but I can see several nurses and care staff still in the room.

"Olivia? A word?"

This is obviously my cue to exit. I pick up the sleeping Emery, and Anna looks back and forth between her mother and me before she grabs my extended hand. Together, we walk outside to the back-porch swing. I can't think of anything to say that will make any of this better, so we lazily pump our legs in and out in complete silence until we hear Olivia wail. Emery immediately wakes up—terrified, and Anna is a puddle of tears in an instant. The tension is too great for the paralysis, and with one cue from Olivia, all of their frozen nerves snap. My mind immediately goes to a dark place. Did my brother just die? —The girl's climb into my lap, and I hold them firmly, absorbing each tremor and shaky breath. I pat their heads and try to soothe them the best I can while I hold my own uneven breaths and begin internally counting. If I release these aching lungs right now, I know they will betray me. I know I will turn into inconsolable tears.

We wait on the swing for twenty . . . thirty . . . forty minutes without hearing another peep from inside which gives me a little hope. Bad news takes time—worse news is immediate. The girls have calmed down a little, and Emery is getting anxious to get off the swing and move around. I want to stay here. I want to be a part of whatever is happening with Gage, but I made a promise that I would take care of them, and right now the girls need to get out of here in order to put a little distance between themselves and the gloom of this morning.

We all pile into my Altima and head to the grocery store; it is Friday after all. I nearly empty out the wine stock at the local Market Street. I find every cabernet I can and dump it into the cart. Whatever Olivia is facing at least now she can face it with copious amounts of red wine. Apparently, alcohol is my love language. I let the girls get almost all the junk food they ask for, and we even grab ingredients to make a hot chocolate bar for movie night. They ask if we can make our typical Friday night a sleepover. I think it might be good to stick around for a little while, so we buzz through the toiletries and pick up some deodorant and a toothbrush.

We linger longer than we need to around town and run a couple extra errands—Pinkberry for Emery and a local florist for Anna—who says we need to get her daddy flowers because they make everyone feel better. At the florist, picking out the simple bouquet, my hand starts to tremble. Flipping through the catalog is just one more punch—reminding me that no amount of distraction will stop this train from crashing. I ask the saleswoman if I can take a catalog with me. Clearly, she recognizes us, Gage is sort of a hometown hero at this point. She not only hands over a catalog, but also wraps up the flowers and gives them to Anna without charging us. Flowers, groceries and frozen yogurt in tow, we head back to the house to whatever news awaits.

Olivia helps us unload the food but never makes mention of what happened earlier in the hallway. She does thank me for the extra wine and informs me, cryptically, that the whole family is coming over this evening for dinner. With that in mind, we all get busy getting the house in order. I clean the bathroom and the girl's room while Olivia tackles her bedroom and the kitchen. We all meet up in the living room to dust and vacuum—four little bodies rotating around each other in perfect sync because we have done this so many Fridays before. My whole life I craved adventure and distraction and the excitement of anything new, but I am learning to be thankful for the familiar. It's solid, and solid feels really good right now.

Right as I get dinner in the oven, my parents arrive and Brec shortly after them. The girls seem to have forgotten the sorrow of this morning as they play with 'uncle' Brec who tickles and chases them endlessly. It's amazing to see this light turn on in them—it makes me realize all the things they are missing with their dad, and all of the things Gage is missing with his family while he's two rooms away.

Dinner is framed with polite tension. Brec asks if I am off tonight and my mother huffs—clearly unhappy that my surgeon ex-fiancé has found out I'm slumming it at the coffee shop.

"You said you didn't tell him about that place."

"I didn't, Mom. He came in to grab a coffee and figured it out for himself—since, you know, I was the one serving him."

Brec interjects to appease my mother and stands up for me all in one obnoxiously charming foul swoop.

"I think it's pretty amazing that Sage took a job she is clearly so over qualified for just because it's a place she loves, and it gives her the opportunity to be here with Olivia and the girls to help out. Honestly, I feel bad that I haven't made it over more often."

This is why my mother loves him so much—that fucking southern charm.

"That's right, Brec. How is the new job now that it's official? I'm sure your momma is so glad to have you back so close to home," my mother says as she glares at me.

"Good. It's nice to work in a place that's a little more my speed. I'm all moved in and settled now—happy to no longer be in a hotel. And yes, my mom is over the moon that her prodigal son has finally returned from trying to be a hippie in California."

Olivia cracks a smile for the first time this evening. "Oh God, that's right. Remember when your mom flipped out about that ridiculous juice cleanse you and Amelia forced on all of us when we came out to visit?"

My parents and I haven't ever spoken about Brec's marriage. I wasn't even sure if they knew who Amelia was, but it's clear by my mother's pinched face and my dad's slow exhale that they are not only familiar with this woman but hurt by the history as well. I'm a little surprised and impressed by the solidarity.

Emery is so much like me. All the pieces that are my favorite and all the pieces I wish I could trade-in for another set of personality traits. With complete earnestness, she breaks the uncomfortable moment by looking from chair to chair as if she's just realized Amelia isn't here. "Where is Aunt Amwelya? I miss her."

Well shit. Every adult seems to be waiting for someone else to speak up. The girls look at me, and I hold my hands up in exasperated defense—I'm most definitely not going to be the one to relay the details of a story I still don't even fully know myself. Brec tries to lock eyes with me, but I just can't. I know his side of the story, but I don't really understand how she went from being one innocent night to his freaking wife. It's just so . . . impossible.

"Actually, Emery, you'll get to see Aunt Amelia soon." Olivia says in a slow, pleasant tone.

Rewind. What the fuck? I now return Brec's stare with one of my own. This piece of shit man must get off on destroying me—but Brec looks just as confused as I do. What are we missing?

"Is everyone done? Why don't we go to the living room? —bring your wine glasses," Olivia calls out as if that were some sort of explanation for the little bomb she just dropped on us.

We're all watching the girls play on the floor when Olivia begins talking in her soft, princess voice.

"Gage is dying."

One.

"His fever spiked last night, and Dr. Russell came over first thing this morning. Gage has contracted pneumonia—double pneumonia. He said these things . . . just . . . happen."

Her glossy, brown eyes tell not only of her pain but also of her strength.

"He's septic, and his renal system is failing."

Brec is the first one to crack. He gets up from the couch, trudges all the way through the house and slams out the back door. The girls, on the other hand, are completely wrapped up in the TV and seem oblivious to everything being said right behind them.

"What time frame did Dr. Russell give you?" My dad asks without looking up from his watch that he continues to clasp and unclasp.

"Time seems to be unique to each patient. He could live for a week—maybe two, or he may not make it through the night."

"But either way, we aren't looking at more than a week now?"

" . . . or two," Olivia states quietly but matter-of-factly.

I chug the rest of my wine because the only way to survive shit moments like this is to numb some of the pain. My mom gets up and retrieves another bottle of before topping off everyone's glasses. —I must have inherited this love language from her. Alcohol aside, I'm incredibly proud of her strength in this moment. Her courage to face the horror and accept the darkness life sometimes hands us.

"The doctor said it's time to call everyone. My parents are flying in late tonight, and . . ." she looks straight to me, "Amelia is coming in tomorrow. I always meant to talk to you about it first, Sage, but Gage told me early on that she should be here . . . that she's family too."

Two.

My first night home, sitting at Posies, I knew this was all out of my control, and the only thing I could do was support Gage, but this stings from his betrayal, and I'm having a hard time not barging into Gage's little makeshift hospital room and demanding answers. As the wine hits my system, it dulls some of the hurt and redirects the blame. *I* was never around—he made new memories. He made a new sister. She doesn't replace me, I know that, but my absence left a hole—room for her to come in. And, I really don't like sharing.

"We need to talk about his service . . ." even Olivia can't keep the wobble out of her warm voice as she sheds a few tears. I think we were all waiting for permission to break because as soon as we see those isolated little drops roll down her cheeks, Mom, Dad and I all begin crying in large silent sobs. I pass the Kleenex around, and we sip our wine quietly trying to compose ourselves. For a moment, I see how ridiculous we all look—red teeth and runny noses. As ugly as it may be, I want a photo of this moment. I want to remember how deeply it hurts to lose someone you love this much. Like somehow the amount of hurt has to balance the amount of love, and I never want to forget how big I love my little brother.

Three.

Mom starts talking as I dig through my bag for some Advil. "Olivia, do you know what funeral home you want to go through? Obviously we have plots for all of you beside ours . . . "

We've never spoken about this. I didn't know my parents purchased plots at all. I wonder when they did that. I wonder if they knew when they bought them that their son's would be the first piece of earth filled. For a sliver of a second, I can understand the hell it must be to bury your child, and then it's gone—like my body can't carry that sort of anguish, so it immediately disappears.

"Yes. Gage and I talked out most of the logistics months ago when this all seemed like a faraway worst-case scenario and not the ending to my week."

Olivia turns off the TV and brings the girls into our conversation. Clearly, they have already talked a little about 'Daddy's Funeral' because the topic doesn't immediately scare them. Olivia brought us here to ask us specifically what we wanted from the service. Anna thinks very hard, and I can tell she is really trying to figure out what Gage would want as his final goodbye. While Anna's thinking, Emery states with absolute certainty, "There should be cake."

We all laugh like it's oxygen to our depleted hearts, and with that, the conversation begins. Dad thinks that his students should be invited and would like to get a chance to honor them and all they mean to Gage. Mom would like a formal dinner catered with close friends and family after the viewing. We discuss open versus closed casket and live music or hymns—it becomes this surreal conversation. I stand up slowly and walk away, down the hall, to the Hospice guard and knock on Gage's door. I'm allowed in without the suit and mask because I guess, it no longer makes a difference—we've already lost.

"The girls think we should serve cake." My words are washed out by the beeps and the monitors and breathing machine. "You're right here, and we're talking about your funeral. It's like this small piece of me just can't believe it—can't accept it. You were the strongest kid. You're a fighter, Gage. Why aren't you fighting?"

I let go of his hand and lay down on the floor beside his bed and imagine, for a second, that we are elementary-aged kids again, laying down together in our tree house looking at the stars—or we're teenagers laying down in my crap hole apartment in New York, listening to music and passing a joint back and forth. We've spent a lot of our lives looking up. I breathe in time with his machine, and it soothes me enough to speak.

"I forgive you —for Amelia. I get it. I don't like it, but I get it."

Beep. Breathe.
Beep. Breathe.

"And I forgive you—for leaving us."

Beep. Breathe.

"Gage? I really, really need you to forgive me. Actually, I need you to help me forgive myself. I'm so scared when you die, I'll collapse and hate myself. I'm scared of my darkness. I'm scared there's no one left to pull me out of it when you're gone."

The day, and the fear, and the hurt and the sounds all begin to pull me under. In this weird place between conscious and, subconscious, it feels like Gage can talk to me. It's not his voice and it's not even really words—it's just a feeling. Like we'll all be okay. Like he's lending me the strength he no longer needs.

And then, together, in that little room, we sleep.

In the morning, my back hurts like a bitch. I don't immediately know where I am and panic. As soon as I realize I'm with Gage, I panic more and listen for the machines and the beeps to tell me my brother is still alive.

One.
Two.

Beep.
Breathe.

I get off the floor and see Olivia standing in the doorway looking at us—that must have been what woke me up.

"Hey. Sorry. I didn't mean to fall asleep in here. I just needed . . ."

"I know."

"Are the girls still sleeping?"

"Yeah. We all stayed up pretty late. I think they'll sleep for a while this morning."

"Are you okay?"

"For now. I have to be . . ."

"Is there anything I can do?"

"Yes. I actually wanted to talk to you about this last night. I was thinking maybe you could make some sort of tribute? I don't know—something with music and pictures seems right up your alley."

"Of course. Yes. Just let me know how long you want it to be, and I may grab some photo albums from you before I leave if that's okay."

"Yeah. Take whatever you need."

Before leaving, I reach out to grab Gage's chilly arm.

"I am." I whisper beside his forehead.

"I'm gonna watch you." I kiss his temple. "Because that's what love is."

As I'm walking out of the room Olivia stops me. I can tell she's off this morning, but I just chalk it up to the emotional avalanche pinning her down. She hands me a slim square wrapped in a festive, metallic reindeer print—very much resembling a Christmas present. I'm openly quite confused. She points one thin index finger to the tag on the front and taps it twice.

Merry Christmas, sis
Love, Gage

The letters are wobbly, and by his poor writing, I can nearly identify about when he must have written this. I don't understand why I'm getting it in March, but I'm so thankful to have one last piece of Gage to cherish—and I'm thankful that I'll have a way to listen to it now.

I have a bit of a hangover. I haven't brushed my teeth, regardless of the forward-thinking toothbrush purchase. My long hair is matted to my neck and hangs in awkward, crinkled waves. My mascara is not only a day old but smeared under and above my eyes [see, Mother, this why it's best to avoid makeup]. I look as homeless and dirty as I did on my first visit to Gage's ICU room, so it only makes sense that after I gather my bag and the photos, I run right into Amelia coming into the house while I'm on my way out. Another greeting in a doorway that I'm not ready for.

CHAPTER *Fourteen*

I don't go straight back to Posies. Instead, I drive around my small hometown and try to pull up every memory of Gage. The park from my seventh birthday, the country club green where he caught me smoking my freshman year, the middle school I used to pick him up from every day. I want to soak it all in, every memory absorbed into an invisible, imperfect camera. Every place I stop, I take out a photo album and flip through the pages. I tag a few and begin to categorize them in my mind—not by time period or by location, but by color. The many colors of Gage. He was a vibrant gold for most of our lives, but he was also great at matching my muted greys, and he was always a soft pink with his girls. He had—*has*—so many different faces of happy.

While perching at the high school stadium the sun begins to set. The colors are a beautiful kaleidoscope that remind me of my brother. How could he be so many things for so many people all at the same time? He's all the best colors mixed together into a piece of artwork—not a harsh Jackson Pollock but something more reminiscent of a rainbow-esque version of The Starry Night. I've flipped through every album at this point, but I stay rooted to the hard aluminum seats until the sun completely falls into dusk. It's such an amazing show of light and color that you hardly realize the darkness is upon you. I quietly hope to myself that Gage sets just like this sun. Something beautiful that softly fades away. I like dusk—when the light is still illuminating the dark reminding you it's still there even though you can't actually see it anymore. There's something hopeful about it being neither light nor dark but some beautiful mixture of in-between.

I drive back to my little one-bedroom bungalow in the black, and for the first time, it feels faintly unfamiliar. As soon as I walk into the café, I realize I'm on shift tonight, and I'm missing it. It's fairly cleared out for a Saturday night, but this is the first time I've ever let Antonia down. I'm not ready for whatever complaint or annoyance she has ready for me regarding my absence. But instead of hearing Antonia's anger, she simply nods her head at me with a sort of understanding on her face as I make my way through the shop to my sanctuary. I'm not sure how, but she just knows. My little Yoda.

Before doing anything else, I go take a shower—a much-needed shower. I stand under the warm spray and cry. Not big sobs but a stream of steady tears that match the water dripping down my body—a release of all today's hurts and confusion and darkness—an acceptance of what's real. I lather up with my girlie soaps and wash and condition my hair with my now favorite lavender shampoo Mom gifted me. Afterward, I feel empty and restored at the same time.

Wrapped in a towel and smelling much better, I boot up my Mac and immediately begin mocking up the design and layout concept I played around with in my head all day. Some of the pictures I can easily inlay from my hard drive and a few others I grab from social media. A lot of what's in the albums will need to be scanned in before I can adjust and layout the photos. I find myself having fun creating each page as a different color and playing with the balance and background to match each shade of Gage. It's beautiful. It's my brother. I play on my computer for hours. It's after 2:00 by the time I fall asleep sitting up, hunched over my laptop with a pile of pictures surrounding me while looking at a collage of my brother's boyishly handsome face.

Sunday morning, I wake up with a jolt of fear as Antonia abusively knocks at my door. She bursts in two seconds later with a dirty chai, a scone and a visitor.

"I wasn't sure whether to send him up here or not, so I figured I better come and check on you first. He followed me. The boy has no patience."

Brec appears behind her, looking comically tall in the small doorway. He looks red—embarrassed maybe? For being here? Which doesn't make sense because he presumably came here of his own free will. None of it clicks in place until I move to grab my chai from Antonia. Only then do I realize I fell asleep in a towel—a towel that has very much fallen off during my restless slumber. Well. Shit.

It's awkward to be totally naked in front of anyone in broad daylight. Make that your ex-fiancé and it doubles the awkward level. Add in a random, extremely opinionated and mouthy bystander, and I want to bury my head under this freaking quilt and never resurface.

"Well girl, we all grieve in different ways, but just so you know—work is not clothing optional from now on. Find some damn pants and for the love of God, eat a real meal."

"Thanks, Antonia." I mumble from my new residence under the covers. "But you could have just left the chai, the scone and the boy at the door . . . You know, before you barged in and embarrassed the hell out of me."

Antonia laughs one of her full belly laughs before she leaves as quickly as she came. She hands the coffee and scone to Brec and closes the door behind her, but I can hear her laughing all the way down the stairs. Bitch.

"So, you want me to, uh, leave you the coffee?"

"Dammit, Brec." I give a muffled grumble from under my quilted fort. "Why are you still here? Yes, give me the coffee and then please leave."

I hear him set my drink down on the small table beside my bed.

"And just so you know—I have the scone. If you want it, you've got to come downstairs and get it."

"I'm not your mouse," I huff out under my breath. Though, I'm pretty sure he still hears me because he immediately chuckles. Besides, the jokes on him, I don't even like those scones nearly as much as I once did. Then again, breakfast is the most important meal of the day.

"I like your place up here, Sage. It suits you."

The door opens and closes for the second time, and I peek from my hideout to make sure the coast is clear. I grab my drink and head to the bathroom to assess the damage. I take a long look in the mirror at my naked body trying to get a feel for exactly how horrifically embarrassed I should be. Unfortunately, the fun house mirror makes my anxiety ten times worse. One boob looks like a 'C' cup while the other is still my trusty 'A'. My ass looks incredibly robust if I turn to the right but turning to the left makes my butt looks like a deflated balloon. Yep, this place suits me—it was intended for carny folk who are used to being mortified daily as a form of employment—that sounds about right.

I quickly get dressed, finish my dirty chai and head downstairs with a bag of photo albums in tow. I grab the scone from Brec, who's sitting in one of the wire bistro chairs with his back to me, and without speaking to him, head toward the long, empty counter to pull out photos and begin laying them in categories. I'm able to finish my work and the scone without interruption and

204 | Unfiltered Sage

almost forget about my morning's shame by the time I'm done. Luckily, my creative mind silences almost everything else. It quiets the pain and the embarrassment. It hushes each insecurity and dulls the darkness. Maybe that's why I threw myself, full force, into my job in the beginning—I needed it. It medicated and numbed the loss of Brec. For a second, Amelia flips to my mind. Not the image of the beautiful women in the doorway from yesterday but the college version of her dressed in Brec's t-shirt with sunshine from the skylight streaming onto her already golden hair. Distractions are a tricky thing.

I dig through my bag for my keys and carefully handle all of the photos I have gathered to scan.

"You coming?"

Brec emerges in my periphery as I make my way out to the car. I drive us to the nearest Staples in complete quiet. I see Brec pick up my reindeer wrapped gift from the backseat, turning it over and over in his hands, without saying anything. As we're walking into the store, he finally breaks the silence—in other words, he loses, and I've just won round one.

"Olivia asked me to help you out with this stuff. I'm not sure how much help I'll be, but I can run the errands for you if that takes something off your plate . . . you know, divide and conquer."

Okay, so maybe I didn't win. His suddenly formal tone and clear explanation that he didn't choose to be here, nor does he want to spend the day with me, is like a knife to the gut. I contemplate letting him get the photos scanned, but honestly, I need to stay busy right now. I need to keep moving.

"Brec, I need this. You're welcome to join and help, but I need to do this—all of it."

My honest answer thaws the tension between us, and Brec unexpectedly wraps me in a hug in the middle of the Staples parking lot. I've always loved Brec's hugs. He's so much taller than I am that it feels like half hug/half human shield. I once read an article about Autistic kids who use weighted blankets to calm their nerves and help them cope. That's Brec—he's my weighted blanket. He kisses the top of my head, releases me and we walk straight up to the counter and attempt to speak with a very hard of hearing, elderly employee who seems to have no idea how to work the store's technology or that he is working the photo desk of an office supply store at all. Brec and I decide to take matters into our own hands and start working through the piles of pictures—scanning and emailing them to my personal account. I finish about 10 minutes before Brec who has to rescan nearly every photo because it's crooked or he opened the cover too quickly. While I'm waiting, I browse through the sample books and brochures laying out on the desk. Staples has a cute little Shutterfly-styled picture book that I ask about. The elderly gentlemen, who is completely incompetent when it comes to technology, is much more helpful regarding the pricing and turn around for the photo book. I take his card and let him know I'll be in touch.

"Where to next?" Brec asks from beside me.

"Well, really, that was all I needed to do today besides actually designing and layering in music and all that."

He reaches for my keys and raises one eyebrow in silent permission. I hand the keys over easily. It's not that I don't like driving, but I think I prefer the ease of subways and public transit more. If Brec wants to be my personal chauffeur, he can go right ahead. I have no idea where we're headed, but the city looks so different than it did 15 years ago. I still lose my bearings around here pretty quickly.

"So, what do you think it is?" Brec asks while tipping his head toward the wrapped gift sitting in my backseat. I don't respond because it seems fairly obvious what it is. "From Gage?" Brec questions.

"Yep, Olivia gave it to me yesterday on my way out." The memory takes me back to the ever-perfect Amelia who I really don't want to be thinking about right now with Brec sitting in my driver's seat.

"Seriously, what do you think is in there?"

"I'm gonna go out on a limb and guess a vinyl, Brec."

"Yes, smart-ass, but which one?"

"You don't know?"

"Nope."

"But you knew about the last one. You were prepared for the fall out at Christmas."

"Gage told me about it . . . months later. So, what is it? angsty teen music or country ballads?"

I think for a few minutes. I wonder if it's another message. I equally hope it is and it isn't. I want to cherish whatever last words he has for me—even if it's through music, but I'm not sure my heart can handle them. Thus, the unopened present.

"I sort of hope it's something really happy like The Polyphonic Spree. *Light and Day* has always seemed like the perfect anthem for Gage. What about you? What do you think?"

"I think if it is an anthem, it will be his anthem for you, not the other way around."

He thinks for a minute—then two. I'm starting to get worried he gave up on the game already.

"I know what my anthem is for you, but I'm not sure what Gage's would be. He admired—*admires*—you a lot, but I also think it might be something silly from your childhood or a local artist to remind you of home. Sometimes, he can be pretty random."

I'm trying to dissect everything from these short sentences. A big part of me wants to dig into Brec's version of a 'Sage anthem', but I know it's not the right time. I agree that this could absolutely be some sort of funny tribute, but I think Gage would be more intentional than random—especially now.

"Where are you taking me?" I ask suddenly unaware of my surroundings.

"You'll see."

"That's a dumb answer. 'You'll see' is for suckers. Are you going to take me to one of these little suburban homes, chop me up and put me in the freezer?"

"Wow. That was really dark. Like *really* dark."

"Dude, I'm from New York. New Yorkers know 'you'll see' is code for I'm gonna murder you, you dumb, trusting tourist."

"You're not from New York, Sage. It was just your home, your comfort zone, for a little while."

I'm no longer sure if we're talking about geography or my state of depression, and he actually may be more right than wrong, so I let the conversation go. We pull into a non-threatening looking driveway in the middle of suburbia. There are literally kids, two houses down, playing baseball in the front yard. I haven't talked to Brec's mom in years, so I don't know if she's moved. However, I highly doubt she would ever plant roots in a non-gated community like this one. We walk directly to the front door. Brec produces a key from his pocket, opens the door and stands aside for me to walk in first. I trust this man, but walking into a dark, unfamiliar house by myself sets off all sorts of alarms in my brain. When the lights are on, the living room reveals exactly where I am. Everything in here screams of Brec. The colors—all blues and greens, very reminiscent of the ocean that he loves—are displayed in all the little accents. The smell is still him. The sun that filters in and casts warm light around the room is him. He's taken me to his house. I've never seen where grown up Brec lives before.

I get the quick tour, and I can sense the old, vulnerable Brec for a minute. The house is pristine—not an item out of place or even dirty clothes in the hamper. The bedroom has some beautiful, high priced artwork hanging on the far wall but no real personal touches. This feels wrong for Brec. He's the sort of man who will display his feelings proudly, not the guy to hide it behind someone else's expensive emotions displayed on a canvas. We're back to the living room, and I still don't understand why I'm here. I'm not complaining about the destination, but it doesn't make sense that Brec suddenly felt the need to take me to his super impersonal home while we're busy pulling together a tribute for Gage.

"Why are we here?"

Brec turns to me, clearly uncomfortable. "I have some pictures I thought we should grab for the slideshow."

Now that makes a lot more sense. "Okay, let's grab them. Are you hiding your pictures in a cabinet or something?"

Brec looks at me then looks to a door off the left of the living room. A door that I assumed was just a closet. Maybe he really does have a cabinet of pictures, maybe that's what normal, non-photographer, people do. He nods for me to go toward the door but makes no movement in that direction himself.

It's a room, not a closet. The room is some sort of den or office. It has a softer, more worn out couch with an old '70s style coffee table and a large TV. The room has a floor to ceiling wall of bookshelves. Most of the space is covered in medical books and old novels but scattered about are framed photos. Some of the photos I easily recognize—pictures of Brec and Gage. Others are moments I always imagined but didn't get to witness—Brec's graduation pic from med school with his diploma in hand. As I study the bookcase, I notice my Christmas gift to him sitting on a small picture pedestal. I'm glad he liked it. Slowly I make my way around the entire room. On the wall above the couch are at least ten pictures all printed in 16x20 with the same basic black frame and white matting. It takes me about six seconds to soak it in—all of these are my pictures. Every single thing on this wall is my work—all my published photos. I'm not sure how he got original prints rather than magazine quality, but those are absolutely my photos hanging on his wall. This is why he was nervous. Here is Brec, the man who wears his heart on his sleeve and loves like a freaking weighted blanket. I finish my tour of the room—of each picture— and choose a few frames I'd like to take with me to scan. The door in front of me is askew, not fully opened or closed, but I can see there is something hanging on the back of the door itself. From here it looks like mostly white space, and I can't make out the image. Out of curiosity, I inch forward and close the door, so I can get a better view.

It's a torn photo put back together and framed. It's clearly over-exposed and it's impossible to see what the picture once was. There is one piece missing from the broken collage, a small triangular shaped tear. A piece I have in my camera bag and have carried with me for 18 years. A one-inch scrap of paper that has a boy's phone number on it. A tiny fracture of paper that was the beginning of something beautiful—and hard—and heartbreaking. I add this photo to the frames I'm taking with me. This one isn't for Gage though. This one's for me.

I head out of the den and close the door behind me.

"You find what you need?" Brec asks looking away from me toward the door.

"Yes, Brec, I found what I was looking for."

We get back in my car and head toward Staples—again.

"Have you thought about the school position much more?"

"Not really. I mean, now it seems silly to stay. I guess I'll talk to Olivia and see what she wants, but right now—it's just not a good time."

"A good time to talk to her, or a good time to be at the house?"

Ah, so he knows his ex is currently staying with Gage and Olivia. I know that none of this is about me, but I really hate that in order to get to my brother, I have to go through her first. Gage better appreciate how much I love him.

"I'm going to the house no matter what. My brother's there. For as long as he's alive, I don't give a shit who else I have to deal with in order to see him."

"Believe me, Sage, she's more scared of you than you'll ever be of her."

Is he taking her side? Maybe I'm feeling overly sensitive right now, but it feels like he still doesn't get how devastating it was to believe for so long that my fiancé cheated on me, left me and then married the woman he cheated with.

"Hey." he knocks his knee with mine to get my attention. "Even if you don't want the job, I think it would be a good idea to head up to the school with the girls and let them see how much their dad is loved. From what I hear, his students are taking this all pretty hard too. It might be good for everyone."

"I think so too. I have the girls every Wednesday. I'll call the principal and see if I can set something up."

I can nearly hear Brec's heart tearing as he looks at me. "Babe, just remember, sooner rather than later."

He takes my hand, and we finish our errands like that—hand in hand in some sort of truce—finding some sort of comfort in the other.

Brec gets a page summoning him to the hospital. It's officially his day off, but as the newbie, he's always on call. I can easily finish up what I'm working on without him, and I'm relieved to have the space to myself—to allow myself to feel it all alone. Before he leaves he tells me to open my gift and see what Gage had to say. Thinking about that leaves me feeling antsy, like I need to get out of my room for a little while and clear my head. I text Olivia to see if it's a good time to come see Gage. It takes her an hour to respond, but she says that her parents are over, and my parents are coming by this evening. So, basically, 'No, Sage, this is not a good time'. I get it. I can't monopolize him.

I run to Taco Bueno for a late lunch/early dinner. On my way back in the café, I go ahead and grab Gage's gift and figure I can decide whether I actually want to open it or not later. It's amazing how much better I feel after a couple party burritos. I flip through my iTunes, but nothing feels right. Either it's too sad and will send me spinning into a pool of emotions, or it's too flippant for the moment. I end up heading toward my vinyl collection and picking something out from there. I separate all of my vinyls into two piles: gifts Gage gave me and random things I've picked up over the years. This gives me an idea.

My senior year of college, I got really into screen printing. I think it was the beginning of my love for graphic design. I love layering and texturing pieces. I guess it just feels right that art should have that sort of depth. What we see is never one thing, it's a lifetime of experience and layers that lead to that one moment— that one image.

I grab my Mac and start playing with the inlay. Quickly, I etch in some of the lyrics from the first album he ever gave me over a photo of us with extra whitespace. Man, I loved Mazzy Star and her beautiful words about finding truth in those around us. I repeat the lyrics over and over in thin wisps of vertical lines covering about 60% of the empty space on the page. I love it. I pick up the next album, a Bon Iver record I've already played more times than I can count and start again. I immediately find the lyrics I want, then flip to a collage of the girls and Gage and begin the inlay. Among the smiling faces are words reminding the girls—all of us—that Gage's love will never end, but soon, it will be a different type of love—a *remembered* love. It takes me the rest of the afternoon and all evening to go through every record, and I still have a couple pages without lyrics. I decide that's good enough. This is what Gage left me, so this is what I'll use. It's late, but I text Olivia to see if there's anything she can think of or a song she wants included. As I'm putting all the records away I realize there is another album Gage left me; I haven't used all the words just yet. I clean up my whole room before I bring the package onto the bed with me and slowly open it. I can tell by the cover art that this is The Avett Brothers. For a second, I hope it's *The Carpenter*. I've always loved that album. However, when I turn it over, I'm surprised and a little sad to see I'm wrong—like Gage and I aren't in sync anymore. This one is *The Second Gleam*. I can't quite remember what's on it.

I put the needle on the record, turn off all the lights and lay down on my back to listen to Gage. I count off each song looking for his words.

One.
Two.

There it is. The second track—*Murder in the City*—my message.

I push the needle back and listen again and again. In the dark, I pull out my Mac and fix the last two empty pages. One page is filled with candid shots of Mom, Dad, Gage and me from over the years. I quickly inlay the lyrics from *Murder in the City*. I repeat the lines over and over a hundred times in a willowy font. Gage's message is a reminder to us of his love and loyalty, and I want him to know I'm listening. The final page is his family—pictures from the day both girls were born, a family portrait, a picture from Anna's infant shoot, and the picture I gave Olivia for Christmas. It's the most painful sort of happy as I type out the last of all the lyrics, and he's right—there isn't anything in this world as beautiful as the people we get to share our love and our lives with.

Done. I close the laptop and fall asleep listening to the rest of the album.

CHAPTER Fifteen

Monday morning I hit the ground running. I dig out Jen's business card and call her at work. Unfortunately, they can't get anything together for today, but she does invite the girls and I to come visit tomorrow morning. We briefly talk about Gage's condition, and she asks again if I'm interested in the job. I honestly have no mental energy left to put toward making life/employment decisions, so I tell her I'll have to get back with her about that after spring break.

Next, I run up to Staples to make the photo books I've decided to give out during the visitation dinner my mother so badly needs to organize. I figure it's sort of a lovely, and morbid, keepsake, but it may help the girls to flip through the photos before the funeral in a smaller, more controlled setting. It's actually pretty easy to transfer my slideshow over into a 10x10 format for the books. By the time I'm done, and the books are ordered, it's still only 10:30. I don't do idle hands well, especially not today, so I head back to Posies and start my shift early.

My shift ends up being incredibly monotonous, and standing still makes me realize I'm itching to go talk to Gage. I haven't seen him since Saturday morning, and I know that every day counts at this point—hell, every hour counts. I shoot a quick text to Olivia asking if I can come in tonight and see my brother. She tells me to bring a pillow this time in case I fall asleep on the floor again. So, before I leave Posies, I go upstairs and grab a pillow and a thin blanket that I keep on top of my bed. She may have been joking, but I think that was some awfully smart, forward thinking on her part.

I'm beat when I finally arrive. I hold Gage's hand for a little bit and tell him about the photo books. Involuntarily, I begin humming the song I had on repeat for most of last night. Thinking about those lyrics I have now memorized, I wonder if he really felt like he needed to make sure I knew that he loved me. Gage loves in violently brilliant colors, so it seems obvious to me that anyone he loves would be fully aware of it, but I also wonder if he's maybe saying, 'make sure my sister knows, in spite of all her flaws, I love her, and she's worth being loved'. I don't know. Maybe I'm reading too much into all of it. I yawn and unroll my blanket and pillow. On the floor beside Gage, I tell him about my photos hanging in Brec's house—pictures, I'm sure, he already knew about. I tell him about all the broken bits and pieces of information I have and can't seem to completely put together. I think about what he told me during one of my first ICU visits—that I needed to ask Brec about why he and Amelia split up. I still haven't asked that, and maybe, if I did, I would finally be able to piece the past back together. Eventually, I fall asleep on the floor beside my brother, which is quickly becoming my favorite place on earth.

Tuesday morning Gage looks nearly green—maybe a greenish blue. He's definitely past pale though and looks like a nauseous cartoon character. I squeeze his hand tightly before getting ready to take the girls today. Fortunately, I can use the tooth-brush and deodorant I left at the house last week before the girls and I head up to the high school. On the way, I'm silently cursing my day-old clothes and lack of shower. This is the worst sort of high school reunion I can imagine.

My teenage memories give me pause before we walk in, but I'm pleasantly surprised that this place is a little nicer than I remember it—like someone polished off all the dust and made it shiny again. These nieces of mine are over the moon with their visitor name badges, and Emery stops everyone she sees to point at her name proudly stuck to her chest. The poor girl has no concept of why each person she talks to squeezes the life out of her and leaves with misty eyes. She doesn't understand what she represents to these people who know and love her dad.

I'm surprised when we don't climb the staircase toward the corridor that houses the history rooms but are instead ushered into the large auditorium. Anna is absolutely horrified by the idea of standing on the stage, but Emery eats up the spot light. Luckily, the attention isn't on us for too long before we're sat in chairs off to the darkened, left side of the stage, and the school begins its own sort of closure—a sendoff for their beloved teacher, Mr. Gilbert.

Once the kids are quiet, we're introduced from our little corner and a slideshow starts of Gage's years at the school—both as a student and as a teacher. Oddly enough, the most ridiculous pictures aren't even from his teenage years. There's a photo of him duct taped to a wall by his students that makes us all laugh. A snapshot of him standing on his desk with his whole class following his lead. There is a soft, candid shot of him smiling with those dimples at someone or something out of view. The pictures are beautiful although the execution of the slideshow leaves much to be desired. They mostly show Gage the teacher, but even then, there are so many shades of his leadership. By the end, everyone is glassy-eyed, even Emery reaches over to me and says, "Daddy used to be so preddy before he die." I decide not to touch that one, not here—not right now.

After the short, shifty film, the superintendent stands up to give a speech on Mr. Gage Gilbert, the teacher. He must be prepped on Gage's condition because he keeps referring to him in the past tense. I don't think either of the girls catch this, but it makes the hair on my arms stand on end. When it's over, we're rushed by students and teachers alike, all of whom want to hug and console us. The fame is overwhelming. The girls are treated like celebrities, and a dozen kids or so ask to take selfies with them. With each new stranger Anna becomes increasingly more clingy and terrified, and I realize I need to get her out here. I spot Jen, the chatty and slightly flirty principal, and ask if maybe there's a place we can go to get away from the masses. She takes us back up to Gage's room where a sub sits, kicked back and waiting for his students to return from the assembly. Oddly enough, this is the first person in the building who has treated us normally—meaning he completely ignores us. Jen—Ms. Nianouris—the principal/not teacher, whatever the hell her name is, tells us that we're allowed to stay up here as long as we want, and it should be a much quieter version of what we experienced this morning down stairs.

Though I have serious doubts about this lady's authority, Jen was absolutely right about one thing, this is much more our speed. The 45-minute class becomes a fractured story of these student's lives and how Gage intervened. The girls and I are snuggled into corner desks as we watch the action unfold in a much more organic conversation than the assembly prior. Every story is completely touching, and without asking, I get out my camera phone and begin filming.

> **Blonde cheerleader looking girl sitting in the front row:** "Mr. Gilbert is the sort of teacher who gives you his cell phone number and tells you to use it if you're ever in trouble—and he means it. I got stuck at a party during football season, and I maybe shouldn't have been driving. My friends were being entirely too extra, and I needed a ride. My parents seriously would have killed me if they caught me partying again, so I called Mr. Gilbert. I mean I kind of assumed he would just let it go to voicemail anyway. He packed his whole family up in the car, woke up the girls and everything, to come pick up my drunk ass. He even took me through the Whataburger drive through. His family was like the cutest ever, and I remember telling the girls over and over again to make

good choices. It was kind of weird, but he was like, for real, the only teacher cool enough to do that."

Anime drawing kid, slumped in the back of the room, with a beanie on: "Mr. Gilbert was the type of guy who always asked questions before he'd judge you. I think it was like the 15th homework assignment in a row I didn't turn in before he called me up to his desk, and instead of yelling at me or telling how I was never going to graduate, like every other teacher, he drew a calendar, handed me a pencil, and asked me to fill in my normal day. Man, I'll never figure out how he just knew. My parents own a dry cleaner and as soon as I get off school, I have to go work there. Between helping out at their place and making sure my little brothers are taken care of, I just never could stay awake long enough to do homework. Every day before school, he let me come up here and work on my homework. Even if it wasn't for his class, he would help me. This is the first year I won't have to go to summer school to make up course credits. That's Mr. Gilbert."

Skinny cool dude with his legs kicked up on the seat of the empty desk beside him: "You know Mr. Gilbert is the first teacher here to realize that I never came to school with lunch. When you're young, teachers see those things, but here, no one notices. I spent my first two years of high school bumming food off friends or just hoping there'd be something at the house when I got home. Mr. Gilbert noticed on the second day of school . . . *the second day*. He never made a thing about it—just always made sure to hand me something on my way out the door. He was the kind of guy who really saw us. I miss him, man."

I'm overtaken by emotion. This is Gage's legacy. The man who spent his life looking after me, apparently, spent his life looking after everyone. I don't want to compare myself, but for a second, I wonder what people would say about me. How many of the villages I've stayed in would even remember my face much less anything I did while I was there? A picture may be art, but what if no one cares about who takes it? Photography will never love me back—not like this.

We stay all afternoon listening to class after class relay these amazing stories. There's never a lull in the room, and thankfully, everyone gives us some space. Before each group leaves, I ask if it's okay to use them in a tribute during Gage's funeral. The girls and I are exhausted as we pack up after the 3:30 bell. The sub quietly nods our way in understanding or apology and is gone before we leave the room. The way the place clears out— how everyone moves on so quickly—feels wrong. Part of me wants to stand rooted to this spot. To camp out. To honor Gage with more than a moment, but right now isn't the right time. The girls are tired and, honestly, my emotions are completely frayed from holding it together all day. Before I close the door and turn out the light, I look around at all the mementos and pieces of my brother on these walls. I realize I'll need to come up here and clean out Gage's classroom. Maybe tomorrow.

Antonia stops me at work to ask if I'm okay. I can tell there is no humor behind her eyes, and she knows how much we are all, like Gage, hanging on by a thread. I let her know that we're looking at days now, and I'll likely need some time off soon. She tries to rush me out the door, but oddly enough, I feel like this is exactly where I belong right now. Alone again, I look to the back table where Brec and I talked about Gage's diagnosis that first night. The first time I'd ever heard of a gliomas or lymphoma—I was so naïve. I was so hopeful. It hurts to stare at those chairs. I wonder how many wrong turns it took us to get from there to here. For a swift second it all presses in on me, threatening my lungs and my heart to give up. Darkness shimmers at the edge of my vision; I feel it there, ready to consume me. I need to get out of here.

As soon as my shift is over, I grab my Mac and a change of clothes, and I fly to Gage—like if I don't get there fast enough I'll lose him, like somehow any of this is in my control. Just like last night, the house is completely quiet—as if everyone has already given up. I'm sure that's not true, but the silence hurts me all the same. I quickly change into some pjs and head into my make-shift bed. For as long as Gage is here, I will be right beside him. Instead of telling him about my day, I pull over a stiff chair and get out my phone. I hold up the video for us to watch, and for hours, we listen to Gage's students tell him goodbye. I know so many pieces of him are already gone and so much color has faded, but I hope with everything I've got in me, that somehow, he hears this. He deserves to know how loved he is.

I don't even bother unrolling my blanket and pillow tonight. I sleep in the chair beside my little brother while holding his frozen hand and listening to all the lives he changed.

I wake up several times during the night fearful that Gage stopped . . . living. He's officially hit multi-organ failure. His renal system went first, followed by pulmonary and now we are waiting for the cardiac to fully take effect—for Gage's heart to give up. I know his heart is the biggest, boldest piece of him, but I'm still sleeping on a precipice of fear and dread. I count the beeps like sheep, each one reminding me of another second my brother is here with me. I get to 7,318 before I fall into my subconscious again.

Gage barely makes it through the night. Hospice hovers around him like the Grim Reaper, and I have to get out of here before I completely detonate on everyone. I grab my laptop and head back to those same old fucking high school bleachers. Something about them makes me feel powerful, and I'll take any strength I can borrow at the moment. I sync my phone to my laptop, put in my ear buds and begin working. It came to me last night while I was counting beeps how I wanted to use the film of the students from Gage's classroom. I open my slideshow to a single shot of the girls and drag in the audio from the first girl I taped. The slide begins with the blonde's profile talking and fades into the shot of Anna and Emery with the girl's voice-over still finishing her story. I layer in music, some of it the actual music to the corresponding lyrics on the page, behind the audio and through the dead moments. It's exactly right—it's Gage. It's an unpretentious sort of complex. I get nearly 20 kids' stories, or a piece of their story, into the slideshow before the afternoon sun and aluminum bleachers threaten to melt me.

I head inside the thick cement building to cool off and wander around before I head to the art hall—to the photo lab. I walk in and no one thinks anything about it. I don't think the kids remember me from yesterday, nor do they seem to think I'm a sub. They just sort of ignore my general presence. I walk the room—the long tables for layout and the cubbies of cameras. I check out the darkroom before I step in, but I still end up walking in on a small girl developing her film.

"Oh, God. I'm sorry. It didn't look like anyone was in here."

She gives a half laugh—literally—half a laugh, like the rest of it was just too much damn effort and goes back to very poorly processing her pictures. I watch her, curious to see if she'll figure out her mistakes, but instead, she stops and looks up at me.

"I know." she aggressively huffs under her breath. "I don't have any effing idea what I'm doing."

"I can see that. Want some help?"

She studies me for a second with hooded, wary eyes.

"You were Mr. Gilbert's sister, right?"

"No. I *am* Mr. Gilbert's sister. I will always be his sister."

She shrugs her shoulders like the verb tense is of little to no importance to her, but I can see the edges of her frown lift to a small smile. "So, you want me to explain how to do this?"

"Sure. Whatever."

The school has definitely stepped up their lab since I was here. It's not state of the art, but it's a hell of a lot better than some of the stuff I've developed with while on location. We spend the rest of the class practicing how to load a reel and check the temperature on the developer. Then I explain how to use developer, stop bath and fixer to expose the pictures. I forgot how much I love working in here, in the dark, away from all the technology and photo "correctors". In this place, photography is simpler—less altered. A place where pictures truly match their memories.

The bell sounds, and we quickly clean up the chemicals together.

"Mrs. Gilbert?"

"Just Ms."

"Yeah, okay. —You're pretty good at this."

"Well, I hope so—it's my job."

"Cool. You're a teacher like your brother?"

"Oh. No, I'm a photographer."

"Really? That's what I want to be . . . but I know I totally suck. It's stupid . . . "

She looks so dejected, so embarrassed by her dreams. I want to fix this, her shame of something that should be really exciting, but I'm not sure what to say. I'm pretty positive adults aren't supposed to cuss in front of students at school—that sort of seems like a no brainer—but I feel like pretty much anyone would let it slide just this once considering the state of my life right now.

"Fuck that. You don't suck, but you're just learning. We all started where you are. Don't give up on the things you love."

By the time we resurface, the room is totally empty as are the halls. School must be over. I lose the girl in the open corridor and chalk it up to some sort of weird fate moment. I look up to the second story and trudge over to the staircase. Time to clean out Gage's room.

The light's still on, but the room is deserted. I take a moment to turn from wall to wall—memorizing the room the way he left it. I take a couple pictures and think maybe one day Olivia might want them. Gage's desk stands out first. I open all the drawers and look through them. He has everything from a set of Emery's hair clips, to *Frozen* Band-Aids and some of my postcards from years ago hiding in there. He also has what seems to be gifts from his students over the years. I find a key chain that simply says, "Gilbert," and a few folded notes from kids. He has three framed photos on his desk—one of his family at the beach in front of a gorgeous ocean sunset. This must have been at least two years ago. Emery is wearing a puddle jumper and one of those weird water diaper things under her swimsuit. Another is of him and Brec snowboarding. Gage's nose is sunburned and Brec's hair is a mess of wet strands, but they are both all smiles. The last is a single shot of Gage—the photo I sent him from his visit to New York when I was in college—his NYC 'postcard'. I stack each frame with his personal belongings from the drawers on an empty desk and move over to the bookshelves.

The shelves and his filing cabinet seem less important, less personal. There is a book on the American Revolution that I grab to take with me; it will always remind me of the kids standing firmly on their desk tops saying, "Oh captain, my captain." There are also a couple of random photography books sitting on the shelf that I place in the take home pile before deciding to leave most of Gage's curriculum books and binders where they are.

One wall has a large collage of photos and keepsakes. It looks like a variety of candid shots kids took in class with some senior portrait pics along with a few professional shots of mine Gage threw up on the wall. There are even a couple colored drawings from the girls hanging among the hodge podge collection. I carefully take each item down and find a large plastic grocery bag to put it all in. I leave the History timeline and a few motivational posters hanging on the walls for whoever comes next. I hope, in this small way, Gage's memory lives on for a little longer. I dump everything I can into the already full grocery sack and carry the few textbooks and frames in my empty arm. With one long, last look around the room—the place Gage inspired kids and changed lives—I turn out the light and awkwardly close the door behind me.

One.

The afternoon and the evening are spent huddled in Olivia's living room—waiting in silence. We're all there. Olivia's parents and the girls. My parents and grandparents. Brec and Amelia.

Dr. Russell even comes in for a little bit to check on everyone. He and Brec talk together in the kitchen before he calls Olivia out of the room. Through the silence, we can make out their private conversation.

"Olivia, are you sure you still want to go with the DNR?"

Two.

"It's what he wanted . . . Yes . . . " she wobbles out the words.

Three.

"Do you have any questions?"

"Just one. How much pain is he in?"

Four.

"Substantial. His body has fought hard. He did well, but it's time. He's tired."

Five.

We all hear Olivia's hushed tears, and I reach out to clench my mom's hand. We hold tight just like that—listening to Olivia's world collapse.

"Olivia," Dr. Russell says in soft, hushed tones like he's talking to a small child, "it's time to say goodbye."

Six.

Brec walks through the kitchen door holding on to Olivia's arm—holding her up. He nods his head for me to come with them, and I pull Mom and Dad behind me. They need to be there too.

Gage looks like death, literally. I've never seen a corpse up close and personal, but somehow, I know this is what it looks like.

Seven.

No one talks as we each tell Gage our own silent goodbyes. His short life flashes through my mind in time-lapse. The infant who I proudly helped feed and change. The toddler I often knocked over or dressed up as one of my baby dolls. The strong little boy who always gave me a run for my money. The curious adventurer who helped me build a tree house. The teenager who kept all my secrets. The young man whose heart broke when he lost a child. The dad and husband who loved so selflessly. The brother who brought me home.

Eight.

We link hands, this fractured version of a family that would have or should have been, and breathe in unison with each beep of the monitor.

Nine.

Until it stops.

Ten.

. . . .

Gage, my baby brother—the best of us all, died at 11:02 pm with his family watching by his side.

Into the devastation I whisper the final lyrics of *What Sarah Said*—the last words. It's true. Gage was right. Love is about being there until the end.

And then Olivia completely crumbles to the floor with an anguish I've never witnessed.

CHAPTER *Sixteen*

One. *Thursday.*

In a way, it's fortunate that we've had so much time to prepare for this day. The moment time of death was called, Olivia ceased being a person herself. Funeral arrangements are practically complete, flowers have been purchased and the pastor is on call, but there seems to be a million little details left to the rest of us who are still able to get out of bed.

Telling the girls is the sort of moment I will have nightmares about forever, and I don't have to tell them just once—we all have to remind them over and over again. Emery is still too young to understand that dying is forever—you don't come back from it. And each time she asks if she can go see, or talk to, or play with, or tell Daddy something, the splinters in my heart turn more cavernous.

Mom steps up and gets everything in order from the viewing and visitation to travel arrangements and hotel stays for some of Gage's college buddies. She's a whirlwind of energy—like a top spinning at full speed—and I'm scared if she slows down, she'll crash. The catering is ready to go, and a space is rented to accommodate everyone for a quiet dinner—an intimate good-bye. Gage's funeral is set for 2:00 on Saturday afternoon at one of the mega churches in the city. The attendance is expected to be over a thousand, but the graveside is friends and family only.

Brec and I write the obituary. If it didn't break my heart so damn much, it could have been a weirdly fortifying moment together. We both cry, and we both laugh while piecing together a synopsis of my simply amazing brother's simply amazing life. I think we're too broken right now to hold our guards up, and without them, it's hard to remember why this didn't work out for us. The hopeful nostalgia is quickly broken because Amelia is everywhere all the time—always helpful, always nice, and always one step away from my tiny fists pummeling her back into the past where she belongs.

Two. *Friday.*

So much has changed in a week. Olivia and I should be snuggled on the couch with glasses of wine relaying our weeks, our stress, our worries—but instead, I'm staring at the black, knee-length, short-sleeved dress laid out on my bed. I hate this dress already, and I've never even worn it. And without a doubt, I know I'll never wear it again. I can put off getting dressed, but I can't slow down a reality that's already smashed everything in its wake.

The visitation is more overwhelming than any of us expect. The line wraps around the entire funeral home, around the building and to the ends of the parking lot. For a second, if I split frame, it feels like one of the overcrowded rides from Holiday in the Park. Although, when I look into the sea of faces, there is no mistaking this for any form of amusement. The crowd is end-less—noiseless. It's a silent assembly line of tears and hugs. Growing up, I was never a big hugger. I don't think I ever really outgrew this—I just became an adult, and adults have far fewer occasions for affection. Either way, this sort of socially demand-ed correctness is an added drain on a day that already feels so empty.

I find it exceedingly awkward, and perhaps a bit odd, that each new set of arms looks to us for comfort. No one warned me that not only would I lose a brother, but I would have to somehow shove my own feelings far enough down that I can play counselor for the hundreds of people who need my shoulder to cry on.

Olivia, with the aid of several pharmaceuticals, has managed to not only get herself out of bed, but also handle the hordes of viewers—and gawkers—and grievers—with a sort of disinterested grace. It's nice that one of us seems to be able to handle the masses with some modicum of patience and understanding. However, her numb is far scarier than my broken. I know I'm not what anyone would call 'emotionally stable', but even I'm familiar enough with the stages of grief to know 'numb' isn't one of them.

When the funeral home empties of the last lamenter, and when my heart empties of its last hope that this was all a really fucking bad dream, we head to dinner. We are all at least an hour late, and by the time I get there, Mom is already having 'strong words' with some poor, unassuming member of the waitstaff. Dinner is left cold and half-eaten. I don't know what my mother expected of this over-coordinated adventure, but I'm positive she's not pleased by the silent scraping of silverware, pushing the uneaten chicken back and forth across the plates along with our acceptance and denial.

Brec's the first to stand and make a speech. He's wearing a tapered black suit that fits him perfectly, and I realize that everything in me hasn't completely withered with Gage's passing—my libido is seemingly still very much alive. This is both exciting and totally pisses me off at the same time because there's not a damn thing I can do about it. From the corner of my peripheral, I catch Amelia's eye, though she's not looking at me. She's staring at Brec with a dopey, girlish grin that awkwardly mirrors my own. My jealousy and pain mixed with the wine create a potent cocktail of confusion that knocks me flat on my ass. In turn, everyone stands and offers whatever they have left in them, whatever the crowd didn't already take from us tonight. I listen to long childhood stories and abbreviated goodbyes delivered to the ceiling. Anna makes a promise, an oath of sorts, to be brave and make her daddy proud while Emery sings a song she seems to have created on the fly that basically says 'I love you, Daddy' over and over again in about seven different keys. The mic is passed to Olivia, but she refuses to extend her hand and take it. I understand that this may be too much—too hard for her right now, but I wonder if she'll regret this choice one day. Eventually, the mic is deposited in my hands, and I stare at it for a second before I clear my throat and stand on wobbly legs. Here goes nothing.

"I wish I knew what to say, but, right now, I'm just . . . blank."

I awkwardly shrug at the many sets of eyes staring me down before I glance from left to right and become increasingly worried that I'm going to do this wrong—this last chance I get to say—something beautiful and poignant about Gage will be totally blown by me being . . . me. Then my eyes find Brec's. We lock in that moment; his eyes shining with hope and something else old and familiar. Something like . . . love. He gives me one single nod, and somehow, I know exactly what he's saying. Being yourself, being genuine and vulnerable, is an exhausting sort of frightening, but running away from sincerity is equally as tiring.

"I've always talked a lot. I've had, maybe, too many choice words for everyone in my path for pretty much my whole life . . . but, I've never had the right words when it counts—never at the times they're needed most."

I clear my throat again, and instead of sweeping my gaze through the room, I look up and talk to my brother.

"Gage. There aren't words that encompass the kind of empty I feel without you. There isn't way to explain the loss. There isn't . . . there is no way you can know how much you'll be missed. There isn't a way to explain how everything, every cell in me, knows that this should have been me—this was never supposed to be you . . . "

I lose my breath. It just vanishes, and I'm left breathing ruggedly through the pain in my chest into the mic.

" . . . There aren't—there will never be—the right words to say goodbye. So, instead, I'll just say, I love you. For always, baby brother."

My heels click in the quiet room as I go to start the slideshow. "The Many Colors of Gage: A Story of Happiness through Pictures," I've titled it. Without another word, I set the mic down on the table beside me and, for a moment, we all enjoy watching Gage's charisma and color one more time. Afterward, I pass out each wrapped photo book, so everyone has Gage's happiest moments memorialized. Olivia neither accepts nor denies my gift; however, I do notice she leaves it unwrapped—at arm's length. I promised Gage I would take care of her, and I feel like I'm already failing. The group begins to dwindle, and I feel, mostly, like I did my brother proud. We are all still pretty silent, but the silence feels a little less like depression. Mom is either paying the caterer or checking the staff's work when Dad comes to kiss me on my forehead. I've missed him. In all of this, from the moment I got the call, my brother needed my dad more than I did. And I let Gage have that—Dad's every worry, all of Dad's strength—but now, I'm realizing how much I need him to get through this—the next step.

"You did good, Sage."

"You think he'd be happy?"

"Oh sweetheart, you always made him happy. His first smile was because of you, and I'm certain, his last one was too."

"He's gone."

"No, he's not. You showed us that tonight. He's always here—in the memories we have, in the stories we tell. He's still here, Sage."

"It's a pretty empty sort of 'here'."

"Sage, remember what I told you in the hotel room when you came home?"

"The first night?"

"Yes."

"You said I was stunning, Dad. You always say that."

"I told you not to look for answers—"

I cut him off and finish the thought. "—you told me to look for peace."

My mom materializes out of thin air and grabs my father's hand. They are complete opposites. He's all calm and she's all storm, and I've never seen two people who love each other more. Dad kisses my head once more.

"Find some peace, Sage."

I nod my head, now tightly tucked against his chest, but, again, I can't find the words. With one last squeeze, he releases me, and they both turn to leave, leaning on each other for the support needed to make it through one more day. I reach down to unplug my laptop and gather all my shit when Dad's voice echoes across the empty hall.

"Sage, you're still stunning."

I shake my head back and forth but smile in spite of the moment—in spite of myself. With my bag over my shoulder, I'm ready. I click-clack softly out of the empty room—each step moving me millimeters toward acceptance, a stepping-stone on my way to peace.

The parking lot houses my beat-up Altima lit under the one lone, bright light, but beside it there's another vehicle and someone waiting outside in the cool March evening. Oh shit. This can't be a coincidence—she's clearly here waiting for me. I'm empty and fragile, but she's the only one with the rest of the story. I can run. I can easily escape this moment and get back to burying my brother tomorrow, or I can find out the truth. Do I want peace, or do I want answers? Fight or flight? I let this all play out in my mind while we both stand outside our cars in starkly awkward tension, and then she makes the decision for me.

"I just wanted to say thank you for the book. It means a lot that you decided to include me."

"It was Gage's request," I reply in a slow monotone.

Her pale blue eyes fall a bit, and I notice how tightly she's holding the book to her chest. I know that stance—I've perfected it. It's the posture of the broken. All at once, the bright and beautiful Amelia looks much less radiant. She doesn't deserve all of my pent up bitchiness, so I try again with some sincerity that I'm sure would please Gage.

"You're welcome. —It was the right thing to do."

She nods her head in a quick, sharp movement. It almost looks strong and assertive, but the wobble to her chin gives her away—that and the loose tears falling down her profile as she twists her face away from me. I can accept this woman's humanity, but that doesn't mean I'm ever going to be her confidant. So, I unlock my door and throw my bag in the backseat—the still clean backseat. My leg is through the driver's side door when her small voice stops me.

"I'm sorry."

She and Brec are cut from the same fucking cloth. Maybe it's that, or maybe it's because this is my least favorite sentence of all time—either way, Amelia, the tender-hearted, just unleashed about a decade worth of rage hidden right below the surface.

"Excuse me? You're sorry? For what—my brother dying or fucking my fiancé'? Both are pretty equally about the worst moments of my life, and both are events I truly wish you weren't around for."

She silently lets the tears fall, and instead of feeling pity for her, I hate that she's the weak sort of girl who fucks up someone else's life and then gets to be the victim because she feels badly about it.

"Whatever. I don't need this shit." I push my weight back into the car and start the engine when her voice, with some strength behind it, stops me again.

"For hating you. I'm sorry for hating you." She yells in one loud, angry burst.

I cut the engine and stare at the steering wheel for a second. I don't think this blonde, Californian, sunshine loving girl can truly understand hate—at least not my kind of hate.

"I can promise you that whatever you feel, it's not nearly as much as I hate you—and I'm not sorry for that at all." I say with a simple shrug of my shoulders and venom running through every intonation.

"I didn't sleep with him. I mean, not when you were together. Not for a really long time."

This girl. She really doesn't understand how to apologize. You don't say sorry and then remind me that you slept with my fiancé. What the fuck? Her honesty is disgusting, but maybe, that's exactly what I've been looking for—what I need. I size her up looking for the truth, and then I jump into courage. I find my strength.

"So, tell me. Tell me what really happened. This is your chance to clear your conscious if you want it, Amelia."

She chews on her lip then walks away and appears at my passenger side door. The door's locked, so she knocks on it for me to let her in. She fucking knocks on my door. Talk about irony. And despite how much I despise her existence, I lean over and unlock it to let her in. After a solid 30 seconds of ear-splitting silence, she begins.

"I knew who he was before he even knew I existed. Ryan, Brec's roommate, —"

"I know who Ryan is."

"He was notorious for hosting parties that catered to the dumb and underage. The first time I went over there was during fall semester. My roommate heard about the party from a friend of a friend. I was shy, people were drunk, and I needed a place to get away. I didn't know who Brec was, in fact, I didn't know Ryan had a roommate, but Brec's room was the perfect sanctuary. I mean, some of the pictures were a little weird, but overall it felt so wholesome . . . so all-American."

She's smiling at this little nostalgic venture down memory lane, and if I didn't want her to get to the end so badly—you know, explain how she ended up marrying my almost husband, I would kick her out right now. She must notice how unamused I am as she quickly wipes her grin away and continues more solemnly.

"There was a picture of him—of you both—on the dresser. God, I hoped so badly you were his little sister. I stayed in his room until the party ended. Then my friend came to get me, and we left. At the time, I just thought it was one of those weird college stories I'd tell when I was older. I didn't even know this guy's name, yet I felt like I spent my first college party hanging out with him, you know?"

I have to stop myself from interrupting this nonsense to point out that this is, in fact, a dumb college story that a much older version of herself is now telling.

"About two months later, I saw him in the library. I couldn't place him right away. At first, I actually thought he might have been a TA from fall semester. He had books laid out everywhere but looked distracted—lonely. He looked . . . sad. I guess that was when I really started to notice Brec. Everyone at Stanford knew him or knew of him, but all the stories I heard made him sound like this golden god. The guy I was looking at, when no one else was watching, seemed hurt. It stuck with me. —I asked around about Ryan's parties and ended up back at that apartment a few weeks later. Ryan and his friends still sucked, but the hope of seeing Brec there made it worth coming back every time."

"Hold up. So, you didn't fuck my fiancé', but you stalked him? Is that where this is going?"

"I told you, I didn't know who you were. No one seemed to know anything about a girlfriend—much less a fiancé'. Of all the stories people told about Brec, none of them included you. I just sort of hoped you weren't something I needed to worry about. Beyond that, I didn't really think I had a shot with him. I knew it was all just some weird fascination with someone I'd never really meet. I think I kind of expected him to let me down if we ever did talk face to face. I had created a fake identity of this person based on the stories I picked up from other people and one random night I spent in his room."

I look away, out the window. We're only a couple minutes into this show-and-tell monologue, and it already feels like my limping heart is going to implode. I honestly don't know if I can do this. What if the answers disintegrate whatever peace I have left? Maybe Dad is right—answers don't always fix the broken things. She waits me out, knowing that I'm on some sort of plateau. Staring at the steering wheel, I slowly shake my head up and down for her to continue. I'm already in this far; I need to see it through.

"The night I saw him next was the weekend you showed up. I had almost given up hope and come to my senses about the whole stupid crusade, when my roommate dragged me back to another one of Ryan's parties. I was bored to death all night, and definitively made up my mind that I was done coming back to this place when Brec walked in. The last time I saw him in the library, he looked hurt. This time there was an edge to his sadness. He wasn't just the lonely boy anymore, he was pissed off, and my dumb 19-year-old heart thought that he was just so hot—he was this all-American bad boy."

I scoff at her description of Brec, who is anything but the all American bad boy—whatever the hell that is, but I do pause long enough on her words to realize that what drew her to him was the very same thing I saw in him all those years ago in the darkroom. Brec wears vulnerability like a fucking medal. He doesn't hide it like I do, nor does he bathe himself in it like Amelia. He pins it to his chest and announces it to the world. He's fiercely vulnerable, and I know exactly what it feels like to be attracted to that.

"I didn't drink. Ever. I knew my only way to have a real shot at actually getting to know this guy I'd been slightly obsessed with was to grab a drink and head to the patio where he was hiding out."

"So, just to be clear, you *were* stalking him?"

"I was curious."

"Yes. Clearly. You tracked him across campus for months."

She turns her whole body away from me and stares out the window for an inordinate amount of time. I assume she's getting ready to tell me the horrible truth—to rip off the Band-Aid—finally.

"I still hate beer. It tastes like horse shit."

Now, I haven't spent any grand amount time with little Ms. Prom Queen over here, in fact, I have mostly dodged her any time we were in the same room, but I am floored by her sudden change in both direction and vocabulary. My eyebrows unintentionally shoot up, and she gives a small, girly laugh in response. It suits her, and I hate it.

"It was the only thing left to drink—some ass-flavored beer, but I grabbed one and tried my best to pretend like I knew what I was doing. I was so nervous. I didn't realize we'd be the only people outside. I had to hold my breath with every sip for the entire first bottle, but the more we drank, the easier it got."

"Yes. That is a general truth of alcohol."

"I've learned. But as a virgin, it was all new to me."

Her choice of words literally couldn't be worse, but I think her brain is on a ten-second delay because it takes her a few beats to realize precisely what she's just said.

"Oh . . . my . . . virgin at drinking. Not a—you know . . ."

"Yeah, I get it. So, to recap, you were a slutty nondrinker that was stalking my fiancé'?"

She pushes her fingers through her hair roughly in a learned gesture that looks just like Brec. It reminds me that this story may start with *my* Brec, but it's going to end with hers. My claim on this man has about another two minutes worth of rambling before he's no longer mine and he becomes some version of her memory—of their life together. God, I just handed him off to this psycho groupie.

"I wish I could tell you that we talked, and I felt nothing for him but a passing friendship. Or that we talked all about his committed relationship, and I backed off immediately. But . . . that's not true. I made him laugh, and it was the best sound in the world. He made me laugh, and it felt like the first time I was able to truly smile since I got to college. Everything clicked—

almost everything. All of his smiles slipped into a two-second frown before his forehead smoothed out again. Even drunk, I knew he was holding something back. That was the first time I let myself acknowledge that you were going to be something more than a little sister. —But, you have to realize that while I was falling for him, I had no idea exactly how off-limits he was. I want to think that if I'd known the truth, I would have left the party that night without looking back. I want to believe that's the kind of person I am."

"Too bad we can't find out now—since, you know, somehow this story ends up with your marriage."

"And my divorce."

This is the first time Amelia's challenged me. And instead of being pissed off at her like I would be with pretty much anyone else in the universe, I'm a little impressed. This is also the first time anyone has officially clarified their status. Gage alluded to it. Brec's missing ring added confirmation, and social media pretty much cleared up any of my lingering worries. But I can't quite explain the relief I feel when she validates their lack of attachment to each other—this three-word sentence that destroys her to say out loud offers me a significant amount of peace.

"So, when did you find out about me?"

"I made a move . . . sort of. Not that I've ever had moves. Either way, it completely failed and he rejected me. It fact, he patted me on the head like I was his pet. The whole night I was busy planning the phone call to tell my mom all about the perfect guy, and he was trying to figure out how to ask for advice about you. All in all, it was a pretty tragic evening. After he was clear about his intentions, this avalanche was un-leashed. We stayed up talking for most of the night. He told me everything about you, and I remember thinking I was absolutely not his type—that I never even had a chance. You sounded cool, but I knew—Brec aside—you'd never be the kind of girl who would like me. We'd never be friends. I wanted the darkroom to be my story and a cute little first date at a place like Posies. In the beginning, you guys sounded so storybook, but by the end of it, I just felt bad for you both. It seemed like neither of you were happy or knew how to make the other person happy. I promise, I didn't take this as an opening, but seeing Brec hurt so much peeled back something new in my heart. Until then, I thought love was this butterfly, bubbly feeling, but what I felt for him that night was something unexpected. I wanted to ease all the hurts and confusion that were crushing him. I thought I was just being his friend, but, truthfully, I was already in much deeper."

"And you guys just talked—for a whole night—alone, you stayed up and . . . just . . . talked?"

"Yes, Sage. We talked in circles for hours until I literally fell asleep while he was still going on and on."

"So why didn't you leave in the morning? Say, you really did just randomly stay up all night talking—or whatever—to this guy you'd been obsessing over for months. You crash—which is semi-believable, but you stayed—and made breakfast in his fucking kitchen. Who's buying that story?"

"He was still asleep when I woke up. I meant for it to be a gesture of friendship—I guess like an olive branch to recover from our fairly weird night. I just made spinach smoothies for us—it wasn't like a full-blown meal or anything. But when Brec woke up to my smoothie offerings, he laughed at it. Literally, he smacked it away and told me that wasn't breakfast. He bragged about big, southern breakfasts, so we made a legit breakfast. I knew it was crossing a line, but I kept thinking he needed the friendship and the laugher as much as I did . . .

When you showed up—I've tried to put myself in your place for 10 years to figure out why it ended right there. I've tried to figure out what really happened. Sure, it didn't look great, Sage, but why would you leave him like that—in one moment of completely confused chaos—and never even look back? He was devastated. To this day, he's never told me exactly how things ended that morning, but all of the charm and golden boy charisma he had left had drained out of him by the time he got back upstairs . . . and he didn't get it back for half a decade. He spent 5 years just waiting for you to look back. And that's when we become best friends."

Reliving all of this with her burns my lungs as I try to control the sob that's formed in my hollow chest. I tell myself at some point we will get to their split and the man who's found and framed nearly all of my pictures but hearing her take his side and lecture me for hurting him makes me—*ashamed.*

"After graduation, Ryan moved on and moved out, thank God, which meant Brec needed a new roommate. He was really buckling down for med school and had to get everything worked out so quickly since his plans had changed. —He hadn't applied anywhere other than NYU medical, and he pulled every last string he had to get into the program at Stanford. He needed someone to split the rent, and I needed a place to live. After that, we became each other's lifelines. I brought him back when he would get too far down his hole of despair, and he helped me with school. It wasn't conventional, and it was nothing like I'd fantasized my freshman year, but we were good at being companions—friends."

"You guys lived together?" My question comes out in a squeak—probably because of the unshed sobs still sitting on my chest.

"Until he started his internship. I moved out. He was, no doubt, the closest person in the world to me, but I had to take a step back. The time brought us together, but I knew, deep down, I wanted more. I was becoming jealous of even the memory of you, and Brec was just as stuck as he was the day you left—standing still—waiting for time to hit rewind."

She's biting her bottom lip as she shifts in her seat and begins with a completely new tone—not nostalgic but frustrated.

"I tried dating. I really did. I didn't want to want Brec because I knew . . . "

Her voice becomes smaller the longer she talks, and I can hear her unevenly stumble through each sentence. I see that she needs to tell this—to shed this story as much as I need to find the missing pieces to my puzzle. She's not here for me, this is the closure she's looking for. I don't want to comfort her, but something in me has to. So, I reach out and lay my hand on her slim arm.

"Brec wasn't even jealous. I tried waltzing these men in front of him, so he could see what he was missing, and he never batted an eye. Actually, he always made sure to ask me about my dating life. It was annoying how supportive he was. Time ticked by like that. When he started his residency, he jumped head first into a new clinical trial. I think that brought him back. I didn't understand it then, but all that mattered to me was that the golden boy resurfaced. I guess I was getting to know the Brec Aldridge everyone had been talking about all those years ago. Every time I pushed for information, all Brec would say is that his work was important—it could fix everything. I remember when I met Gage for the first time, and it all clicked. I finally got Brec's obsession with MS and the children's hospital. But looking back on it, now that I can see the full story, I think he always meant you. He was trying to fix everything with you. *Still.*"

It's a weird thing to feel my heart slowly inflate—like a balloon that someone is breathing life into again. The muscle memory is still there, but the stretching and pulling is an unfamiliar feeling all the same.

"By then, I had graduated from grad school, and my mom kept telling me I needed to move on. She loved Brec, but I guess she could see what I couldn't. I had a job offer in the bay area, but right as I was ready to leave it all behind—things changed. Something in Brec shifted. Not slowly, but all at once. He became desperate to catch up on all the life he'd pushed to the back burner and, amazingly, we were engaged within a year."

There. It. Is. The other shoe I forgot about.

"All the butterflies and bubbles were there, and I was so excited about the dresses and venues and flowers that I forgot that loving Brec should have felt like more than that. Being loved by Brec should have felt like more. God, I watched him love you for so many years—I knew firsthand what that should have felt like. I think part of why I wanted him so badly was because I knew what kind of love he was capable of. For a while, the excitement of it all finally coming true—the engagement party and the photo sessions and the wedding decisions—covered my sadness, covered what was missing—but it didn't take long for bitterness to catch up with me. We bought our first place together and were supposed to move in before we left for Italy—our honeymoon, but everything got so hectic right before the wedding. We hired movers to take care of it while we were out the country. It felt so glamorous. Suddenly, I was a surgeon's wife—jet-setting and letting other people take care of life's pesky details. Everything I'd wanted came true—until we came back from Europe. We'd been home for less than 24 hours when I found the boxes, carefully packaged, of all your work. It was a fucking shrine. He had framed pictures from high school and some from your senior exhibit at NYU. He had boxes of photos that took extensive work and money to find. He'd just married me, but there you were. While he promised to love me, he never promised not to love you—I guess, I thought it was sort of implied in the vows."

Her tone becomes harsh—cynical—very un-Amelia-like. When I try to pat her arm, she jerks it away in a defensive gesture, and I start to feel that hate she warned me about.

"From day one in that house the precedent was set. I got him—just not all of him. There was always a piece of himself he kept for you. We argued about it, but he still hung the damn photos in his office. When he wasn't at the hospital, he was in that freaking office. Every secret he kept—every bad day he refused to tell me about was shared with a glass of scotch in his office. It's like he couldn't break the habit of coming back to you. After a couple of years, I stopped trying to compete. New pictures showed up out of nowhere like clockwork, and we never discussed them. I would hear him hammer a new nail in the wall and each sharp point punctured my heart again. That's when I started to hate you. And over time the hate just grew and grew. I made him move to Santa Cruz. I wanted a more lavish life; I wanted a reaction. Instead I got compliance. He would rather tank his career at a second-rate hospital than to just give you up. The house in Santa Cruz was huge. It was beautiful, and it was all fake. We moved into different bedrooms, and we both stopped pretending that what we had was a marriage."

I expect her to cry big, weepy tears, but instead her voice grows frigid as she digs her nails into her skin.

"You know, I wanted kids. I always thought I'd have them by now. Brec would have made a great dad, but he refused to even talk about the idea of children. I saw him with Anna and Emery, and my hate grew a little more. He never said it, he never had to, but you were why we didn't have kids. Why have kids with the runner-up if you're still waiting on first place? . . . Olivia's the one who mentioned splitting up. She asked me if we'd tried counseling and what I was willing to compromise in order to keep my husband. That's when I realized I was already done. I didn't want to compromise anymore. Second best is the most defeating sort of love."

I don't know what to think or say, but as her hate grows, I start to feel mine slip away.

"When I packed a bag and told him I was leaving, he didn't even ask me where I was going or try to fight for me. Instead, he just said that he should be the one to leave. God, I wanted him to get mad—to do something, but he calmly packed his stuff and said he'd be away for a little while. He gave me everything in the divorce He met every outrageous demand, but he wasn't even in the country to sign the damn papers. He was already half-a-world away—looking for you."

This is beautiful and heartbreaking at the same time. My humanity hurts for her, but with every puzzle piece that clicks into place, the picture in front of me becomes harder and harder to deny. It was always him and me.

"I told you that I'm sorry for hating you. And I am. But that doesn't mean that the hate has disappeared—I'm just sorry for it now. You deserve my hate about as much as I deserve yours. We made choices. I knew—*I knew* he was still in love with you, and I gave my heart to him anyway. You knew that if you let him go, he wouldn't stay single forever. One day, I'll heal from this.

One day, we'll all be okay. Until then, you'll just be the girl who took my best friend away from me."

All of the truth settles between us before I speak.

"Well, I was wrong; you definitely know how to hate."

I can see the tick of her jaw, but she doesn't open her mouth to agree or disagree, so I try again with a little more empathy.

"Hate me. If that makes it better, then hate me forever. But I can tell you from experience, hating you didn't make it any easier for me to forgive myself."

She closes her eyes and lets out one very long breath before she reaches for the door handle.

"Sage, don't fuck this up. Whatever happened the first time . . . just don't repeat the past. I may hate him, but I still love him too, and I don't want to see you hurt him—again."

"I promise. And Amelia, I'm sorry. I'm sorry that he—we—hurt you. I'm sorry about your best friend."

"Life never promises not to abuse us. You lost Gage; I lost Brec. I think we can call it even."

I understand her sentiment, but I don't really think Gage's death is the same loss as her divorce. Either way, I'm not going to argue the point. To her, it feels like something died, and that's all that matters. She gets out of the car and closes the door softly behind her. I wait for her to start up her car and leave the parking lot before I crank my engine again.

In the dark, the highway feels open, and endless and full of possibilities. I pass my exit for Posies and keep driving.

CHAPTER Seventeen

It's somewhere past midnight—maybe 1:30? I don't know. My car's clock hasn't worked in years, and my cell phone's been dead all day. His house is completely dark and completely quiet. I'm not actually sure what to do next. Do I knock on the door and scare the crap out of him? Do I MacGyver my way in a window? Do I find a Bose speaker and stand outside the window playing cheesy '80s music? I finally decide that it doesn't matter how or what I do at this point. I finally showed up for him—that's all that matters.

It turns out it's not all that difficult to get in the house—the front door is unlocked. I smile at the knob as it twists in my hand. This man. I grew up under constant lockdown with alarm codes and gated entryways, and here Brec is, in the middle of the night, with his house pretty much wide open. God, I find this man's ability to trust everyone and everything in the world around him so fucking adorable.

The door gives a barely squeak as it swings open, but when I stop and listen, it doesn't seem to stir anything in the house. I try to visualize the layout of Brec's house from my quick tour. I turn right and head to where I remember the bedroom is. I'm not sure if I'll just hop into bed with him, or fling on the light and surprise him. Maybe I'll take off my clothes first? God, no, that's a horrible idea. I drop my heels in the carpeted living room because they hurt like a bitch, and they'll make too much noise if I have to click around on the tiled hallway with them on. For a second, I realize that my unexpected intrusion may not be welcome. I mean, I don't like to be woken out of a dead sleep—even if it's for a beautiful reunion from an ex-lover. Brec's always been a more pleasant person in general, but that doesn't ensure that he won't be annoyed or even completely unhappy to see me here at this hour.

The door is open, but his bed is still made. I quietly tiptoe into the bathroom and the closet off of Brec's room, but there's still no sign of him. His clothes aren't in the hamper—nothing. For a second, I'm fearful that he didn't come home tonight. Or what if he and Amelia are having their version of the conversation we just had? I guess it makes sense that she'd seek closure from him if she sought it from me. Was his SUV even in the drive-way?

It takes me two tries to find my way back to the living room. The house is still soundless. I guess he's not here after all. I can wait him out and hope that when he gets here he'll want to see me, or I can leave a note.

Hey Brec,

Just came to say that I'm still in love with you and am banking on you reciprocating those feelings. Give me a call so we can figure our shit out.

Sage

Yeah, that seems like an exceedingly poor idea. Timing sucks. I'm standing in the dark, carpeted living room twisting in circles while trying to figure out how to best tell my ex-fiancé I think I never stopped loving him. Oh, and sorry—I need to work that in there somewhere as well. Then I hear a small sound. It could be the foundation shifting, the ice machine, a strong wind outside— but a part of me knows it's him. He's waiting for me to find him, but I've looked everywhere—everywhere except his room of photos. I forgot it was there. I thought it was a fucking closet again. My heart is beating rapidly as I slowly pad across the plush flooring to the simple door. I'm standing right there—

hopefully a matter of feet from my future, and my hands are shaking. I'm not sure if I can open this door. I'm not sure what it means or what I'm committing to. I'm not certain that he wants me the way I want him. I close my eyes and begin counting. One. Today I've survived leaving my brother in a closed, cold casket to be buried in the ground somewhere. Two. I spoke in front of a semi-full room of people without turning my worst pain into a joke. I allowed myself to be genuine and fragile. Three. I didn't immediately run away from Amelia. Four. I listened to her story—I stopped talking and stopped judging [mostly], and I listened. Five. I acknowledged that this thing with Brec and me was largely my fault and 100% not over. Six. I drove here—without a plan and only a strong dose of hope. Seven. —Fuck it, I'm going in.

I open the door quickly, anxious to see if he's really in there waiting me out. It's dark, but I can immediately make out his silhouette on the couch holding a glass of scotch. He's looking down at his almost empty drink, and my heartbeat falters. Maybe he didn't want to be found after all.

"It took you long enough."

"It took me 14 fucking years, but. I'm. Here."

He looks up immediately, searching my eyes through the black that surrounds us. He looks through me, studying my posture and my expression. I feel completely stripped bare, completely vulnerable and totally terrified. I stand there for what feels like forever weathering his scrutiny, and then I see it—the light that turns on in his eyes. Without either of us breaking eye contact or a single word spoken, I know, without a doubt, that he sees I've found the missing pieces, and I'm here to stay.

I launch my petite body at him and land semi-straddling/semi-sitting on him like he's Santa, and I'm about to give him my

Christmas list. Our mouths collide in something painful and beautiful. I can taste the lingering scotch on his lips as they mix with the salt of my tears. Odd, I didn't even realize I was crying. His fingers from one hand are roughly pulling through my hair as his other finds my leg and the hem of my dress. This isn't us dancing around some new beginning, but an acknowledgement, that for us both, this is it. We are the end. His lips find my neck and my hips begin to move against him involuntarily. The ice cubes, still rattling in the weighted glass between us, are in the way of me finding the friction I'm desperately seeking. I stop the kisses for a moment and reach between us for the drink but find something else altogether. Brec smirks at me and kisses the side of my lips.

"Whatcha ya looking for down there, babe?"

I grab the glass in my right hand and shake it in front of him as a way to answer his question. He roughly grabs the drink from my hand and downs it in one big gulp then sets the empty glass on the coffee table before resuming a slow, teasing kiss. I'm surprised when he pushes a small ice cube into my mouth. In fact, I nearly choke on it before my gag reflex saves me. I can feel the vibrations of his chuckle through his throat that's now pressed against the side of my face.

"God, Sage, you're perfect."

"You find my choking sexy, do you?"

He raises one eyebrow at me as he nips my jaw line.

"You get kinky on me, babe?"

Oh shit. I guess, for some, that may actually be a turn on. I really don't get S&M. It mostly seems like sex gone really wrong, and now I'm worried that maybe Brec and I aren't sexually compatible anymore. Brec can feel my momentary paralysis, and he laughs at me—again.

"Just to be clear, I'm not into choking or ball gags or whips. Maybe I could get into some good spanking, but, no, as a whole, you choking isn't a turn on. It actually reminds me to brush up on the Heimlich."

The Heimlich? Oh God this is embarrassing. I don't think there has ever been anyone less sexy in the history of humanity. "Fuck me. I'm so bad at this."

Brec pulls my hips down to him and grinds into me with needy desperation as he growls near my ear and whispers in a rush of full breaths.

"I warned you about that."

It was an accident, maybe a reflex—my go to phrase when anything goes slightly awry, but suddenly, I'm liking this game. I tease him with kisses to the shell of his ear and whisper back to him between nibbles.

"Fuck. Me."

Before I even get a glimpse of victory at taking the upper hand, I'm flipped over and laying with my back on the couch. Brec has both my ankles in his hands, and he forces me to still my struggling movements. He kisses the small tattoo of a camera on the top of my foot and raises my legs slowly so my knee length dress rides further and further up until I can feel the air brushing the edge of my panties.

"Say it." Brec halts the ascent and locks eyes with me. Some of his fire is masked, and instead, his cobalt eyes are shining with admiration and hope. "Say it," he repeats.

"Fuck me?" I'm honestly not sure if I've answered him correctly, but by the look on his face, I'm fairly certain I just failed the test. He rests my right ankle over his shoulder and moves his free hand up the inside of my leg. I'm still rather immobile, but his hand is almost there—almost where I desperately need him to be.

"Say it, Sage."

I really don't wait to get this wrong again, but I have no idea what I'm supposed to say. This isn't some sort of cat and mouse moment—I legitimately don't understand what he wants from me. Brec's left hand grasps my ankle with more authority as his right fingertips dance along my panty line. If I don't get this right, I'll never get an orgasm—that's clear. Brec's eyes plead with mine as I search them for the right answer.

"Please say it, babe. I need to hear it."

It clicks. I know what he wants from me. He wants reassurance. He wants me to connect his broken pieces. Without hesitation, without any thought about the consequence, I ease his worries.

"I love you, Brec."

"Finally."

The look on his face is pure joy, and I feel euphoric knowing that I put it there. Quickly, he releases my ankle and adjusts my weight to pick me up. He pushes the dress back down and carries me to his bedroom—though, I rather liked the idea of having sex right underneath all of my life's work. For the first time in 14 years, Brec and I are officially back together. We spend all night reconnecting the fractured shards of our hearts.

Three. *Saturday.*

It's morning and it's sunny which is reason enough for me to be in a bad mood. Add to that my lack of sleep, my current lack of caffeine and the realization that today is the day Gage is gone forever, and I quietly slip into a dark, foul place. Luckily, Brec wraps his long body around mine and reminds me of much happier recent events. He knows and understands the dark irony of life somehow giving me the most impossibly perfect night followed by the most impossibly treacherous day. Brec's always allowed space for my moodiness, and today is no different. As much as I would love to show him my thanks for his ability to deal with me, I know today is going to be long and it will take the whole family's strength for us to survive it, so we need to get moving. Brec helps me zip up my simple black dress and walks me back out to my car. I need to get to my place, shower and then grab another new, black ensemble my mother picked out that I'll add to the pile of things that will never be worn again. After a simple kiss, I'm back on the highway driving headfirst toward the disaster that awaits me today.

We're supposed to meet at the church by noon, and by the time I get to my little efficiency, I have about an hour and a half to get ready. I quickly shower and get dressed. Today's dress is three-quarter sleeves with a snug fit that hits right below my knees. When I rip the tag off in a hurry, I laugh at the fact that this must be some sort of designer outfit my mother has arranged for today. Pretty clothes and pretty pictures won't change how this day ends. In fact, I find it repugnant that Mom can find the energy to care about photo ops right now. I text Olivia to see if she wants me to come pick her up—not so much for right now, but I imagine, later, she'll very much want someone else to drive her home. It's half past 11:00 before I hear back from her. She and the girls are already on their way with Mom and Dad. Now, I'm realizing, maybe I didn't want to ride alone as much as I didn't want her to be by herself. I stare at my reflection in the fun house mirror. My hair is coiffed—held in a tight updo. My makeup is in place, and the pearls are secured around my neck. God, Gage would hate this version of us. He never cared for perfect pictures. Mom and Dad paid thousands of dollars for our braces. Two months after he got them off, Gage came home from Lacrosse with a chip in his front, right tooth. Mom insisted that he get a veneer to fix his perfect smile, but he refused. I loved Gage most like that. He never yelled or raised his voice, but he had a lazy defiance about him—the ability to blow off the fake things Mom held so close to her heart. If he was here today, he'd find a way of blowing off these stiff outfits and celebrating his life the right way. Gage was always a jeans and t-shirt kind of guy.

It's time to go, but I'm still staring in the mirror—lost in my subconscious somewhere between a memory and a dream when someone knocks on the door. Brec pops his head through the oak doorframe and takes a long look at me from my heels to my head and down again. He confidently saunters toward me and kisses my forehead but turns to the opposite end of my bedroom where my clothes are hung. He pulls outs a simple pair of black skinny jeans and a sheer black button down blouse and shoves them at me. I stumble back into the bathroom to quickly change into a much more comfortable outfit. Before I have my pants up and buttoned, I hear Brec on the other side of the door.

"Keep the heels, Sage. I like the heels."

"Fine. You can have the heels, but I at least need a camisole to wear under this top, or this will quickly become a very inappropriate afternoon."

Brec twists the handle and jams his arm through the door with a simple black tank top in hand. After I'm dressed, he joins me in front of the mirror, and we stand there together taking in the reflection of us. In a way, this mirror is a perfect representation of who we've become. Complete imperfection—blurred and distorted from time and age, but the love is still the most visible part of the image.

Brec and I arrive right at noon. My mother appears to be too busy to even notice my wardrobe switch. There are mounds of food everywhere as we're ushered into some sort of reception hall. Other than an Americano I grabbed when entering Posies this morning, I haven't had anything of substance to eat in the last 24 hours. My amazing appetite fails me once again as I pass over all of the casseroles and southern baked goodness and head to the coffee bar for a cup of straight black caffeine. While we're all shuffling around and waiting for the actual funeral to start, Amelia takes notice of our interlocked hands. I can see the pain on her face, and I'm fairly certain Brec sees it too. I loosen my grip to move away and put some distance between us, but he holds on to me tightly. I don't want to be rude, Amelia doesn't deserve for us to shove this in her face, but I know how important this is to Brec. PDA has always been his thing, and while I don't want to hurt her, it's more important that I do this for him.

20 minutes later, we're lined up to enter through some side entrance of the church. Funerals are hushed events, but there is still a rather loud hum of voices on the other side of the heavy, wooden doors. I'm unexpectedly nervous. So many eyes pitying me or judging how I grieve is pretty fucked up thing to carry on my shoulders.

The service feels like it's in fast-forward. I only catch bits and pieces of proverbs read and songs sung. It doesn't feel like goodbye at all, and I'm terrified that I'm missing out on the last memory of my brother. The slideshow is shown again, and Olivia looks anywhere but at the screen. Anna has silent tears streaming down her beautiful, porcelain face as she grasps the pew in front of her tightly, and Emery is digging through Mom's purse for either snacks or entertainment. I wonder which one of them this will screw up more—the one who aches for the dad she knows she's missing out on, or the one that won't even get it until it's too late to say goodbye properly.

The funeral ends, and we're paraded through the long, silent pews following Gage's casket. People stop the procession to pull on Olivia and give her a hug, and you can physically see her shrink away from each new set of arms. I'm beyond worried about her. A couple of attendees pat me on the back or reach out to squeeze my elbow. I can see a shorter girl several rows away crane her neck out into the aisle to look for me. She's the girl from the photography lab sitting with, who I presume to be, her high school friends. From the distance, I see her mouth, "I'm sorry." It feels oddly surprising that these unspoken words from a stranger mean more to me than half the hugs or pity pats I've received in the last several days. I think it's special because she isn't here out of obligation. This girl couldn't give two shits what I think about her. She's here—they're all here—for Gage. They're here for us because Gage was always there for them.

It literally takes my breath away to look out into the sea of faces, into the balcony, and see how many of Gage's students are here. It's inspiring. God damn, what a life well-lived. There's some sort of orchestral music playing in the background as we walk toward the exit, but someone above us begins singing the school song. By the end, hundreds of voices join in and finish this weirdly beautiful ode to my brother. Looking at the audience, I think of the Death Cab song again. What an honor to have this many people love my little brother this much.

The graveside is almost 15 miles away in some upscale section of the city. There are only about 30 people invited to be here. The awkward folding chairs are set up under an awning, and it feels remarkably like the funeral we just left and the visitation from last night. I know, in ten years' time, all of this will blur together. I won't remember it in pieces but in one hellish onslaught. And I'm okay with that. I don't want pictures of this when I think of Gage.

Olivia and the girls sit in the first row on the right side. Brec, Mom, Dad and I sit directly behind them while we wait through another speech given by the same pastor we just left. Gage is in front of us. The casket is closed now—thank God. I don't want to remember him as anything other than my strong, fun, loving, selfless brother. —a man filled with color—not a man stuck here for the rest of eternity.

When we've gone through all of the motions and every last person has spoken or read or talked at us—when all of my tears are completely used up, we each take a flower and lay it on top of Gage. I feel like I've said goodbye—my last words—so many times, but I guess the only good part of today is realizing that none of this is really 'the last'. Just because he's gone doesn't mean I can't still talk to him—just like it doesn't mean he's any less my brother.

Like the night he died, we gather around him in a circle, holding hands as he's lowered into the earth. Mom cries into Dad's shoulder. Brec holds my hand fiercely. Anna and even Emery get the significance of the moment, but it's Olivia that slays us all. With each descent of the pulley, Olivia shrinks more and more until she's on her knees—reaching out for the casket—reaching out to Gage.

"I can't do this without you," she cries in a staccato hiccup at the ground over and over.

My parents take the little girls away, and I follow shortly behind them. And, after a long while, Brec goes to the still hysterical Olivia and carries her to the car.

It's horrible, absolutely horrible, to see her this devastated, but it's an absolutely beautiful reminder of how much love they shared.

Four. *Friday (four weeks after).*

Time becomes a funny thing. I work at Posies. I check on Olivia. I spend most nights with Brec, and life moves forward. It feels like years since Gage's death, and at the same time, it hurts like the minute he stopped breathing.

Mom and Dad take the girls away on a trip to Disney. Olivia still hasn't put them back in school, and I'm anxious about what's going to happen next. Olivia was supposed to go to Florida too but backed out at the last minute. In all fairness, I wouldn't want to grieve for a week in an amusement park littered with animated cartoon characters either. Olivia's grief is scary. She's ceased to be a person since Gage's funeral, and she's clearly surviving on an endless cycle of uppers and downers. When I confront Brec about this, worried that he may be the one prescribing her the avoidance, we get into an argument about what we each think is best for her. I can fully admit that I don't know how to fix this, but I know from living too long in the dark that it's a dangerous place to get so comfortable with.

I still go shop and clean for her on Fridays. We pour the wine and sit on the couch, but we never talk now. I want to tell her about Brec, but I can't find it in me to force her to celebrate the happy ending to my story while she's weathering the hell of her own. Maybe one day we'll get there, but this Friday, like the several before, isn't the time. I have a bad feeling about leaving her when it's time to go. With the girls gone—with Gage gone— it feels like it would be entirely too easy for her to slip away too. So, when she silently gets up to go crawl into bed, I stay put. I clean up the glasses and put them in the dishwasher as I hear her turn on the TV in the bedroom—the bedroom that she sleeps in alone every night. I know she didn't invite me, and I don't know if it's what she needs, but I pad down the hallway, push the door open and crawl into bed with her. She sleeps on Gage's side of the bed now, and I scooch into her old spot. She doesn't acknowledge my presence with a word or a glance, but after a few minutes, I feel her reach out for my hand. We fall asleep with the lights on and the TV going hand in hand.

Five. *Saturday.*

My phone ringing from the living room wakes me from a startled sleep. Olivia is still snoring, so I take the phone call outside.

"Hello?"

"Yes, is this Sage?"

"It is. Who is this?"

The person on the other line giggles, pauses, then answers. "Jen, of course. It's Jen."

Jen? Who the hell is Jen?

"I'm sorry, Jen who?"

"Oh, don't you play with me like that, Ms. Jokester. I ran into Brec a couple days ago, and he suggested that I reach out to you about the photography job one more time since we still haven't been able to fill the position."

"Ohhh, Jen. The principal."

"Yes. Did you really not know who this was?" She asks in a clipped, miffed tone.

Oh shit. I've offended her. "Uh, kidding. You caught me," I lie into the receiver.

"Well, we really wanted to have something more permanent put in place by the time the kids came back from spring break, but this sub position seems to be cursed. No one stays for more than a couple days. I think it's just too hard without much help from the department and being an elective and all."

I think it over. I do miss photography. I haven't done much of anything creative in the last several weeks, and I've pretty much given up all hopes that Ty will ever write me much less give me my job back.

"When do you need an answer?"

"As soon as possible would be nice. What if you just came in on Monday to sub? It may give you a better idea of what the job entails, and you could help give us some advice on how to get the yearbook finished. God, that's such a mess right now."

"Wait, you don't have a yearbook laid out, and it's already April?"

"It's been a tough year. Education is not so glamorous these days and with your brother's passing . . . We've just had a lot going on this year."

"So, if I come on board to help out with the yearbook, I can help design it and lay it out—make it whatever I want?"

"Well, within reason. It can't be one of your racy Times pieces—we do live in a conservative community, Sage, but if you'll take it on, you can have the final say, yes."

"Deal."

"Really? Oh my gosh, this is perfect. Okay, there is sub training that you're supposed to go through, but I can sign off on most of that on my end. I may need you to take an e-course or two during your conference periods. Otherwise, we'll see you at 7:30 sharp on Monday morning."

"7:30? Isn't that pretty early to start school?"

"Well, I guess so, but that's when school starts."

Fuck me. "Okay, 7:30 it is."

I end the call, smiling as I text Brec. While waiting for his response, I realize I'll also have to deal with telling Antonia. Without working for her, I'm not sure what new deal will be made about rent. Posies is at least a 30-minute drive into town, and that means even earlier mornings for me starting Monday.

I formulate an idea. If I can get Olivia on board with me taking the job at the high school, maybe she'll let the girls go back as well. Lord knows they need it. They can reinstate the old system where they get dropped off at the high school after their school day is over. I can handle the afternoon childcare and maybe, just for now, I can move in here to help out. Olivia needs more support than me dropping in once a week, and the girls need someone who can really look after them until their mom is ready to be a person again.

The sun is already mid-way through the sky, and I can feel its warmth. Finally, it's starting to feel like a southern spring.

Somehow, I know this is what Gage would want—like he's here guiding my steps. I made a promise, and I'm going to be here to take care of them now that he can't.

CHAPTER *Eighteen*

Six. *Monday.*

Forget active warfare and dodging landmines, that all seems like child's play after my first few class periods of 'teaching'. Now I can see why no one stays in this position. Half the kids in this class have zero interest in photography and the other half are relentlessly bullied. I've done nothing more than play referee today. By 7th period, I desperately turn to my flimsy sympathy card. I'm hoping I'll get some pity as soon as the class finds out I am Mr. Gilbert's sister—and a professional photographer—but instead, they seem to see this as an opening and, together, gang up on me.

"Miss, if you're so famous whatcha doing in this hick town trying to be a teacher?"

"Right? You sure you're old enough to be a professional anything? I think my 10-year-old sister's bigger than you."

"I bet she's making it all up. Subs are always desperate to impress us—like we give a shit."

The kids are total assholes, but two can play at this game. I pull out the class' portfolios and plan to absolutely annihilate each of the artists. I open the binder on top to the first page, pull the first photo out of its sheet protector and hold it in front of the class.

"Okay. Can anyone tell me one of at least ten things wrong with this photo? Bonus points for anyone who can get two in a row. And go."

The kids quickly turn on each other and raise their hands to point out the technical inaccuracies in the photo. It becomes brutal. The students mock everything from the composition, to the artist, to the concept. We go through several rounds of this sort of Russian roulette with the portfolios before I feel like I've made my point.

"Now, who feels better after having their art critiqued? Was it helpful? Did it make any of you better photographers?"

One of the kids in the back huffs under his breath without raising his hand, "It makes you feel like shit."

"Ah, it makes you feel like shit. Who agrees?"

Several of the kids slowly raise their hands. I can see some of them begin to get the metaphor, but I go on to explain it for those who haven't quite connected the dots.

"And what if that photograph was a person, let's say a sub, that you endlessly critique. Does it make them a better teacher to have endured your many criticisms? — I'll be straight with you. I don't know if I'll be a good teacher. In fact, you guys have already annoyed the hell out of me all day, so I'm fairly certain I'll be pretty bad at this job. But, I'm a kick-ass photographer. Get out your phones. Yep, you heard me—get them out. Google me. See what your all-knowing devices have to say about my work."

The kids are instantly on all sorts of smart phones and pull up everything from magazine articles to collections of photos to early installation pieces I did at NYU. They talk over each other and pass phones around to the students near them. The murmur continues to grow louder and louder with every new browser they open or detail they find out about me.

268 | Unfiltered Sage

"Miss, some of this stuff is straight up dirty. Who let you be a teacher?"

"Well, *Mr.*, that's art. It's really more about how *you* interpret a piece than the piece itself."

"Dude, she just called you out. You dirty, bro."

The small girl from the photo lab and the funeral speaks up for the first time.

"Can you teach us to do this?"

"I can teach you what I know—if you'll let me."

The bell rings, but I feel like we've reached an understanding. The ball is still in their court . . . or whatever—I don't really do sports analogies. They have the choice whether they want to learn or not, but I'm pretty sure I won't have to prove myself in that class again tomorrow.

I've spoken with Antonia about my job and living arrangements at Posies. She gave me one stern nod and said, "If that's what you feel you need to do." That woman is forever evasive. All of my things are still in transition between both places though. I have most of my clothes at Posies, but my bedding and toiletries have been moved over with Olivia and the girls. Olivia was surprisingly on board with everything I proposed. She agreed to let me stay. She agreed to let Mom enroll the girls back in their schools first thing Monday morning. She agreed for them to come hang out with me after work. Her compliance seems like another facet of the denial she's cocooned herself in. Maybe she needs someone else to make the decisions for now, but this isn't—it can't be a long-term solution.

The girls arrive right on time. I'm drumming on the keyboard listening to another one of the asinine e-courses when they bolt through the lab at full force. I catch Emery as she launches herself at my lap, and Anna stands behind me running her fingers through my hair. I've learned over the last 6 months that this is called 'beauty shop'. And although you look like a freaking troll afterward, it is *actually* a sign of affection. We talk about their first days back, and both girls are all animation. I'm so glad that coming back to school has been a step in the right direction. I don't want their excitement to end, so after I get the classroom prepped for tomorrow, we head to Pinkberry and devour entirely too much sugar.

The girls still think my staying at the house is like a never-ending sleepover, but I have a feeling this will quickly change as I'm the only one doing any of the disciplining right now. It's all fun and games until someone gets timeout. I put the girls to bed and talk to Brec on the phone for a little bit before watching Olivia head off to her room with a bottle of pills. The guest bedroom is made up for me, but I can't quite force myself to sleep in there yet. For months, that was Gage's headquarters, and though I desperately seek anything that makes me feel close to him again, sleeping in that room once more is just too depressing right now. I make up the couch as a little bed and set my alarm. Brec and I have been hit and miss for about a week now. The newness and some of the shine has worn off, and now, real life is becoming a bitch as far as our schedules are concerned. With my family and the added distance between his place and my work, I just don't see this getting easier any time soon. Unsure if he'll still be up, I type out a text and hit send.

Free to grab dinner with me Saturday?

Less than a minute later his reply comes through.

270 | Unfiltered Sage

Are you asking me out on a date?

I don't know? Is it called a date after 14 years? It's less me asking you anything and more me telling you I miss you.

I miss you too, babe. How long do you think you'll stay at Olivia's?

I don't know. I guess as long as it takes. I need to be here, you know?

Sure. You need to do what's right for them — for Gage.

I'm so relieved he gets it. It would be incredibly easy to get swept away in 'us', but I'm thankful that all of this adulting is forcing us to slow down and live a little more independently—outside of each other. That's one of the things I want to change from the past. We were such codependent teenagers. I don't want to be a codependent adult.

So, is that a yes to Saturday?

It's an always, babe. As long as you're asking, I'll be there.

This man. His cheesiness is surprisingly genuine and a constant reminder of how real—how rooted—his feelings are. That's another thing that's changed—I don't mock all of his soft edges anymore. Without them we would just continue to sharpen and puncture each other, but instead, his softness dulls the razors I've spent a lifetime building around my heart.

Seven. *Friday.*

Each day at work gets easier and easier until Friday when we actually dig into the disaster that is the yearbook. There's a rough collage of overly posed and lit 'professional' photos on one of the light boards and backed up in the system, but that's it. There isn't a theme. There aren't students even assigned to certain sections. I mean, most of the sports seasons are already over and somehow no one got a single fucking picture. This is bad—really bad.

We take a vote on who actually owns and likes yearbooks— traditional yearbooks at least, and over half of the yearbook staff refuses to raise their hands. This starts the first really productive conversation we've had so far.

"Okay, so you guys don't like traditional? I get it. It feels stiff—unrealistic. So, how do you guys want to set this up? Let's say I gave you totally free reign, and you could do whatever you wanted, what would that look like?"

"Ditch the formal class pictures. Everyone hates how they look in those anyway."

"Do we all agree? We're in favor of ditching class pages as they've been set up in the past?"

There is a resounding yes from the whole staff.

"Okay, Jose, will you do the honors?"

Jose looks like he might shit his pants, but he goes to the very little we have uploaded for the yearbook and hits delete. And just like that we're a blank slate; I've always loved a clean canvas. I push the class for more decisions since we need to get the ball rolling.

"What next? We got rid of something. Now we need to get some ideas."

"What about searching student Instagram and Snapchat accounts to find their profile pictures? I mean *typically* these are pictures the student would approve of, and they are a hell of a lot better than the awkward ones with that baby blue background."

"I like it, Chloe. It definitely has a more urban and authentic feel, but what if students don't have a social media account, or what if their profile pics aren't school appropriate?"

"Um, no offense, Ms. G, but everyone has social media—like, everyone. As far as appropriate goes, what's off limits? Like if they have a nose ring, but it's not a close up of their face is that school appropriate even though it technically violates 'dress code'?"

Jose, the 'dirty' kid from my first day can't help but chime in.

"Chloe, we all know what you're really asking. No, you can't use that damn profile pic of you in a bikini. Even Ms. G won't go for that."

"Jose's right—bathing suit shots are a no go. How 'bout this, you guys use your best judgment to pull pictures that are flattering and that don't break the school dress code policies, and I'll do the last pass to okay the spread before signing off on it. If there is anything we need to throw out, we'll deal with it at that time. Now, I need five students to cover the senior section. Do I have any volunteers?"

I dole out jobs and assign a few people to each class of students then give them a week to get the assignment done. In the yearbook world, I basically just asked for the impossible, but I'm hoping they will put some real effort into this since it was their concept—and a damn good one. At this point in the semester, the yearbook should have already been sent to the printer, so everything we get from here on out is borrowed time.

With that, the bell rings, and it's FINALLY the weekend. This has been the longest week of my life.

The girls arrive at 3:30 on the dot. I already have my lesson plans together for next week, so we immediately head out of school and to the grocery store for my regular Friday shopping. Everything goes slower with them in tow. We spend double the amount of time and money that I normally do and have a whole bag of snacks that Emery insists I keep in my desk drawer for them at school. When Anna tells me it's what Daddy used to do, my heart caves. We get stuff for an easy dinner, and we even plan on baking cookies tonight. Easter came and went with none of us realizing it, so we make a plan to decorate egg-shaped cookies before movie night. We pass the wine section, and I hesitate to pull any off the shelf. I don't want Olivia to think that I'm taking this away from her—or that I don't want to keep our little tradition—but I am seriously concerned about her constantly mixing alcohol and pills. Do I really need to encourage it? Maybe I can just explain to her that I didn't want to grab wine while having the girls with me. Brec and I talked again on Wednesday about Olivia's downward spiral. I think he personalizes the conversation because he remembers what his mom went through after his dad died. I don't point out how he's projecting. I don't really want to argue about anything with him, but my gut keeps reminding me that this is bad and getting worse.

I'm on full-time parenting duty all weekend. I almost cancel on Brec, but we haven't seen each other in two weeks at this point. I know it's not a good idea to leave Olivia alone with the girls, so

I call Mom and Dad. We've spent quite a bit of time apart after the funeral. I don't know if it's intentional, or if it's just nice to not all be crowded around Gage's bedside day in and day out anymore. Either way, they are more than willing to help me out, so I can get a night off.

I meet Brec at his place at 7:00. It may be untraditional for a date, but, hey, that's us. I've had a long week and, from the looks of it, so has Brec. We decide to go old school—we pull up one of our go-to, vintage dates. No matter where we were or where we lived, we would have 'tour' date nights. We've had a tour of New York and a tour of Stanford, Maui, Steamboat and Cancun. The objective is to see who can eat the most without getting sick or passing on a plate. The driver starts by selecting a place to eat—otherwise known as round one. At the res-taurant, you have to get an actual food item, but it can be an appetizer, dessert, main course—whatever. However, the rule is you have to finish whatever you order. After round one, you switch drivers, and the next person chooses the location for round two. Brec took me to some of the nastiest places San Jose has to offer on one tour. I remember in one night I ate pig's feet, pickled edamame and jellyfish tentacles. Needless to say, I lost that tour. The first person to tap out, or not finish what they ordered, loses. It may be the least sexy version of a date night, but, for us, it's perfect. In fact, I think Brec fell in love with me when I wasn't trying at all, and it was during times like this that I got to know his sense of humor—his likes and dislikes—the lines he would cross and the lines that were firmly in place. It was our way of being adventurous together without jumping on a plane or taking a road trip. We were just kids—limited by curfews and wallets, but we've always been our best when we're jumping feet first into life together.

We used to play where we went to each actual restaurant, but as Grubhub and DoorDash have become more prevalent, it seems smarter for us to order in each round one at a time, rather than battle traffic and wait in lines on a Saturday night. I come over in jeans and a semi-clean tank top but go into Brec's closet to change into my competition clothes. I pull on a pair of Brec's pajama pants and my old, favorite Stanford shirt—which he eventually stole back from me one night when he came over to Posies. With stretchy pants on, I lay down on the couch and sprawl out. I'm ready for round one.

Brec's up first. He chooses barbeque. Easy. He must have really been craving this, otherwise he never would have started out so simple. High protein is the way to go if you want to make it to the end. Go for dessert first or carbs, and you won't make it past maybe round three. Start with protein, though, and you're golden. I order a brisket sandwich—no bun, and Brec gets ribs. The food should be here in 30 minutes, so we turn on the TV while we wait.

It feels so comfortable here, relaxing my legs on Brec and curling up on the sofa. I'm thankful for the comfortable—especially tonight, but I'm also worried about what the comfortable means. Are we going to fall back into the same old habits? Are we going to become the same past tense versions of ourselves? —The girl who's too insecure to love, and the boy who doesn't know how to fail.

"Brec?"

"Uh-huh?" he responds, half-listening, while flipping through his DVR.

"Don't let me become her again. Okay?"

He halts his motion and drops the remote. He grabs my right foot, the one that's in his lap, and begins rubbing it—all without actually looking at me.

"What are you worried about?"

I have to think about that for a while. In so many ways, I feel so distanced from that girl who ran away from here—the girl who walked across the stage so defiantly, the girl that left him without a single question—and at the same time, this feels incredibly familiar. I've already resigned myself to the fact that we don't get a new beginning—not really. But what if we're only fooling ourselves into believing that we can create a new middle and a new ending? Do we ever truly get a chance to fix all that we broke both as a couple and within ourselves? The longer we're together, the more opportunity we have to fall back into the old folds and creases.

"I don't know. I guess I'm worried that this feels—maybe—*too easy*? We get to skip the worst part about dating and jump right into the good stuff. We don't have to figure out how to have great sex. We don't have to learn each other's buttons—you know, what will start a full on fight vs. what we can work through with a little privacy and a bottle of wine. It's just so . . . comfortable."

"Babe, I don't understand why any of that is a problem. I think it's amazing. We already put in that work, and now, we get to enjoy it."

I think he's right, it makes sense that this is so good now because we already learned from our mistakes—all of the things in the past that made us bad. But, just because he's right doesn't mean I can't also be right.

"What if it becomes so comfortable that we fall into old rhythms, old patterns, old versions of us? What if we autopilot this because it's so damn easy, and we wake up in a year or two and I'm her all over again? I'm all darkness. What if this—our life together—folds us back into those people?"

Brec yanks on my leg and pulls my body toward him on the couch. He leans over me and gives me a long, simple kiss.

"Life doesn't give promises, Sage. There is no way to know that with or without me you won't go back to that place. But, now we know the path that took you there—that took us there—so we know to try a different route this time."

He wants so badly to make this better—to ease my worries, but if we're traversing a new path, then why does this one feel so fucking familiar? I give up on my anxiety for the moment and let him kiss me. We have sex on the couch, and I don't know if it's new or old. Is this our 'old love' or something we've created since we've been back together—or, maybe, a recycled mixture of both? I love this man so much, but do I love him enough that I'm willing to go back into my shadows? Can I gamble my sanity for his love?

The food arrives shortly after we finish and find our clothes. We have simple fun eating together and making empty bets. I laugh so hard I have to run to the bathroom before I pee in Brec's pajama pants. We watch old TV shows—things we both found in our years away from each other. We're both Arrested Development junkies. We make it through the first two seasons of Arrested and 6 rounds before we both pass out into food comas. We each finished our plates though, so for the first time in the history of 'tours', we tie.

I wake up to the strong aroma of coffee close by. When I open my eyes, Brec's holding a cup just out of my reach.

"Talk first. Coffee second."

I grouchily grunt out my response. "Have you learned nothing about me in all these years?"

"Fine. Drink the damn coffee but listen. I woke up thinking about what you said last night. I think you're right. I think comfortable is potentially hazardous for us, but I also don't want to take all of that for granted."

"So, you're saying it's a blessing and a curse?"

"Something like that. God, I hope a little less cliché though."

"So . . . where does that leave us? It doesn't solve the problem. It doesn't keep us from crashing and burning."

"No. It doesn't."

Brec reaches over to grab my coffee and takes a long pull before handing it back. He trails his tongue over his top lip. This is his thinking move.

"Honesty."

"Honestly, what?"

"No, H.O.N.E.S.T.Y." Brec says again more slowly. "Honesty is the difference between us now and then."

I think back to high school and the beginning of college. I never felt like I had a secure hold on him. *Honestly*, I don't think I ever quite understood why he chose me out of every other girl available to him. Brec always knew more of my truth than I told him, but he's right—I kept so many secrets. Secret hurts and secret insecurities. Secret anger. Secret fear. I nod my head at him and take a sip of that damn Americano with two raw sugars before I nod my head and agree, "Honesty."

We kiss with coffee on our lips and morning breath, and somehow, that feels more solid, more sexy, than the sex last night. We aren't brushing problems under the rug or blindly following some old road map. We're moving forward with a plan and a little more wisdom.

Eight. *Monday.*

Monday morning we're all back at it again. I'm headed on my way to work after dropping the girls off at school. I hate leaving Brec after the weekend, but once I'm here—back in my life with Olivia and the girls—I have to compartmentalize everything else. Brec doesn't deserve the back burner, but I don't know how to juggle it all at once. It's not perfect, but it's working—for now. As I pull into the staff parking lot, alongside a spot Gage may have used many times before, I wonder how he did it. How he had enough of himself for Olivia and the girls and his students. For maybe the ten-thousandth time in a month, I wish he was here, so I could get some help—some advice from my little brother who made living life look so easy.

I'm blown away with how much the students have accomplished over the weekend. Give students essays to write or a test to study for, and they'll never even open their backpack; however, assign your students to cyber-stalk their classmates, and it's pretty ridiculous how much they can get done in two short days. I am so excited by our momentum and progress that we all stay late on both Monday and Wednesday to arrange and finalize the student sections. By Friday, we not only have a solid start to the yearbook, but I assign the remaining school events to the senior photographers. I've also been able to do a couple mini lessons on shooting and composition—you know, my actual area of expertise. Because the kids are still so new to decent photo-graphy, I decide to pencil myself in and tag along for some of the bigger ticket items left like prom and senior breakfast. I don't want to micromanage them, but I know some of my best lessons were learned out in the field and not in a classroom. We are still left with a pretty big conundrum of how to somehow piece together nearly a year's worth of school activities that, mysteriously, no one seems to have any footage of.

"Can't we just take pictures from last year's book and re-caption them? I mean most sports wear helmets, right?"

"Chloe, are you serious right now? How are you even a senior? Seriously, you give all of us a bad name. Ms. G can we vote her out?"

"Out of yearbook, out of the graduating class, or out of the gender, Mia? —Some of those might be harder than others."

"That's what she said."

We all yell in unison, "Shut up, Jose."

"Okay. FOCUS. I know it's Friday afternoon, and we're all tired. You guys have accomplished so much this week, but I feel like we need to get some ideas going before we leave today, so we can get just as much work done over this weekend. We need to have everything from the fall locked down no later than the last week of April. IDEAS, people. We need ideas."

Lily, the girl from the photo lab with the seriously shitty developing skills, is chewing on her lip. I've only heard her speak out loud in class once—on my very first day, but I can tell she has something in her head that she's not sharing with us.

"Lily? What's up? Spit it out . . . Jose, don't you say a damn word, or I will let every girl in this class smack you upside the head."

Jose ducks his head and covers his body to prepare for the assault, but none of the girls even move toward him. Sadly, they are totally used to his antics.

"Well, I was thinking—what made us work so well last week? It was social media, right? We were on our phones, which you can do pretty much anywhere. What if we made the whole yearbook pieces of social media—even the events we have coming up? It sort of encompasses our generation, right? We wanted it to feel different, so why go back to the 3-5 photo layout with borders and captions for only some of the occasions? I mean that just feels—incongruent."

I can tell as soon as she's done that she doubts the validity of her comment; she's physically closing in on herself. I'm silently hoping that one of her peers will agree with her before I have to step in. She's right—she's absolutely right, but I'm learning that other kids can't see very well past social stigmas. If this comment had come from Chloe's big mouth [and bigger boobs], half the kids in this class would already be signing up for which events they would be researching over the weekend, but because it's from Lily—and because she's a wildcard—the room is dead silent.

"You know, I think the squirt is right."

Thank God this didn't have to come from me. However, now, it's up to me to prove it to the rest of the class.

"Why do you think so, Landon?"

"I don't know. Because it would look like shit if we mismatched the whole thing. It would be like someone wearing leather pants with a freaking Vineyard Vines shirt."

Other than relating to wine, I have no idea what the hell a vineyard vine is, but Landon just made the point clearly enough that I don't have to pipe in at all. Obviously, this analogy only works for people born after 2000.

"Yeah, I think they're right. We need to keep it the same." Chloe adds in her super bubbly, super helpful high-pitched southern accent.

Now that Lily has gained momentum and some respect, she keeps going with her idea.

"We could assign people to specific events, but that would take a lot of time and I think we would get pretty distracted going through people's feeds and stories. What if we made an account just for yearbook and posted that we needed people to tag us in certain activities? That way, we could sort through everything one at a time. Maybe leave the post open for 24 hours, so we can pull some of the best shots and then go on to the next thing."

"Wow. Good job, Lily. This could really work. Now, you know if we take this approach, we have to give photo credits to wherever we pull from—it also means a lot less time behind the lens. Are you all okay with that?

The staff agrees with one rather noisy, resounding yes. They also decide that they may need to market the picture campaign before starting it, so we spend the rest of class thinking of ways to spread the word and maybe even add in prizes for the craziest or best pictures tagged. This weekend, Lily will open up an Instagram and a Snapchat that all senior staff members will get the login and password to, so we can filter through the work faster. This may slow us down a little bit right now, but I think the approach will actually save time in the long run. And the end result will definitely look like a 'millennial' piece. It has a voice; now we just need to lock down a theme.

By the 4:00 bell that releases the teachers, I am totally beat. The girls and I rock, paper, scissors it to decide who gets to choose what we order tonight for dinner, and I shoot a text off to Olivia telling her that I will shop tomorrow morning instead of heading to the store with the girls again. By the time, I pull into the driveway it's only 4:30. The girls still have time to play outside, so they dump their child-sized backpacks off with me and run around back to their swing set. Brec's SUV is here parked along the street. He didn't tell me he was coming over tonight, but it suddenly feels like 100 years since I've seen him. I bust through the front door with bags in hand but stop still when I see Brec and Olivia talking. At first, I wonder if this is a private moment that I should walk away from, but then I notice Brec handing Olivia a couple familiar orange bottles. Olivia hugs Brec, which is the most affection I have seen from her since I moved in. Then she scurries away—back toward her bedroom.

That asshole.

We've talked about Olivia's dependence on both pills and alcohol no less than 10 times in the last few weeks. I mean, I thought he was making excuses for her because it hit close to home, but I didn't think he was the one drugging her. Prescription pills and I have a pretty sordid past, and Brec knows how I feel about numbing a situation vs. fixing it. I move to set the girls' bags down, and the movement catches his eye. He can instantly tell that I'm not happy, and I'm sure it doesn't take long for him to realize how much of that I just witnessed.

"You better start talking. Outside. Now."

Brec's long legs carry him to the front door in 5 big strides. He holds it open for me to pass and tries to rest his hand on my back in a soothing gesture that only proves to annoy me further. Once we're alone in the front yard, I lay into him.

"Honesty. The last time I saw you weren't we talking about honesty?"

"Sage, loo—"

"I'm not finished yet. If you want honesty, you have to give it. So, what is it Brec? I'm taking your lead here. If we're going down this road, and we're sincerely looking for a different outcome, then we have to be different people. You can't just tell me the pretty details that you know I'll be happy with. You have to tell me all of it—the shit too. If you aren't really in this, let me know now. I just . . . "

I really must be tired because I begin to break down. It's been weeks since I've allowed myself to cry, but here I am with a Hello Kitty backpack around me and big ol' tears leaking down my face.

"I can't lose you too, Brec."

This is when Brec and I work best—when we somehow move and think and live in unison. He doesn't fight back. He takes all of my abuse and pockets it. Instead of getting defensive, he comes right at me and cradles me in a hug. This man gives the best hugs. He moves his big hands under Hello Kitty and rubs circles into my lower back.

"You're right. I should have told you. You're right."

I'm so glad that Brec's old go-to, "I'm sorry" has now become, "You're right." Maybe we are creating new, better habits.

"So why didn't you?"

"Tell you? Because I was afraid it would turn into something like this."

"You don't trust me? Not even to listen to you?"

"Uh, Sage, you have some rather strong opinions about . . . well, pretty much everything."

"I thought you found that adorable."

"Most of the time, I do. But when it's related to my job . . . well, it's different."

"You're a neurosurgeon, Brec, not a psychologist. Should you even be prescribing her stuff? Is that legal?"

"Shit, Sage. You think I prescribed those? I could lose my license for that. No, she's coming up to the hospital once a week to talk with a friend of mine who's a psychologist; I just picked up her meds and brought them to her. They are lower dosages. Rashida is trying to wean her off. I was just going through the side effects with her and talking to her about the difference in milligrams when you walked in."

I hug him tighter to me.

"She's getting help?"

"She's trying."

"And you didn't tell me?"

"I should have told you. I was worried that Olivia didn't want me to say anything. She stops by sometimes after her appointments, and we grab lunch. She's opening up—just a little each week—but I wanted to keep her confidence. It's the doctor thing."

"But she's not your patient."

"No. She's not. But even if she was, that confidentiality informally covers spouses too. I should have said something."

"So, you can tell Gage about whatever she told you? That seems somewhat useless. Are you sure that's right? Nearly every medical show—"

"No. I mean, I could tell *my* spouse."

The taste in my mouth turns bitter. How did we take a turn back to Amelia? We talked about any last questions I had weeks ago, and I'm as at peace as I'll ever be regarding her existence in our lives. But why bring her up now?

"Sage? I'm not officially asking—yet, but think about it. Okay, babe?"

Huh. Asking me what?

"Oh. *Me*—spouse?" I ask lamely while waving my index finger wildly between the two of us.

Brec laughs at my incoherent sentence.

"Yes, I'm talking about you, spouse."

Oh my. This gets very real very quickly. I'm pretty sure my ex-fiancé just sort of proposed to me—*again*—after an argument with a Hello Kitty backpack resting squarely on my shoulders. I can't even make this shit up. And sadly, it's completely par for the course in my life.

CHAPTER Nineteen

Nine. *Monday.*

I'm seriously in love with these kids. Even Jose is turning out to be an asset to the staff. We have two more weeks until graduation, which means we aren't just cutting it close to deadline, we've completely missed the ship for printing. Surprisingly, Chloe's the one that came up with the idea that saved everyone's asses. It was pretty brilliant, really—release the millennial yearbook digitally, and to everyone, free of charge. The copyright laws and restrictions were a pain in the ass to figure out, but we got there. At 12:01 am on May 26th, graduation day, the yearbook will go live to all 1,400 students and staff. We made a deal with Jostens to still get printed copies out to the students who ordered them sometime during the summer. It isn't ideal, but I'm incredibly proud of my team who totally kicked ass in the last two months of school and got the job done.

This thing is a straight-up piece of art. I taught the students to screen print at the end of April, and they then, replicated this idea throughout the book. It's a graphic design dream. Because we are releasing digitally, we were also able to add a whole media section with student interviews and clips from everything to pep rallies to the winning shot for basketball playoffs and the crowning of the prom king and queen. Top songs from the years since the senior class was born get layered in over class pages and sports collages. It is seriously one badass yearbook.

The kids wanted to do a page for Gage—Mr. Gilbert. I fight to keep my shit in order as we worked through what the students wanted to say about him. Every day it hurts. Every fucking day. But everyday I'm thankful for his life as well. The kids let me have last pass on the page, and I add in a couple of stolen photos of Gage with his family. He wasn't only a teacher after all. But, mostly, the kids did a really good job. They made me proud with the hard work and sincerity that they've poured into this small memorial. All we have left to add now are a few of the senior moments and a title. We've been bouncing different ideas back and forth for weeks, but nothing seems to stick.

"What about The Millennial?"

Everyone sort of hems and haws over the suggestion. No one hates it, but no one loves it either.

"Let's play on the digital aspect—like, Digital Footprints. You know, like life brought us through all the shit so we'd end up right here."

"Not a bad idea, Jose, but I'm worried the idea of a digital footprint tends to have a more negative connotation. It makes me think of the kid who's trying to cover their browser history. What do you guys think?"

"Ms. G's right. It sounds like we have some erotica or some shit that we're hiding."

"Okay. So what makes this yearbook different? What sets this apart? Let's just brainstorm here."

I take out an expo marker and begin writing their responses on the whiteboard.

"Social Media"

"Profile Pics"

"Candid photos"

"Graphic inlays"

"Digital disbursement"

"Reality vs Staged work"

"A true picture of our generation"

"It has our voice. It really looks and sounds like who we want the world to know us as."

I include Chloe and Jose's comments from earlier and hand out expo markers to all of the senior staff members.

"Start by crossing off what you don't like. Something that sounds too wordy or doesn't truly capture our purpose. Everyone gets to choose one thing to cross out."

After about 10 minutes of careful choosing, here is what we have left:

The Millennial
Digital ~~Footprints~~
~~Social Media~~
~~Profile Pics~~
Candid ~~photos~~
~~Graphic inlays~~
~~Digital disbursement~~
Reality ~~vs Staged work~~
~~A true picture of our generation~~
~~It has our voice. It really looks and sounds like~~
~~who we want the world to know us as~~

I love it. I erase everything off the board and rewrite what we have left in the exact same order. Now we're left with a pretty decent title, "The Millennial: Digital, Candid, Real". I can't help myself from throwing in my two cents as I add one last word to the end.

"The Millennial: Digital, Candid, Real & Unfiltered"

That's it.

"Wait, I don't get it. Most of these pictures are filtered. I mean, people have freaking Snapchat filters of cats as their class photos. How can we title it unfiltered if this is nothing but constant filters?" Chloe asks as she pans the room looking for support.

"Because the title isn't about the photos, it's about the people in them. This is our generation unfiltered—it's who *we* really are."

"Good job, Lily. The title shouldn't ever explain the art itself or even the process—it should explain the subject."

And with that, we're all but done. It will go live in 12 days. I think we're finally ready.

The rest of the week is spent going over some basic photography lessons. We take a field trip to the local park, where I used to come in the afternoon, and learn how to shoot in direct sunlight. There are a lot of small children that want to pose as models for my burgeoning photographers, and the students get a second lesson in how to shoot moving targets. I also teach them how to work the exposure process to best aid them with overly lit shots. It's fun putting my hands back in the chemicals and spending some time in the dark room again.

On Friday, I take them to the football stadium—their graduation arena. I tell them to shoot anything, obvious or obscure, that they want to help them memorialize this adventure—their success. I take out my own camera and shoot a whole roll of film—just for me.

Being back in my old high school, where Brec and I began and where Gage worked, has been a complete mind fuck. In a way it's forced me to deal with my ancient hurts and my more recent ones. Mr. Willmers left at semester—Gage was already in the hospital, already fighting for his life, but I still wonder if he didn't somehow set this whole thing up. It feels like Gage—always meddling in the background.

During my conference period, Principal Nianouris comes in to visit me. I don't have papers to grade or lesson plans to prepare for anymore, so when she enters, she catches me mindlessly playing on the internet. I'm actually looking at message boards for job listings—seeing as I'll be unemployed, *again*, in a couple of weeks.

"I didn't catch you at a bad time, did I?"

I can't tell if she's toying with me, or if she is really that dense. Either way, I decide to play dumb.

"Oh, no. Not at all. I was catching up on some new photography techniques—it's always important to stay fresh, right?"

"Of course. I do the same thing. I watch Gossip Girl and Riverdale to make sure I stay relevant with the students. It's important to be able to speak their lingo."

Lingo? This poor woman.

"So, what did you think of your time here as a sub? The kids seem to love you, and we're impressed, if not just slightly worried about all you've done to help guide the yearbook along."

"You know, surprisingly, I've really enjoyed this job. My first day was tough though."

"Yes—I heard about that. You know, we really do frown upon cursing at students."

"Ah, Jen, I wasn't cursing *at* them; I was cursing *with* them—learning the lingo."

"Still, boundaries need to be set. I haven't heard of any more explicit language from you, so I think I'm safe to assume you've dropped that habit."

"Yeah . . . Sure."

"Well, let me cut to the chase. We posted this job in March, but I've only had a couple interviews for the position and none of them have your expertise. I know you're, supposedly, some fancy photographer in New York, but I was wondering if you'd be interested in staying on here—long term—for another year."

"You mean becoming a teacher? Like a *for real* teacher?"

"What's wrong with being a teacher? Teaching is the noblest profession in the world."

"Well, aside from your job. Principals are definitely more respected."

She totally misses my sarcasm and takes the comment as a compliment. She even blushes with quiet pride. Idiot.

"Honestly, I don't know. I've never thought about teaching as a career—I mean I went to art school. Can you give me more specifics? What does the contract look like? Can I subcontract on the side if I want to shoot over the summer or on my own time? Can I create my own curriculum? How much freedom would I have here?"

"You're free to work on your own time as long as it doesn't violate your contract with the school. Be careful. Racy pictures of half-naked Cambodian women won't be tolerated. You have an ethics clause to uphold as a teacher. If you take the job, people will start watching you. You become like a celebrity—everything you do or say becomes big news. So be *extra* careful."

"A celebrity?" I ask dubiously.

"Are you interested in the job or not?"

"I'm interested, but can I take some time to think it over? I need to talk to Brec about it before I jump into any big decisions.

"Ah, Brec. Brec Aldridge. How's he doing? I heard he's moved back home. I know a lot of girls from high school who are very excited about that little piece of gossip."

"Good. *We're* good."

I try to make my point without being too big a bitch to my boss, but the girl better back the fuck off.

"*We're*?"

"Yes. We." I emphasize.

"Too bad. That's such a bummer."

"Excuse me?"

"Never mind. Take the week to make a decision, but I need to know one way or the other by graduation on Saturday."

"Got it. I will let you know by then. Thanks for stopping by. And, for real, the job has been fun. These kids have a lot of potential. I'm sorry they didn't get more time to explore that. Thanks for giving me this opportunity."

"Well, it wasn't like we had any better options."

Nice. She flops her hand at me in slow motion to wave goodbye like she's practicing to become royalty or something.

"Have a good weekend, Sage."

"You too, Jennifer."

Olivia is picking up the girls this afternoon, so they can do the weekly shopping together. Which means I'm free as soon as the bell rings, I jump in the car and head to Brec's. It's amazing to get away for the whole weekend. I truly love those little munch-kins, but I am more than ready to begin phasing myself out of the parent role. Olivia is healing with time. She is still on low doses of Pexeva, but she's part of the world—our lives—again. I have reinstated wine Fridays—and Mondays and Wednesdays to help us all get through the week in one piece. I can tell she's truly happy when I tell her about Brec and the road we're quickly heading down. She never offers information about Amelia, but I know they still talk on the phone from time to time. It must be really hard to be in her position. I know she cares about all of us, but it's difficult to root for one team without feeling like you're rooting against the other. Somehow, she makes it all work, and that feels the most like old Olivia—the Disney princess that makes all of life's hard pieces look incredibly easy.

Brec's on call tonight, so we decide to stay in and make dinner at home. He's a phenomenal cook, at least according to my standards, and he patiently spends each week teaching me how to make oven-browned potatoes or skillet-fried chicken. In the future, I foresee myself being the one to shop for the food and maybe dice a tomato here or there more than making pulled pork or a nice pot roast. I have Brec here—do I really need to relearn what he already does so well?

We're doing much better with the whole honesty thing, but I don't know if I should bring up the job proposition tonight. If he has to leave, and we don't get to really discuss it, wouldn't it be better just to wait? We have all day together tomorrow, so I decide to sit on it for the night. I know some small part of me is afraid to tell him about the job, but I don't know why. This is Brec's dream—our dream—we'd finally be together in the same place for good. So why is it so hard to get the damn words out of my mouth?

Saturday is perfect. The weather is all sunshine, and Brec and I head out on the boat with a couple of his friends from work. I didn't realize today would be a group date, or maybe, I would have brought up the teaching job last night after all. Out on the lake with good beer, good food, good music and good friends is not the time for us to jump into a big discussion about our future, so I postpone the news just one more day.

Sunday Brec is called into work before I even wake up. I slept restlessly last night, so I'm all about having this queen-size bed to myself for a couple more hours. As much as I love spending

296 | Unfiltered Sage

my weekends here with him, I still haven't gotten used to sleeping beside someone else night after night. It's not that I'm nervous of what I'll do or say in my sleep, it's just the annoyance of another body being in my way as I'm trying to get comfortable. Brec is a tall man, and he takes up a lot of my much-cherished space.

When I finally make it out of bed in search of a cup of coffee, I'm hit with the guilt of not telling Brec about the job opportunity yet. If he got called in for surgery, it will be hours before he gets home, and I have to leave this afternoon in order to get ready for the last week of school. That doesn't leave us much time to talk anything through. And I already know he's going to be upset that I didn't say anything until now. I finish my breakfast and type out a quick text to Brec as some sort of damage control.

> Hey babe. I miss you this morning. I hope everything's okay at the hospital. When you get home, there's something I want to talk about. XOXO

I grab my laptop and open a Google doc to make a quick pro/con list about the teaching job. I figure this conversation with Brec will go much smoother if I already have a solid idea of what I want out of it. In 30 minutes, I have a pretty meaty pro column and a few puny cons typed out in front of me. This seems easy —here's the answer right in front of me, but I'm not sure that every piece of me wants it to be the right answer. In my typical avoidance, I flip over to my personal email that I haven't checked in a couple of weeks. Most of this is trash. I have a couple short notes from old friends sending condolences for Gage, and I have one from Ty. I've written him almost ten times with no response, and now here he is—showing up in his own, inconvenient, timing.

> Sage - long time no see.

The word got back to us about your brother.
Life's a bitch, you know? I remember when I
lost my mom, the whole world stopped. I hope
your world is still rotating. Speaking of,
I've got some work for you.

I know I've been MIA lately, but this is a big
one, Sage. I'm not giving it to anyone else
until hear back from you. Pack your bags,
cupcake, you're heading to Venice. We're doing
a piece on Venice Biennale - this year's theme
is, "All the World's Futures." But get this,
it's curated by that Nigerian dude you love -
Okwui Enwezor. It's a once in a lifetime
opportunity. Don't miss it.

Ty

Fuck Me. I delete my entire pro/con list. This is a total game
changer. I head to take a shower in hopes that the steam will
help me clear my head.

Right as I start shaving my left leg, Brec storms through the
bathroom and rips open the curtain. This could be a really sexy
overture, but I can tell by the look on his face that nothing the
least bit romantic is on his mind.

"What the fuck, Brec?"

"That's exactly what I was going to say."

He holds up my laptop in his monster-sized fist, and I'm afraid
he's going to smash it to smithereens on his bathroom floor.

"What. The. Fuck. Sage?"

Dammit. I've got to stop leaving my shit out for him to completely misinterpret. I don't even bother to finish shaving my sad, prickly left leg. I turn off the water, grab my towel and step out onto the tiled floor.

"Please let me get dressed, so I can talk about this in something other than a towel. And leave my laptop in here—I don't trust you with it right now. Brec, just give me a chance to explain this before you rush to your own opinions. I want to be honest with you if you'll just give me the opportunity."

"You've got five minutes, Sage, and then we're talking about this."

He storms back out of the bathroom, no less angry than when he came in. After my hair is towel-dried and my teeth are brushed, I pull on some yoga pants and one of his t-shirts and open the door to what will likely be a deal-breaking fight. Brec's sitting on the couch in his office area with all of my photos when I find him. I sit down in the chair across the room from him in order to give each of us some space.

"When I text you this morning, I hadn't even read that email. I'm sure somewhere in cyberspace there's a time stamp for when I opened it if you'd like some evidence. That wasn't what I wanted to talk to you about at all. But, I did want to tell you that I've been offered a full-time job at the high school teaching Photojournalism. It looks like it will be a pretty big pay cut, but it's still something I want . . . us . . . to think about."

Brec's posture and his whole demeanor immediately change. He's suddenly golden again.

"Really? You'd do that? You want to stay here and teach?"

"Don't you want me to?"

Brec runs his hand through his now unruly hair and looks at me before he speaks.

"Sage, I want it to be what you want. Maybe it's not teaching—maybe it's something else, but I want you to want to be here with me. I want you to put us first and everything else second."

Damn. Talk about some brutal honesty.

"What if I need you to put me first over your career? Could you do that?"

"Yes. I've done it before, and I'll do it again. If you want to go work in Italy long-term, then I will do what I can to find a job in Italy. We'll figure it out."

"So you read the email?"

"Of course, I read the damn email. I trust you, Sage, but he's a hard line for me. Whatever really did or didn't exist between you two is in the past—I get that. But I need him to be out of your life. I need you to work for someone else."

Even I can see that's fair. If Amelia was somehow in his life—work related or not—I would flip my shit. Ty needs to be gone. Even though I don't have any lingering feelings for him, I need to do this for Brec.

"Deal. After Italy, I will cut all ties with Ty. I'll find a different agent."

"After Italy? That isn't a deal, Sage, that's a compromise —and one I'm not willing to make. If you're going to Italy associated with Ty in any capacity, then I'm out. I can't do this waiting for you to come back to me bit for the rest of our lives."

"Is this about Ty or is this about Italy? Are you saying I can't travel anymore?"

"I'm saying I want us to put down roots together. I want a family, and you want to run away still."

"A family? As in kids?"

"Yes. As in kids. I'm almost 36, Sage. You always knew I wanted kids. I haven't changed—I was just waiting."

He doesn't have to say the rest. I know it's supposed to be incredibly romantic that he was waiting—he put his life on hold for me, but all I feel right now is pressure. Like I have to sacrifice my future because he sacrificed his past. It's not that I don't want kids with Brec. If I'm doing the whole mommy thing, there is no one else I want beside me. But right now? Am I ready to be that person? Are we ready for that added layer of complication?

"So, what can we agree on? If I want to live in Europe, you're on board, but so long as I stay in one place forever? Do I have a time frame for when I need to start popping out babies? Have you scheduled our whole future without even asking me?"

I can see that this isn't where either of us hoped this would go. Earlier this weekend I thought this would be some pretty damn good news, but now I'm scared it's only going to reveal how shaky our foundation really is. Brec pushes his long body up and walks toward me. Instead of touching me he reaches around me to open the desk drawer. He pulls out a tiny key with a small red bow wrapped around it and lays it down in my lap.

"If you'd check your texts, you would have seen that I wrote you back. I had something I wanted to talk to you about as well."

I pick up the cute little key and roll it over in my hand. He wanted to ask me to move in with him. If I had told him Friday night, before the fucking email, this all would have gone down very differently. But, now, instead of us moving forward together, I'm not sure where we are. Brec leaves the room and I hear him grab his keys off the counter. He isn't often the one that needs space, but if he does, I'll respect that. I pack up my stuff and shove it all into my messenger bag. I take the key with me —not sure if it's still meant for me or not—but I'm worried it would do more damage to leave it behind.

When I pull up to Olivia's around 2:30 in the afternoon she and the girls are playing with a sprinkler in the front yard. Anna has grown so much since I got here in October. That girl is all legs. Emery is still short and petite like me but with a never-ending supply of energy. They look happy—all three of them—their family. God, Gage should be here to see this, to be a part of this. I don't know that I'll ever be able to feel like he isn't missing. I think the hurt reminds me of the love. Love isn't just the pain of losing someone—it's missing them, and it's living for them every damn day once they're gone.

I know everyone in the house can feel my moodiness from the moment I get home, but Olivia doesn't ask about it until the girls are asleep.

"He asked you to move in didn't he?"

"You knew?"

"Of course, I knew. That man is incapable of keeping secrets. He was really excited when I talked to him on Wednesday, so what happened?"

"Ty happened."

"Oh shit, Sage. I didn't even know you two were still in contact."

"We weren't. But there's this job—it's a dream job in Italy with an art historian that I've followed for years. It's a universal piece. It's a career-making assignment."

"And Brec doesn't want you to go?"

"Well, it turns out Brec wants a lot of things. Chiefly he wants me to leave Ty and find work elsewhere—which I get. It's pretty shady to work with an ex. Oh, and by the way, I was offered a full-time job at the high school teaching photography."

"Okay. So, you have door one—go to Italy and live out a lifelong dream but lose Brec to his macho jealousy or whatever, or door two—you can stay here with Brec, not to mention the girls and me, and live a different sort of dream. I guess it depends on which dream matters most, Sage?"

"He wants kids."

"And you don't?"

"I don't know. What if I totally fuck them up? Or what if they get my genes and end up in counseling—or spend their whole childhoods hating me like I did with my mom? What if I'm a really terrible mother and wife?"

"Oh, Sage. Look at all you've done for us. All you've conquered with my family. You did the hard part. You were a single parent at so many points over the last year, and you did it really well."

"I don't know that I did it 'really well', and I only did it because I had to."

"That's parenting. There isn't a rewind button with kids, so you just keep pushing forward because people are counting on you. And when you get stuck sometimes, you pray that you have an amazing sister-in-law who will pick up the pieces for you. If and when you and Brec get stuck, I'm here. And you know you'll have free babysitters pretty soon. Anna already feels like a teenager."

"Oh God, I'm never letting Emery near my kids. She'll kill them if she ever babysits."

"Remember the beginning, at the hospital, when you asked if you could keep the girls?"

"Oh God. You really thought I was going to kill them, didn't you?"

"Sort of. Not seriously, but the control freak inside of me was so anxious that first day. And you know what? You couldn't have done a better job. I wouldn't want anyone else to raise those girls apart from me or you. Oddly, like it or not, you are their other parent. In Gage's absence, you stepped up."

"And I'll do it again. Anytime you need me, I'm here."

"So, Sage, which dream matters most?"

Fuck me.

Brec doesn't write or call all night, and I continue to give him space. I know my answer, but it will come best when he's ready to hear it. After Olivia heads to bed, I pull out some old boxes from the garage to begin packing—hopefully for the last time.

Graduation week is freaking crazy. We are pulling pictures and turning them into layout in the same day. On top of that, I'm still packing up my stuff from Olivia's and Posies. It's beginning to look like I live out of my car again.

I run up to Posies late one night to gather the last of my personal items. I box up my record player and all the vinyls from Gage. I grab the picture frames and Mom's old albums that I still have from Gage's funeral. I add the picture I took from Brec's house the first time I went over there. Which dream matters more? Brec and I text back and forth but mostly about surface level shit. I don't want to get into anything serious over the phone, and this work week is like a Tsunami. Stupidly, I thought this week would be so simple since most of my kids don't need to take finals and are released from class for a various number of senior activities. In reality, it's my hardest week on the job. My students have become maniacs, and there are a million colored pieces of paper to check off and hand in to the registrar before anyone can go home for the summer. Add to that the final touches for the yearbook and grades, and I'm beat.

During the senior breakfast on Thursday morning, the valedictorian talks about Gage. Apparently, Gage had this kid in his class junior year. Mostly, at work, I've been able to be professional about the loss of my brother, but today I'm all emotions. I can't help it. I'm not even hiding it well. One of the moms leans over and hands me a Kleenex to wipe my running mascara. The loss of my brother will never stop hurting just like the legacy he left behind will never stop amazing me. One day, the last of his students will leave this place, but he's changed them—who they are—on such a fundamental level that wherever they go, he'll go with them. Again, I'm reminded of Olivia's question: which dream matters most? At the end of my life, looking at the whole scope of what I leave behind, do I want to be known vaguely as some name or idea of a person no one's ever met, like Okwui Enwezor, or do I want to be known on a personal level as a mentor, a role model, a friend?

Afterward, the valedictorian, Eli, comes to give me a hug.

"Hey, I saw you out here. I didn't mean to upset you Ms. G."

"Eli, that was one hell of a speech. I can't wait to see what you say on Saturday night. I'm glad that you, that the whole senior class, has commemorated so much of graduation to Gage. I'm sure he'd be so proud."

"Actually, Ms. G, that's what I wanted to talk to you about. I think we—most of the seniors—would really like to give you a chance to make a speech in honor of Mr. Gilbert at graduation. Typically, he emceed the event. No offense, but I don't really think that's your thing. I talked to Principal Nianouris, and she's on board with it . . . She also told me to remind that you're not allowed to curse at the podium."

"Aw, Dammit. You're going to make me cry again."

"So, that's a yes?"

"God, Eli. I really hate public speaking, and under any other circumstance I would say hell no, but I of course I will. I have to—for Gage."

CHAPTER Twenty

I have two days to figure out my employment, write a meaningful speech that will be delivered in front of thousands of people, talk to Brec and move. Seems reasonable enough.

Friday is a half day for the kids. THANK GOD. All of the equipment is cleaned and stored for the summer, every checklist is turned in and my grades have been verified. I have just survived my first, *partial,* year of teaching.

Olivia takes the girls over to Mom and Dad's for dinner, so I can finish packing and get some work done on my speech for graduation. I'm already nervous when I stand in front of the mirror and read back the three measly sentences I have written down. When the words stop coming, I switch gears and get up to grab another box from the garage. My car is nearly stuffed to the max, ready for the move—somehow, I've acquired a lot of shit since I've come home. I have three more boxes lining the perimeter of my room—Gage's old hospice respite. I fold open the last box and begin throwing in the final odds and ends—everything except what I'll actually need to get ready tomorrow. I find the amazing dinosaur t-shirt from our trip to the Science Place along with several other field trip themed items: a plastic cup from Holiday in the Park, a humongous straw with an elephant's head at the top from the zoo, dried flowers from the Arboretum. I also find the items I was saving from Gage's classroom. I dump both of the photography books in my packing box but save the rest to give to Olivia when she gets back tonight. I think now is the right time to give it to her. I go ahead and leave the box untapped, so I can add in my toiletries after I shower tonight. After scrubbing the room clean, and when I can no longer avoid my writer's block, I sit back down on the couch with a glass of wine to finish my speech.

When the girls come home, I've finally hit my stride. I've switched over to my laptop and it seems that the words come more naturally there. The girls must be pretty tired, or Olivia must warn them not to mess with me because I barely hear a peep from anyone once they walk through the living room. I'm spell-checking and revising the last pieces when Olivia walks in with a new bottle of wine.

"You up for round two?"

"Are you asking me if I'm willing to drink some more? Olivia, the answer is always yes."

She laughs and tops off both our glasses. She nods her head toward my laptop in a silent question.

"Sure, go ahead. Are you guys coming tomorrow afternoon?"

Olivia reads my entire speech before she responds to my question.

"Sage, that's amazing. Seriously, amazing. Gage would love it. And yes, now that I've read your speech, we will *all* definitely be there."

"Good. I'll need the support."

"Yeah, I thought you hated public speaking."

"I do."

By her second—my third—glass of wine, I go grab the bag of stuff from Gage's classroom. Olivia takes her time looking through the bag gingerly. It reminds me of victims of a fire looking through the last remnants of their homes in search of their memories. In a way, I guess that's pretty accurate. Cancer is like a fire—eating through every last piece of oxygen. She's lost in her own thoughts and pain, so I give her a hug goodnight and head back toward my room. I trust Olivia to be able to hurt now and find her way back toward the light. *Strength*.

My last night here feels solemn. At first, this room gave me the creeps, but over time it really did feel like I was closer to my brother in here. Our last conversation was in this room—his last breaths. I don't believe in ghosts, but if I did, I can easily imagine Gage chilling on my bed, kicked back, catching up on all he's missed out on. I'm oddly not tired considering the long week I've had, so after I blow dry my hair and add the dryer to my open box of junk, I grab out the photography books from Gage's classroom. They are pretty cool—sort of retro and not really the kind of thing I would expect my brother to have at all. I flip through the stiff pages and read all about New York's architecture. This book is definitely straight from the '80s—all clean lines and framed shots. It's beautiful but not exactly my type of photography. I like to shoot color—humanity. These are black and white shots of buildings. I carefully put the book back in the box and reach for the next one. As I'm carrying it across the bed, something falls out. It looks like an aged envelope. When I flip it over, my intrigue grows. It's addressed to me, but it's an address from years ago, and it's from . . . *Gage*. Is this letter from my brother? God, it must be at least 5 years old if this address is accurate. I know what I'm looking at, but my brain won't fully process it. I drop the stiff paper immediately like it wounds me. And it does. A pain builds in my chest, and my heart beats out a frantic rhythm. I stand up and pace around the small room. This would have been early in my career. A year, maybe a little longer, after I joined Ty. This could be anything, and it clearly didn't merit sending. My brain tries to reconcile that it's meaningless. That's not how Gage worked though. He saved this for me to find. I don't know how, but he knew. He knew I'd be the one to clean out his classroom. He knew I'd take the books. He knew exactly how to leave me one last message. A message that's stamped and addressed and meant to look forgotten. A message from our past that I'm terrified will fuck up the present. With trembling fingers, I reach for the slim package on the bed and bring it with me to the floor. I lay on my back and look toward the ceiling, to Gage, for guidance. Unsure of what to do, I begin counting my heartbeats, much like counting Gage's breaths so many months ago. When I get to 2,375, I flip over the delicate paper and run my index finger across the seal. Still laying down I carefully open the well-worn folds and read.

Happy 27th birthday, big sis! You're ancient, man. Sorry if this gets to you a little late—your address was a bitch to find. By the way, thanks for telling me you moved.

I love you, and I hope you find some of these boring photography books useful. You know you can take pictures without leaving the country—novel idea. I'm pretty sure we even have some buildings you can photograph around here. hint, hint.

Seriously though, there's something I need to tell you. Okay, maybe a couple of somethings. Before you judge me or hate me, I need you to know that I love you more than just about anything else in this universe (other than Olivia). Also remember, for a second, that I'm your baby brother—I'm learning, and sometimes I get things wrong. This is one of those times.

First. Brec and I are still close. I know you'd punch me right now if you could. He was the big brother I always wanted, and after you left, he kept in touch. I think he kept us close, so he could still feel connected to you. I know you came down when Olivia and I lost the baby, but Brec was also there for us during all of that. He became this metaphorical uncle to little baby no name. He became my best friend, Sage. I know this will piss you off and hurt you, but Brec's a good dude. I hope you can be happy that I have people in my life that will support me even when life gets hard. That man will be with me one day on my deathbed. He's the real deal. He's the closest thing to a brother I'll ever have.

Next. I fucked up. When you and Brec split, I was still in high school—I was so young, sis. It all seemed like a lot of unnecessary drama. I'm not saying that you both weren't really hurting, but I think we all saw it coming. Not to be a dick. You two were so young. I guess, I thought love was something only adults could really understand, and since you guys were still kids it must not be real —it couldn't be lasting. I never told him anything concrete, but I did spend a lot of energy encouraging him to move on. In fact, I may have exaggerated the whole thing with you and that Ty guy to help Brec see it was time to let go. I'm sorry. It was wrong. And now I don't know how to fix it.

Shit. I don't know how to admit how bad this has become. Sage, Brec's engaged—he's getting married at the end of the summer. It's a bad move—I know he's fucking up. He's never looked at her with half the love he had for you, but I don't know how to stop it. Maybe I set this in motion, or maybe not. But you know Brec—always the gentlemen. He won't leave her just because I tell him it's the right thing to do. I think you're the only one that can stop him from this. I know you still love him. Hell, I think we all believe that somehow, despite the odds, you two will end up back together one day. You guys are just meant to be. And now I mean that. I really think that no matter how hard you guys fight life, you'll find a way back to each other. I just want you to be happy—wherever you end up and whoever it's with. I want you to be happy, sis. I want you to smile.

which brings me to the last thing. About a year ago Brec gave me a letter I was supposed to get to you. And I didn't. And so much has gone wrong since then. I don't know what it says, but hopefully it will be some extra encouragement to come stop this shit show of a wedding. I'm sorry. I love you more than life itself. I know I screwed this one up.

Please forgive me.

Gage

This can't be fucking happening. This was five years ago. There is so much to process all at once. I mean, I've already dealt with the whole Brec and Gage are best friends fiasco, but what was Brec trying to tell me, and why didn't Gage ever send these letters? What the hell happened? How could my brother do this to me—to us? Gage, the golden child, royally fucked up. I wad up the letter into a tiny ball—twice—but smooth it out both times and reread it. This is it. The last of Gage. No matter what he put into motion, I can never rip up his words. We both let each other down. We were both disappointments. And now, it really doesn't even matter anymore. He's gone, and no one's keeping score.

Behind Gage's scribbled note, I find Brec's neatly handwritten one. I don't want to read it—I'm terrified of how this threatens every thread of trust between our nearly united futures, but I can't keep my eyes from devouring every word on the page.

I get the meaning of the words, but I can't quite place them. I feel there must be some added significance, I'm just not getting yet. It definitely sounds like a poem, but it's not EE Cummings—my favorite. In desperation I find my cell phone and begin to Google the words. Then I find it. These aren't just words—they're lyrics. I turn up the sound on my phone a couple notches and listen to the pleading desperation in the music. Somehow, this completely encapsulates how those first years without him felt.

It's a song; he was trying to speak my language.

I listen to the song over and over and over again and let Snow Patrol's *New York* retroactively break my heart with every repeat. Brec and I have talked through the rundown of the time after we split, but this is like hearing the splinter of his heart in those moments—before our memories altered the hurt. Before Amelia. Before Ty. Brec was just as broken and just as desperate as I was. This is his version of darkness.

Every time I listen to the words, I find new phrases to catch and hold on to. It's three am, and I must have listened to the song *New York* no less than 50 times before it's enough. I pull everything I can from this letter meant for the 26-year-old version of me and let my 32-year-old self-process it. He just wanted me to meet him fucking halfway. Halfway between my dark and his light. Halfway between my dreams and his. Halfway between New York and California.

And here we are—living in the halfway. Gage was right; we were always meant to find our way back.

I finish taping the last of the boxes with renewed courage. I know what I need to do now, and tomorrow will take strength.

Ten. *Saturday.*

Saturday morning is a complete rush. My phone starts going off at 6 am with all sorts of texts and tagged social media messages about our digital yearbook. So far, it's been a hit, and all the work is paying off. Olivia and the girls open my Mac and browse through the pages, and I realize again just how much we were able to accomplish in a few short months.

All of the teachers have to be at the field today by noon to begin prepping for graduation, but I leave a little early to go talk with Principal Jen. Today's the day I have to let her know my decision. I easily find her alone in her office checking through the stacks of diplomas for this afternoon's proceedings and let her know my plan.

Once I make it to the field, I'm put to work helping the tech team get everything set up. Setting up mics and running 100-foot extension cords is a blast in this 100-degree heat while wearing a dress and heels. I'm melted and pissed off in less than thirty minutes.

The graduates show up about 2:00 full of infectious energy, which calms my anger and gives me a second wind. I shoot off a quick text to double check with Olivia that *everyone* is coming today, and then I find Lily in the sea of faces and hand her my phone with some vague instructions, "When I get to 10, push send. Okay?" She nods her big eyes at me with her graduation cap wobbling wildly.

Every teacher in the district is here—even the ones who have retired. We line the field where the seniors enter. The first row of teachers, closest to the graduates as they enter, are the kindergarten teachers from the many elementary schools around the district. Following them are first and second grade teachers all the way up to where I stand with the other 12th grade teachers. Many of the students jump out of the processional line to hug former teachers' necks, and tears already begin leaking from the corners of my eyes. I'm a ball of raw nerves today. As if it isn't enough to just watch this display of joy, knowing that I have to get up in front of this group in about 15 minutes and pour my soul out on a microphone has me ready to either combust into hysterics or spontaneously vomit. Lily spots me from her place in line and jumps out to come talk to me. I assume she's lost my phone or needs the passcode, but instead she fiercely hugs me with those big, dumb eyes shining and says, "Thank you for believing in me—in all of us." *Now I can see it, Gage. This is why you did it.*

We all take our spots and go through the pledges and prayers before I'm up. Jen, herself, introduces me. As I begin marching awkwardly up to the front—past the sea of students, some of whom I now know most of whom I still don't, I see Gage. Not like a floating apparition in front of me, but some past tense version of him crossing the stage. For a second, I stop still on the dry grass creating a memory that should have already existed.

I never made it home for his graduation. Talk about a shitty sister. It was too soon after Brec and, at the time, my hurts mattered more than his accomplishments. He was different then. Gage had never been one to hold a grudge, but back then he still had hope for me. He called me up with boyish enthusiasm, certain that he could charm me into flying home to see his big night. I could hear him smiling through the receiver—so confident and so unaware that this would be the beginning of a series of times I would break his heart. When he was born, I knew, without a doubt, it was my job to protect him. Yet somehow along the way, what he needed protection from was me—the sister he could never count on—the friend who taught him about disappointment. If I were a true masochist, I could catalog each and every time I let him down, and I could bury myself under the pile of my selfishness.

He graduated top of his class. Literally, he was valedictorian. He was captain of the Lacrosse team. He was voted most likely to succeed. He was a class favorite every year. He was golden. Even now I can see the shine radiate off the vision of him.

I see him take the podium to give his speech—his parting words to his friends and classmates. He would have tilted his head slightly to the left and smiled at the crowd with that one dimple, and then he would have poured out his heart. Gage was good at charming, but what really drew people to him was his sincerity. He had an ability to see and speak to everyone as if they were the only one in the room.

I'm sure his speech was the perfect mixture of wisdom and humor, and I'm sure he meant every last word of it. He made his moment on that stage matter; he made all his moments matter. And now, his legacy is left to me. I wonder if he'd approve of the speech sticking to my sweaty palm. The pressure of it sags my shoulders but reminds me to keep moving forward. I pull my heel from the sunken ground and begin walking toward the stage— toward my brother—toward light and strength.

The scratchy pops of the mic pull me back into present tense. I'm embarrassed and suddenly aware of the silence and students and whispers around me. My momentary paralysis must have stopped the proceedings, but I gain momentum as Jen finishes announcing me.

"We are pleased to announce that before we start with the official acknowledgement of this year's graduating class, we will hear a quick commemorative speech from our newest full-time member of the faculty, Ms. Sage Gilbert."

The vision of Gage holds as I approach the final steps to the stage, and with one more breath, I close the distance between us until we stand at the *podium—together*. Here we go. I unfold the wrinkled and revised speech, close my eyes to feel one last time for Gage's presence and begin what will likely be the most devastating five minutes of my life.

"A long time ago, someone special taught me to handle stress by counting to ten. Well, folks, I can tell you that being up here is pretty dang stressful. So, bear with me, while we count to ten together—

Many of you know that Gage Gilbert, the beloved history teacher, was—and will always be—my brother. Even when we were kids, he was an old soul. I can say, without a doubt, a lot of who I am, and whatever wisdom I possess, is owed to him. For whatever it's worth, here is my unfiltered and unsolicited advice—here are ten things I've learned through knowing and loving my brother.

1. From a young age, Gage showed me that imperfections are what make you beautiful, so wear your scars proudly. Imperfections tell the stories that make us who we are. Embrace them, own them, because they are the most magnificent pieces of all of us. They are the proof of a life fully lived.

2. More recently, Gage showed me that life is unpredictable. No matter how long you prepare for it or line up the shot, no matter how many times you test the aperture, nothing—NOTHING—works out the way you thought it would. Just remember, messes often end up being the most beautiful pieces of art. I would give anything to get my brother back, but I can absolutely stand here and tell you that I wouldn't be the person I am today without losing him.

3. Gage was the proverbial golden child, so his choice to stay in our hometown, become a teacher and start a family came as a bit of a shock. What his life said, and what he wanted people to understand was that adventure and success come in many forms. It may be becoming a foreign correspondent or becoming a mom or dad. Learn which adventures you can't live without and don't compromise.

4. I hope I would have learned this one on my own— eventually. Gage was just there as a constant reminder that it's okay to mess up even when it involves someone else's heart. He once told me, "Love is a messy thing, and Sage, you're going to get it wrong—a lot." He was very right. The only thing I know for certain about love is that without a doubt you will disappoint the people you love, and without a doubt they will disappoint you. What makes it love is the ability to forgive the disappointments.

5. This one I'm still learning and could only see after Gage's death. Selfless lives leave legacies. We all want to be remembered. We all want our lives to mean something, but it takes work to matter. If you don't love and nurture the world around you, however big or small that may be, then it won't remember you when you're gone. Gage— Mr. Gilbert—will be remembered forever.

6. Though my brother was amazing, he wasn't perfect. This is one we both got wrong. This is one we both had to learn. Always choose honesty. Be honest with yourselves. Be honest with the people you love and those who love you. Be honest with your dreams and ask for nothing less. You'll only ever get what you're willing to ask for.

318 | Unfiltered Sage

7. Gage loved this job. He loved you—all of you—and he believed in you—his light touched everyone he met. Millennials, be the light—be the change this nation and this world so desperately needs. Take it from a girl who spent way too much time in the dark: sadness takes no effort but choosing joy—even when it's hard—that's strength. Be strong and shed some light on a dark and fragile time for humanity.

8. Not many people know this, but this is the first time I've been home in 15 years. Gage brought me home. And by coming home I've learned this—soak up wisdom wherever you can find it. Whether that be from an old, sassy café owner, an impromptu photography teacher, or your boyfriend's ex-wife—listen to what others have to teach you. If you listen well enough, you can learn from just about anyone. People fall into three categories: the ones you aspire to be, the ones who are just like you and the ones you never want to become. All three groups have knowledge to give.

9. Gage's light was infectious; it was beautiful. But sun and light also create shadows. You can't have one without the other. Gage spent so many years and so much time teaching me to embrace the broken. There are people and moments in life that won't value your whole worth. Employers who will pass on you for the job you're perfect for, fiancés who will disappear and break promises, mothers with expectations you can never meet, and brothers who will betray your trust. This doesn't make any of them bad people because it's not a bad thing to be broken. If our hearts were never broken, then we would never have built the strength to weather life. Broken

pieces are like your heart's immune system. It's vital for us to break in order to for us to truly survive.

My voice is past wobbly, and the tears that have welled up in my eyes are one second away from cascading down my cheeks. Speaking these words into existence—acknowledging their truth—is like shedding the layers of armor I've built over the years for protection. It's liberating.

"Thanks for making it all the way to ten with me, you guys. We're almost done."

I look out to Lily who nods her head at me in understanding, and I shade my eyes to search for Brec in the crowd. When I spot him, I don't look away, I don't look at the sea of faces in front of me or the brown field I once despised. I speak boldly into the mic and get to ten.

10. The world is at your fingertips right now. This is the most exciting part of life. Today is the start to one of your greatest adventures, but, remember there's an end to this beginning. So, somewhere on your journey, stop long enough to find out where you belong and plant some roots. Congratulations graduates!

During the applause, Lily gives me a quick thumbs up to verify that the text was sent. I move to the end of the receiving line on the stage to shake hands with each student as their names are called. As soon as we get to the M's, my palms begin to sweat again. I take a quick peek out at the crowd to help calm my nerves, and all I see when I look out is color. Vibrant colors. Every shade of happiness is here walking across the stage or sitting in the stands. Pride. Joy. Celebration. Confidence. Laughter. Inspiration. Relief. Anticipation. Nostalgia. This—this is Gage. I'm pretty sure this is how he saw life, and it's beautiful.

"Lily Metzger," The superintendent announces.

All 5 feet of this girl waltzes across the stage, poses for her picture and shakes hands with the rest of the line. When she gets to me at the end, she slips the phone back into my palm as we shake hands. She wiggles her eyebrows at me and whispers, "Smooth moves, Ms. G." And then she's gone.

I know as of four hours ago I became a super professional teacher, and we live by a 'higher code of ethics' or whatever, but I can't help it. As discretely as I can, I open my phone to see if he's replied. Lily must have sent the message at least 20 minutes ago now with how slowly this line is moving. I take a breath and open my messages.

Marry me?

As long as you're asking, I'll be there.

Every piece of me smiles and radiates with relief. It's the perfect response from my perfect man—simple, a little bit sarcastic and completely unfiltered.

When we leave the stadium, we leave together. He's driving my car, filled with all my shit—a lifetime of baggage. Before we make it out of the parking lot, I make him stop.

"What—you're backing out on me already?"

"No, idiot. I want a picture."

I can tell he doesn't fully understand it, but he humors me anyway. We both climb on top of the hood of my car. Brec is taking up nearly the whole damn thing, and I'm sitting between his legs. The sun is beginning to set behind us, and with my wide-angle lens, I can get nearly the whole field in the background. There are royal blue-gowned students littered all over in uneven clumps—not paying any attention to the selfie they are accidently about to photo bomb. We don't have a ring to commemorate the moment, but we will have a picture—which is really better anyway. A photo to remind us of our many shades of happiness—all the shades that it took for us to get right here. Right as I snap the photo, Brec leans in to kiss my cheek, which makes me involuntarily close my eyes for a second. It's perfectly imperfect. I'm smiling directly into the camera with my eyes scrunched, and Brec is smiling through his kiss while watching my reaction. It's genuine, so I love it. Tomorrow, I'm going to get the photo printed and hang it in a frame right beside our first photo—the one he saved from the darkroom. And, together, we'll hang them up in our house. The end beside the beginning.

Home.

LETTER TO THE *Reader*

Thank you—thank you for taking a chance on this book. If you'd like to keep up with all my things—writing and wandering related, be sure to visit and subscribe to my website, www.celinahilbrand.com. I hope you each found a piece of yourself—your story & your truths— somewhere in these pages.

Acknowledgements

First and foremost, to Nikki and Sarah. You two were my rocks. You patiently read every draft. You bravely gave me suggestions, edits and opinions. You listened to voice memo after voice memo and never complained. This book would not have happened without you both. From the bottom of my heart, thank you.

To my many beta readers who sped through this book and gave me everything from hope and support to corrections on typos. Thank you for being my extra eyes, my proofreaders and my cheerleaders.

To Lauren and Stacy. I brought you both on so late in the game when I realized I couldn't do it all, and you both jumped in and got to work immediately. Just so you know, you're stuck with me now. This book would still be a really long word document sitting on my laptop if it weren't for you two. Bless you both for dealing with my crazy, especially at the end.

To my readers and bloggers. Thank you for taking a chance on this first-time author. It's said that any writer will be most embarrassed by their first book, and the truth is, I hope that's never true. It took 35 years for me to gain the courage and strength and vulnerability to accomplish my first novel. Never be ashamed of your dreams or the journey it takes to get to them. Whatever your dreams are, go be it.

To my family who will probably think this is about them, **but it isn't**. Thank you for not having a communal heart attack when I decided to leave a well-established career and chase this long-ago fantasy of becoming an author. Thank you for allowing me to be me—the performer, the dreamer, the author.

To all my 'pebbles' who helped create the rocky path leading me toward today. Thank you for your inspiration and for helping me find the belief in myself that I can do big things. Your voices, collectively, are the foundation to these characters that I love so much.